RON RICHARD

GROUP SIX
AND THE RIVER

OF WATER AND BRIMSTONE

GROUP SIX SERIES

GROUP SIX AND THE RIVER

RON RICHARD

GROUP SIX AND THE RIVER

OF WATER AND BRIMSTONE

CHRISTOPHER MATTHEWS PUBLISHING

Group Six and the River, *of Water and Brimstone*
by Ron Richard

Christopher Matthews Publishing
Gleneden Beach, Oregon
ChristopherMatthewsPub.com

ISBN:
   978-1-944072-61-2 (pb/Amazon)
   978-1-944072-62-9 (hc)
   978-1-944072-60-5 (pb)
   978-1-944072-67-4 (epub)

Library of Congress Control Number: 2022903476
Genre: *magic, fantasy, adventure, humorous, mythical creatures*

Cover design and formatting by Suzanne Fyhrie Parrott
Cover art by Gaurav Srivastava (@hephaestusart, Fiverr.com), © Ron Richard

Please provide feedback

10 9 8 7 6 5 4 3 2 1

Printed in U.S.A.

To My Love,
My Lady,
My Lifesaver

TABLE OF CONTENTS

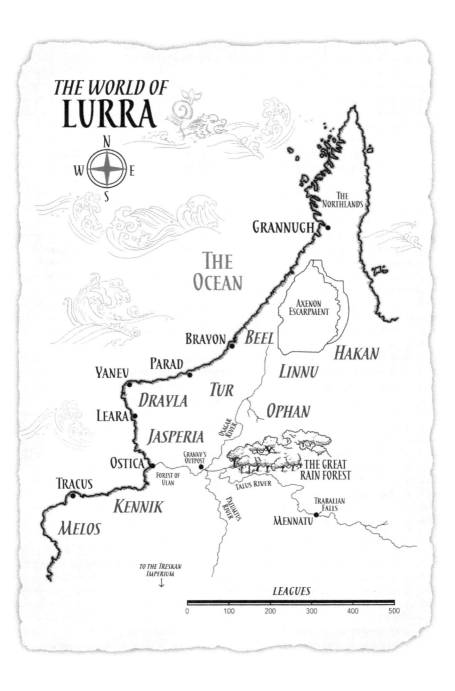

MAJOR CHARACTERS

GROUP SIX

SERENA
A 27-year-old Macai Northlands Warrior. A fierce fighter, she values honor in battle above all else.

ORCHID
A 30-year-old Macai forest steward. Raised by Eryndi foster parents, she practices Worldly Magic, which is unusual for a Macai.

FOXX
A 33-year-old self-taught Macai Magician. Inventor of the Knowing Spell, which allows him to read moods and influence others.

TRESADO
A 45-year-old Eryndi Magician who practices Absolute Magic. Chubby and out of shape for an Eryndi, but a first-class Magician specializing in kinetic spells.

LEADER
A mysterious and impassive figure who appears to be a Macai.

OSTICA

BUNKY BOATWRIGHT
Eryndi boat builder who created *Enchanter*.

JENNICK
An Eryndi professor of Life Empathy at the Melosian Academy of Wordly Arts.

SAGE MARISON
Magic instructor with a maddening sense of ethics.

PROFESSOR ABADIAH GENERAX
Owner and operator of Professor Generax and His Traveling World of Wonders. A shrewd businessman, if not a completely honest one.

THE NORTHLANDS

BATA
Enigmatic Eryndi woman who seems to have strange powers, including some knowledge of the future and illusionary skills.

EYMON SKAGSGARD THE RANK
Chieftain of Grannugh and Belzar Fjord Environs.

IBARR THE SCARY
Northlands Warrior who survived a nasty encounter with a berg bear.

GUNNAR AND HULDE BRIMSTONE
Parents of Serena.

EGGBERT AND OGGDEN
Twin cousins of Serena.

PARSOMAL
Eryndi traveler from whom Serena received her diamond.

ANCIENT MENNATU

JARAYAN
Eryndi Elder mostly responsible for creating the Great Hearth, which resulted in great change for the Mennatuan Domain.

ZAROSEN
Son of Jarayan.

THE CRYSTAL PALACE

JAKUNDARANA SLIVERSHKANAT TRYSTELLIAR
Steward of the Crystal Palace and a powerful Magician. She enjoys the fast-paced style of life within the Palace.

JAKKI
Short, plain, dumpy, and a terrible waitress. She always chews gum and calls everybody "hon."

SUNSHINE AGNES
Eryndi martial arts fighter who competes regularly in the Dinday Night Fights in the Palace's competition center.

SPARKLY
Assistant to the Steward. His clothing and even his teeth are sparkly.

MARCELLA, DRANIA, AND CERVANI
Previous stewards of the Palace.

DEMENTUS, THE MAD TRESKAN
Legendary (and some say mythical) traveler of the world.

PART I: THE RIVER

CHAPTER 1

Ostica, a large port city on the Talus River, (pop. 187,309; 72.1% Macai, 27.9% Eryndi) does not seem to live up to its potential. Despite the prominent, broad highway into the rich interior, the content Osticans limit their trade to countries reachable by the sea.

—*STARFISH* ARCHIVAL SPHERE 342

Today – Kevoday, Tono 30-21876

Tresado plodded down the filthy alley, wondering if the pouring rain would lessen or add to the filthiness. His question was soon answered as the delicately blended mixture of soil, grease, urine, and fish scales that was the road beneath his Eryndi feet embraced the rain water like a long-lost family member. The happy reunion produced a substance as slippery as owl poop on a brass sword pommel. While Tresado's face plant into the slime was not physically damaging, the emotional scars would be with him for some weeks.

Rather on the pudgy side for an Eryndi, Tresado liked to think that his lack of grace made him a better Magician.

Let's see those thick-headed jock captains of the boingball team back in cram school try to cast a decent levitation spell.

Not everyone was good at or even capable of using Magic. There was subtlety involved, finesse. One just didn't say *hanketyblank* and turn a guy into a frog. The idea of reciting bad poetry to bring about Magical means was a myth amongst the unenlightened. One needed skill, endless study, commitment, professionalism, an ambitious nature—but most of all, a sense of *style!*

Tresado rose from the muck and peered through the rain to face the cruel world.

Someday I'll make 'em all pay, the bastards.

His foul mood was slightly eased by two items. The first: the immediate relief gained by spitting out the rat turds that his open mouth had scooped up in its watery dive to the ground. The second was the never-to-get-old sight of one of his traveling companions, the lovely Serena.

The lady (and there was no doubt that such was the case) stood at the end of the alley, her female form softly silhouetted by the orange glow of the setting sun over the tranquil ocean behind her. How it could be raining in the alley and balmy where she was didn't matter. It was just part of her pure nature, one would suppose. Her hair, a waving symphony of golden promise, flowed about her angelic face like a hundred beckoning fingers, drawing him irresistibly into those lapis-colored eyes. Her lips, luscious purveyors of what must certainly be the perfect kiss, parted sensuously.

"Hey Tresado, whaddaya doin', humpin' a dead monkey? Why don't ya get your ass outa the mud, and let's get goin'! We don't have all friggin' night, for crap's sake!"

Such a delicate flower!

* * *

Serena is a bright girl if she chooses to apply herself. Excels at Basic Weaponry and Wrestling, but has difficulty paying attention during Tactics and Strategy class. Fights well with others.

—Hrolvad the Berserker Elementary School; Third Grade student evaluations; Miss Herkimer's homeroom

Last month - Serena

Serena hefted the tree limb in her feminine hand, wondering if it were stout enough to cave in the average skull. Maybe if she hit this guy just right.

"But Serena, you don't understand. I love you! You are the sun of my day and the orb of my night. You are everything I've ever dreamed of: beauty, grace, the epitome of femininity. You are life itself. You are . . ."

It was unclear whether the Macai's nose was broken by the initial blow or by the fall. The important thing was that it was broken. It shut him up for a few beats, anyway. At the very least, it kept him from following her like a puppy.

"Serena. Wait, my love . . . WAIT!"

The man's words had a bubbling tone as they filtered through the blood gushing from his nostrils. Serena found the effect aesthetically pleasing as she stomped away, still annoyed.

"That's it! Something's gotta be done about this crap!"

She didn't know what, exactly, but that was okay. The silent figure watching her from the shadows did.

Last week –
The Maimed Moose Inn of Ostica

"So what do I . . . *we* call you if you won't give us your name?"

Foxx's question produced no reaction from his dining companion. In fact, during the three hours he had known the man, he'd observed only stone-like emotional responses.

"If a name is necessary, then *Leader* will suffice."

"Leader? . . . Okay, fair enough."

Foxx had purposely inserted a smidge of sarcasm into his response, but it was a carefully crafted test. He studied the face of the man who had just hired him and apparently several other people for a job. There was no look of indignation or evasiveness . . . no embarrassment or guilt or anything written there. He never even flicked an eyebrow. Foxx had never encountered the like before and was troubled by his inability to read the man.

Foxx was a Macai of many talents. Chief among them was his ability to read others' moods and intentions, even their demeanors, enabling him to 'fit in' to any situation. It was a quasi-Magical/hypnotic skill that had served him as well in diplomatic negotiations as in Four-Card Blitzkrieg. With most people, Foxx was very perceptive and persuasive . . . but this fellow was different.

Just then, the Eryndi at the next table puked up his dinner of sheep's eyes on a shingle. The other customers in the inn fled from the projectiles. *Leader* simply flicked the chunk of eyeball off his boot and then used his napkin to restore the leather to a brilliant shine—as if nothing had happened at all.

Impressive, thought Foxx.

"Now, as to your mission, here is a list of names and their probable locations." Leader handed Foxx a piece of thin paper.

"Nice penmanship."

"Temporary penmanship. Please memorize this information now, and then give me back the list."

Leader regarded Foxx impassively as the three names, one of which he was familiar with, were assimilated. Two minutes later, the paper was burning to ashes in the candle holder on the table.

"Good," Leader said. "We will meet back here at the same hour in eight days."

Foxx drained the last of his makara juice and set down the mug. He shoved back his stool and stood.

"One week, it is."

Last year –
Yaneva Research Laboratory
For Alchemic Sciences - Drayla

"Shall we try this one more time?"

Tresado's question got an over-the-nose look from Cheltanek, the lab technician assigned to assist him.

"I think you mean one *last* time. You do know what day this is and what the administrator said."

"Yeah, yeah, I know what the evil queen of bean counters said," Tresado replied testily. "And if I had the money, I would rent more lab time. But I don't, so I can't, so we have to get the formula right this time."

For the past three weeks, Tresado had been trying to perfect his idea. It involved rented time and space in the research center. He needed access to a transmutation oven, different chemical compounds, Magically sealable containers, and the services of the specialist Magicians employed there. Cheltanek's specialty was the ability to analyze the category and power of certain types of Magic infusions. The lab technician produced a spell that, combined with chemical experiments, measured several factors. The special analysis strips changed color when dipped in test material, providing the answer.

Today's round of tests involved mixing different types of acids of varying strengths with limestone and powdered coral. The substance was then infused with a binding Magic and, finally, baked in the transmutation oven.

The preliminary assemblage of components was completed with no problems. That in itself was progress. The first two attempts had resulted in an uncontrolled reaction that required Tresado to wipe down the entire lab with neutralizing agents. The solution was stable, and the crucible was prepared. Two dozen coin-shaped molds stood ready. Cheltanek held a small funnel over each one as Tresado carefully poured the solution. With all the molds filled, they slid the rack into the oven. Its spell was activated, bathing the experiment in Magical heat. As the chemical bonds reacted with the binding spell, Tresado counted two-hundred-forty-two beats, then shut down the oven and removed the rack of molds to cool. Cheltanek performed his test spell and made the announcement.

"All checks are nominal."

The next three minutes felt like an eternity. Finally, the required cooling time elapsed, and the molds were broken open. Before him lay twenty-four ceramic coins with his own personal, embossed symbol on them—a vanity he couldn't resist. The top of the mold had a couple of beads of hardened material that had dripped from the crucible onto the mold's outer part. He picked up the pea-sized piece with a pair of tongs and held it over a beaker of water.

"Let's give it a test, shall we?"

He dropped the bit of ceramic into the beaker, and the solution immediately overflowed with a fountain of bubbles. The little particle continued to fizz furiously, maintaining its rate of bubbliness for the next twenty minutes.

"Success!" Tresado breathed gratefully. "Now, all I need is the boat."

Cheltanek gave him a confused look. *"Boat?"*

Seven weeks ago –
Corsairs' Wharf - Ostica

"Now you understand, these plans aren't carved in stone."

The old Eryndi looked oddly at Tresado.

"Well, no . . . they're drawn on parchment. Anyone can see that."

Pause . . . pause . . . pause.

"You're right. What I mean is it doesn't have to be built exactly according to these drawings. You're the shipbuilder; you know how a boat needs to be designed."

Bunky Boatwright stroked his pointed beard and perused the plans.

"With a few minor changes, she should sail just fine," he said, pointing at the drawing. "It seems to me though, that this tubing on the side of the pontoons will slow her down a bit."

"That tubing is one thing you can't take liberties with, Bunky. It has to be exactly as drawn; every dimension just as it indicates."

Bunky moved his often smashed finger along the drawing. "And this . . . canister thing on the platform?"

"That canister thing I have right here." Tresado reached into his saddlebag and pulled out an object wrapped in fabric. It was a peculiar-looking doodad; brass and steel with one end of the cylinder covered with a hinged lid with heavy screw-down clamps. There was a lever on the side that opened and closed a kind of internal flue.

"The piping attaches here," said Tresado, indicating a flange on the other end. "And the other thing I have to insist on is the materials. The platform and mast can be any material you think is suitable, but the hulls and tubing must be constructed out of monkeywood. The sail and rigging can only be made from Treskan flax. The bladders have to be made from stickfish stomachs."

"The monkeywood I can get, but it's expensive. Treskan flax has an import tax . . . huh, huh." Bunky loved a good poem. ". . . so it's expensive. And stickfish stomachs, I can only get from a couple of deep-sea fishermen I know and, well . . . also expensive."

Tresado did a quick mental calculation of his available funds.

"How expensive?"

The figure that Bunky gave was about three times more gold *tormacs* than Tresado had in his pouch. He doled out everything he had minus the cost of a modest meal.

"This is a down payment. I'll give you the second third when you start construction and the rest of it when you finish."

Bunky looked at the coins on the table before him. It was enough to start this weird-ass project, but not enough to finish it.

"I'm gonna need half down just to get the materials."

Tresado sighed and glanced over at his horse, who was staring back at him with a look of betrayal. She knew.

"All right, half it is. I'll need to . . . go to the bank. I'll be back in a couple of hours."

* * *

Magic is neither good nor evil. It is not a divine gift or a hellish curse. It is not a philosophy or a belief. It is a tangible, measurable phenomenon with which to conquer a world.

—IMPERATOR MERAK,
COMMENTARIES: BOOK 13, CHAPTER 7, PARAGRAPH 2

Two and a half days ago –
The Forest of Ulan - Orchid

Orchid watched from the hiding branches of a flapper bush as the poachers snuck through the forest. The six men were a scurvy lot . . . literally. The stench from their rotting teeth alone was enough to alert every animal for leagues around. They were trying to move silently, but these guys had as much woodcraft as a pod of sea swine. Every twig and leaf snapped and rustled beneath their feet, further warning their quarry. The flock of flightless mica cranes leisurely strode away on their long legs at what for them was a slow walk, but far faster than their Macai pursuers could even run.

Orchid nodded to herself and smiled.

"These clowns are the worst ones yet."

She was about to let them off with a warning until gargling cackles began coming from where the birds had disappeared behind the hill.

Oh twigs, she thought. *They've walked into Emmet's Gulch.*

Mica cranes are one of the more stupid of bird species. That was why there are relatively few of them left around these parts. Their dimwittedness, combined with their prized feathers, made them common targets for hunters. This flock had walked up a blind alley. The fissure only extended about fifty paces into the cliff face, but the cranes were too dumb to turn around and go back out again. They just stood there, staring at the wall and clucking at their predicament.

A minute later, the poachers caught up to them. The head scumbag, named Broon, signaled his pals with some bizarre silent hand gestures. Orchid didn't recognize the language but assumed it translated to something like: *I say, the creatures are trapped; let us kill them, shan't we?* The men began fitting arrows to their bows and flanking out across the entrance to the gulch.

Orchid let out her breath, letting the image of what the men deserved form in her thoughts. She allowed the Magic around her to coalesce into focused energy. Nothing forced; nothing manipulated; merely allowed. Once sufficient power was gathered, Orchid directed it on the grove of *seramin* trees through which the poachers were sneaking.

The archers were now in a position to loose their shafts on the helpless cranes. Broon was within a beat of giving the signal to fire when he suddenly found himself upside down and suspended above the forest floor. He felt and then saw the reason for his predicament. Several strands of tree vines were coiled about his waist. Before he had time to think about how such a thing was possible, more tendrils from the nearby tree lashed out and snaked around his wrists and ankles. His longbow was also entwined and wrenched out of his hand.

Broon managed to twist his body around and looked up. What he saw made him cringe.

The seramin tree had come alive. Its stringy, hanging branches had twisted together into a shape of a giant Macai. Its 'arms' held Broon in a grip of steel. The tree's twisted trunk formed itself into the semblance of a pair of crossed legs. The whole tree now resembled a giant seated being, holding Broon facedown over its knee like a small child about to be . . .

"Oh, no!" Broon yelled, struggling against the force holding him.

The rest of the poachers were in similar trouble with other trees. In perfect sync, each of men had their trousers yanked down to their knees. Six bare butts reflected in the sunlight.

As Orchid's spell took full effect, she mimicked the trees' movements as they performed the spanking. It helped the efficacy of the Magic, and it was vicariously damn fun. With ready-made, thorny switches built into their 'hands,' the seramins punished the naughty boys until their butts were crisscrossed with welts.

"Six apiece should do it, my friends."

The trees obeyed, but not because they were friends or even because they understood. Trees don't understand anything. They're just trees.

Orchid allowed the spell to dissipate, and the trees returned to normal, dropping the poachers to the ground. The men pulled themselves to their feet, whimpering about sore butts. Orchid stepped into sight.

"Did we learn a little lesson, boys?" Orchid said, scolding them like children.

The poachers looked at the slight figure confronting them. Orchid was a petite Macai with long, chocolate brown hair. Despite her unthreatening appearance, two things commanded their respect. The first was her intense green eyes, which blazed like the brightest stars, except green.

The second thing was the ornate staff she carried. A head taller than Orchid, the carvings of floral patterns and bird wings adorned the rod from base to coiled tip. It pulsated with power as miniature lightning bolts crackled around its head, shooting off sparks; all in all, a thoroughly imposing looking and obviously powerful Magical weapon. The poachers quaked with fear at the sight of that stormy stick, especially when Orchid brandished it in their faces.

"All right boys, you know this is the Duke's territory. Now I'm not going to see your faces around here again, am I?"

Five heads shook side to side in fear. Number six stood his ground.

"Drop dead!" Broon tried to maintain a tough front.

Orchid's patience grew thin. "You shouldn't make me angry."

The seramin tree re-animated in a flash, and once again, Broon found himself at its mercy. By the time it was done with him, the poacher was blubbering like a toddler. The other poachers tripped over each other in their haste to leave. Their abandoned bows dangled from the highest branches of the trees that had disciplined them. Broon was again dropped to the ground, right into a massive pile of lumba poop. Over two hundred maggots lost their lives in the impact.

"Get out of here."

Broon limped painfully after his buddies, whimpering little ooh, ooh sounds.

Orchid watched the poachers leave, but her woodsy instincts told her she was still not alone. She spun, staff at the ready, to confront the new intruder.

"Nice touch with the trees, effective, yet no harm done."

Orchid regarded the well-coiffed Macai that stood before her. There was another one, a blonde woman, holding a couple of horses down the hill on the road. Neither was making any threatening moves.

"The arrow up the butt on the last guy was kind of . . . nasty," the stranger said, wrinkling his nose.

"It went in feathers first," she replied defensively.

"Merciful." He suppressed a smile.

"I think so," Orchid replied. The stranger continued to regard her.

"Can I be of service, somehow?" she asked, warily.

"My name is Foxx. That's with two *exes*. I have a proposition for you."

CHAPTER 2

Perhaps the most non-biased thing and the only thing I can think of that one could envy about the Eryndi race is their longevity. Living two or three times longer than Macai can have its advantages, one would suppose. Think of the knowledge and experience you could gain in all those decades. However, it is an unfortunate truth that the balance of them cannot or choose not to learn from all that knowledge.

The problem with a race that lives so long is that it takes a great deal of time for cultural change to occur. Eryndi leaders that are in power for centuries keep the same ideas, the same misconceptions. The Macai, on the other hand, with lifespans of only eighty years or so, tend to get things done at a much quicker rate. Knowing they're going to die soon creates a kind of impatient desperation in the Macai psyche.

I suppose that could explain why Eryndi Magicians tend to limit themselves to Worldly Magic. It is passive and mild and hence ineffectual. Macai, on the other hand, recognize that the wise use of Absolute Magic can ultimately change this world for the better.

—JOCULAN THE THIRD – MUSINGS DURING THE LAST DROUGHT – 21655, NEW CALENDAR

Today - Ostica

"There it is," Orchid said, pointing to an overhead sign. A painted wooden depiction of a big, legless deer swung gently in the breeze.

Serena wrinkled her delicate little nose at Tresado. "What a turd pile. But even this joint might not let *you* in. You stink like a diseased buzzard on a honey barge."

Tresado *was* still a bit slimy from his alley face plant, but that was of no matter. The personal observation from Serena was like a rose petal bath. It showed she cared.

The door was open at the Maimed Moose Inn. Out of it came the sounds of drinking, eating, laughing, yelling, farting . . . all in all, a typical tavern.

Tresado, Serena, and Orchid made their way through the crowd to the back, where the innkeeper was busy filling several bowls with an oily fish stew. He was also rather oily looking, with a perpetual frown draped across his jowls.

"Yeah?" he snarled as the three travelers stood before him.

"We're looking for a guy named Foxx," said Serena.

"Inna back," he swung his head to the side to indicate the door to the private room behind, giving his visitors the briefest of glances. But he suddenly froze, his dripping ladle suspended in space. His eyes returned to Serena, who stood before him lit with an internal glow of purity, the very essence of innocent femininity radiating from her like the sun itself.

In truth, Serena was a bit rank from the trail and smelled like her horse. Her jerkin was stained, and her hair was a tangled home to an extended family of lice. But to the innkeeper, she was the goddess of beauty herself. She stood on the other side of the bar from him, fingering the pommel of her wicked curved sword and getting more and more pissed by the beat.

"O-oh, m-my," the stammering man could do nothing as he stared open-mouthed at the angry Serena. A long stream of drool slowly drained from the corner of his mouth, dropping into one of the bowls he had just filled.

Serena half drew her sword and probably would have leapt over the bar and beheaded the man were it not for Orchid's firm grip on her arm.

"Don't you start that crap!" Serena yelled. "Don't you do it or I'll split you from crotch to collarbone. I swear!"

Orchid and Tresado managed to maneuver the furious woman away from the bar and into the room beyond. The innkeeper sighed and mooned after her with probably the first happy expression he had worn in decades.

"The next guy that does that to me is a dead man. *A DEAD MAN!*"

Serena screamed the last part of that just as the door was closed behind her. The man named Foxx was seated at a table with another Macai she had never seen before.

Or *was* he a Macai? The man with Foxx did not have the long, pointed face and conical ears of an Eryndi, but he didn't quite look fully Macai, either. His smooth skin had not a wrinkle or a blemish. His clothing could be described in the same way.

"Come in, sit down. Would you care for some honey wine?" The man's movements were smooth and efficient as he tilted the swiveling amphora and filled three mugs.

Serena had not entirely calmed down yet. Her wild eyes shifted between the two men at the table, daring either to idolize her at peril to their lives.

Foxx was a master of controlling his outer demeanor, as anyone who had played cards with him could attest. The trickle of sweat that ran down his temple was the only indication of the internal pressures he was feeling.

The other man regarded Serena, Tresado, and Orchid with equal attention. He was apparently unfazed by anything. Serena glared angrily and snapped her sword all the way back into its scabbard with a scary *click*. The threat of violence apparently over, they sat down at the table.

Foxx stood and made introductions in his best diplomatic tone.

"May I present Serena, Orchid, and Tresado?" They gave little nods as their names were announced.

Foxx continued. "This is . . . *Leader*." The pause in his voice conveyed, *'Yes, I know it's dorky, but whatever.'*

If Leader caught the dig, he showed no reaction.

"Please, enjoy," Leader said as he slid the mugs forward.

Orchid leaned her ornate staff against the wall. The motion caused it to spark and then vibrate with an ominous rumble. She sat, took a sip of her mead, and smacked her lips in appreciation.

"Excellent, smooth with a touch of *griffleberry* flavoring."

"You have a very discerning palate," Leader said.

"I know my berries," Orchid replied.

Leader looked around the table. "Well, perhaps you were wondering why I've gathered you here today."

Tresado rolled his eyes at Foxx and returned his attention to Leader.

"As Foxx has undoubtedly explained to you, I have an expedition in mind."

"Up the river?" asked Tresado.

"Up the river," replied Leader.

"Is it true what they say, about the Magic guy?"

Leader said, "Your question, Serena, is a bit broad, but yes, most everything *they* say is true. There is a man who dwells far upriver. He is possibly the most powerful Magician in the world. His Magical abilities are nearly without limit. There is little he cannot do."

This final statement perked up everyone's ears. Serena inquired about clarification of the details.

"Is he a good guy or a bad guy?"

Foxx, the diplomat, quickly interjected, "I think what Serena means is . . ."

Leader interrupted, "What she means is, will he give each of you what you want? The only answer I can give is that he is certainly capable of it."

"What I *mean* is," Serena said, glaring at Leader, "I've fallen for this goat crap before—some Magic miracle worker that'll solve everything at no charge? Been there, done that."

Orchid drained the last of the mead in her mug. "So you say this guy will give us what we want? Just what exactly is it that *we want?*"

Not batting an eye, Leader replied, "The most honorable and noble of goals for each one of you. You, Orchid, seek *understanding.* You practice Worldly Magic, as do most Eryndi Magicians. But as a Macai, there is always something that eludes you. You feel not quite connected to the world that you love so much, not in the way an Eryndi is. Perhaps this powerful Magician can enlighten you."

Leader turned toward Tresado, who was idly levitating a salt shaker. "Tresado, to you Magic is everything. Therefore, you seek *more.* New *methods,* new *forms* of Magic, ways sometimes frowned upon by your kind and by your peers. You are an Eryndi, though you practice the limitless Absolute Magic. This super-powerful Magician could teach you much.

"Foxx, you look for *adventure* and to go places you've never been. You have been told of wonders far upriver. You have also been warned of all manner of dangers upriver. What actually *is* upriver, no one here can tell you for certain; therefore you have no choice but to find out for yourself . . . to see what is over the next hill. You wish to know the world.

"And Serena, my friend. You seek none of these things. Your need is different. Rather than enlightenment or knowledge or even treasure hunting, you wish more than anything to rid yourself of the treasure you keep next to your heart."

"Treasure?"

"You have treasure?"

"What treasure?"

Apparently, the group's goals weren't entirely limited to just *honorable and noble.*

"I thought you said you were flat busted," Orchid said, directing her comment toward Serena.

With a fearsome glare, Serena growled, "I'll show *you* who's flat busted."

She quickly unlaced the front of her jerkin and pulled the lapels apart. An audible gasp came from Tresado. He tried to choke it back, but it only turned into a pathetic whimper.

A scintillating glow came from the center of Serena's chest.

"Is that a . . . ?"

"No, it's way too big to be a . . ."

"But it is . . ."

"That's right, numb nads," snarled Serena. "It's a diamond."

* * *

In the immense expanse of time since the Gods created Lurra, the races of people that have inhabited Her have come and gone like needles on a scarum tree. They grow and thrive for a few seasons, only to eventually wither and have their dried remains pushed aside by new growth. No one can say how long the Eryndi race has existed, but ancient burial sites deep in the Spektros Mountains indicate that other forms of men pre-dating the Eryndi lived and flourished eons ago.

The race known as Macai is difficult to catalog from an anthropological point of view. Studies indicate their appearance is relatively recent, somewhere between thirty-five and sixty thousand years ago—a mere grain of the hourglass on the grand scale of time. Although a newer form of man, Macai appear to be physically inferior to the more ancient Eryndi race. Their lifespans are much shorter, they are less agile and slower than Eryndi, and they seem to lack much of the innate wisdom of their older cousins.

One could suppose that Macai are a mere evolutionary dead end, a kind of failed experiment that the Gods tried and then discarded. How then does that explain the fact that the Macai population is five times greater than that of Eryndi? A gloomy prediction might be that in the far future, Macai will eventually dominate Lurra completely, leaving the extinct Eryndi race as nothing but bones to be studied and speculated on by men such as myself. But perhaps another race will emerge to replace the Macai. Life is, after all, in a constant state of change.

—Professor Hariel, Dean of Kadizio
University – 21056 to 21172 - New Calendar

Today – The Maimed Moose Inn - Ostica

The stone was as big as a hobo clam and embedded deep in Serena's sternum, flush with the skin. It was not faceted but smooth. A close-up examination would have revealed tiny pore-like depressions that matched the contours of Serena's skin, but a close-up examination would have resulted in a jawbone driven into a brain.

The innkeeper poked his head into the room to ask if anything was needed. Serena immediately covered up before his gawking gaze could linger.

Leader quickly said, "Bring us another amphora of mead and a tray of sweet meats."

The man hesitated and sighed, then withdrew and closed the door.

Tresado mopped the perspiration from his brow. "So this diamond is the source of your . . . *troubles?*"

"That's right. It's what turns harmless rubes like you into . . . *such dorks!*" she snapped.

"It is a diamond to be sure," Leader said. "It is also . . . a *receptacle.*"

"A receptacle? For what?" asked Tresado.

"For a powerful spirit," replied Leader. "A form of intelligence unlike our own."

"It lives in the diamond?" asked Foxx.

"It only inhabits the diamond," Leader replied. "It *lives* in Serena. This spirit exists in a symbiotic manner with its host. Serena provides a living home for it, and in return, it grants the host the gift of being adored by all who meet her. I believe it actually thrives on being loved."

"It's not a gift!" Serena snarled. "It's a big pain in the ass, and I don't want this *gift* anymore! And how do you know so much about my diamond, anyway?" she demanded of Leader.

"That's amazing," Tresado interrupted, ever curious about Magic. "It's not easy to Magically influence emotion."

"Unless it's some kind of delusion," Orchid offered. "Certain Worldly spells are designed to fool the senses, the way a dragon uses Magic to lure in a victim with hallucinatory sensations."

"You're suggesting that people around Serena only *think* they love her?" Foxx replied.

Tresado angrily stood, knocking over his stool.

"I don't *think* anything! I know *exactly* what it is I feel for Serena! My emotions haven't been compromised, my senses haven't been manipulated! Serena, can't you tell? Don't you know I would do anything for you? Serena, gem or no gem, *I love you!* I only . . . OOOF!!"

Serena's snap kick to Tresado's chubby midsection doubled him over, forcing the air out of his body like a summer whirlwind.

"When they start freakin' out like that, it's the only way to handle 'em," Serena calmly said. "See why I need to get this thing out of me?"

* * *

Oh yah, there's a bunch of non-physical forms of belt intelligence that exist here. There's as much diversity among them as there is among proper life on Lurra, ya know. They dwell in the air, the water, plants, animals, even the rocks themselves. But these 'spirits' are an unpredictable bunch, ya know. Once I encountered one who passed by my place in a herd of migrating bergalos. It could have helped me, but I had nothing to offer in exchange, doncha know. The being, which I learned was female in a sense, did pull up long enough to chat for a few hours, though . . . oh yah, that was a welcome diversion . . .

—Mama's notebook – day 28434

Today – The Maimed Moose Inn - Ostica

"You seem to know much about us," Orchid said. "You know what we all want . . . that we all have reasons for wanting to go on this expedition up the river. Why do *you* want to go there?"

"And why did you recruit all of us to go along?" Foxx added.

Leader impassively answered, "Because I need you, all of you. I need your abilities and resources. Tresado, when you ask the locals what is up the river, what do they say?"

"They tell me a bunch of ridiculous stories about cannibals and monsters."

"There was also the one I heard about some castle in the mountains filled with evil witches," Orchid said.

"I heard that one too," Foxx added, "but I was told the

castle was deep in a swamp surrounded by quicksand for leagues in all directions."

"That hillbilly at the stable told me about lions the size of horses," said Serena.

"That should answer your question. Cannibals? Witches? Monsters? If these stories are even close to the truth, I will need the protection of a mighty sword arm," Leader said, nodding in Serena's direction.

"I also need Tresado's formidable Magic skills and Orchid's Worldly talents to protect me from the beasts of the wilderness. I need Foxx's diplomatic flair to protect me from the beasts of civilization and negotiate safe passage through other lands. These things I cannot do myself."

Leader looked at his prospective employees. "So, shall we consider ourselves banded together in common cause?"

To punctuate his offer, he heaved a heavy bag upon the table, which nearly collapsed under the weight. From the bag spilled a carpet of large coins, some of which fell onto the floor, musically tinkling in the way that only gold can.

The four faces at the table looked at each other and quickly nodded their affirmatives.

"Excellent," he said. "From now on, I will refer to us as *Group Six.*"

Four voices answered as one: *"Group Six?"*

"Merely a designation of mine—an *eccentricity* on my part, if you will."

What other eccentricities are in there? Foxx wondered to himself.

"I have another question," Tresado asked. "Just how are you taking us upriver anyway?"

"My dear Tresado," Leader answered, "it is *you* that is taking us . . ."

CHAPTER 3

Love is all there is, but you can't have love if you got no friends, and you got no friends if you fart in a covered wagon.

—Travelogue of Dementus, the Mad Treskan

A few years ago - Tresado

"You don't understand, My Lady. I need to know these things beforehand. If I don't have time to screen the guests, there is no way to . . ."

"I told you. Prelate Marmaduke and his sons are coming tonight, and they *are bringing their servants!* I would expect to do the same if it were me!"

"But I didn't find out until just a few minutes ago, and he has a retinue of over thirty people. The Prelate's order was in revolt only last year. There still may be some bad feeling among his followers. What if . . . ?"

"I don't care what your stupid problems are; just get out there and do your job, fat boy!"

The ornate door slammed in Tresado's face, leaving him in the hall to stew in his own juice. He had taken this job only three weeks before and hated it already. Watching over the security of the Princess's keep paid reasonably well, but putting up with her petty moods was like eating wasps. He could hear Her Royal Highness ranting at one of her body servants from behind the closed door. There was a crash of glass and something about *finding yourself scouring toilets!'*

At least I'm not the only one . . .

With an astounding amount of self-control, Tresado calmly made his way down the stairs to check on things. Princess Pamperia was a social animal, and there was another in an endless stream of parties scheduled for tonight. She had no compunction about spending piles of her mommy's gold on cotillions and grand balls. The keep would be packed with johnnies looking to marry into money. It was their only inducement, as the princess had the face of a dugong. It was Tresado's job to make sure she stayed safe and secure while she played with her boy toys.

It was actually Queen Drucilla who had hired him. She had told him in no uncertain terms that anyone who might seem like they were making headway with Pamperia was to be tossed out. Tresado, with his paunch, was not really the tossing out sort, but his Magic abilities more than made up for his lack of physical prowess. Just the other day, he ousted a fellow who had a ring, flowers, the whole bit. While proposing on bended knee, the johnnie suddenly found himself levitated out an open window and dumped unceremoniously into the moat. Luckily for him, he managed to swim out before the sewer eels took too many bites.

The upper floor and main hall were secure. The guards were in place, and there were no traps, Magical or otherwise, to be found. Tresado headed for the kitchen to check the food and drink for anything harmful. He didn't think that was all that necessary, but carried on anyway. No one really wanted to harm the Princess, only take advantage of her. But there was always the possibility of a kidnapping. The Queen would probably pay handsomely to get Pamperia back, though he couldn't imagine why. Drucilla did have eleven other daughters, after all.

Surely this one wouldn't be missed, thought Tresado.

Oddly, there was no one working the kitchen when he entered. Voices were coming from outside. Tresado flattened himself against the wall and worked his way toward the open door. As he got closer, he began to make out what was being said. He froze just out of sight and listened.

"Comin' around, comin' around, next shooter."

"Five *paleens* on a fourteen, two *paleens* on the hard way and a *tormac* on rock the boat . . . be good to me, now . . . here we go, here we go . . ."

Venture cubes rattled in a cup, followed by howling and laughter.

"HA HA! Pay up, sucker!"

"Ohhh, you sharks are too good for me. That leaves me busted."

"Hey dude, come back any time; your money is always good here."

"If I come back here, I'll be wearing a barrel. So, the Princess pay you guys pretty good here?"

"Cah-rap, you kiddin' me?"

"The Princess is tighter with a gendrin than a beggar's bookie."

"She keeps a close eye on things?"

"Like what?"

"Oh, you know, I bet there's a lot of money and royal goodies in a joint like this."

"Oh yeah, oh yeah. You should see the sparklies that she decks herself out with."

"What, like jewelry and stuff?"

"Bracelets, necklaces, rings . . . she gots a tiara with a big ol' ruby on the front."

"She likes that kind of stuff, does she?"

"More like she needs it. Keeps 'em from lookin' at her face."

Laughter.

"She must got a bunch of goons to guard that stuff."

"Yeah, there's a couple dozen soldier-boys that watch things."

"I wonder how good *that* job pays."

"Why, you lookin' for work?"

"Hey I need to do somethin' to get back on my feet after losing my lunch money to you guys."

"Well, we hope you find somethin' here at the keep. We'd kinda like to have you around here, ya know?"

"Yeah, I bet you would. So who's the person in charge around here? I might just have to ask about a security job."

"Well, there's a new guy that just started . . . an Ernie. He's one of them *Magicians.*"

It was at this point that Tresado decided to move in. This slick talker, who had obviously lost on purpose, was using these kitchen rats to find out about palace security. Tresado had learned that nobody knew more about the inner workings of an establishment than the hired help. He stepped out the door into plain view.

"Evening, boys. Nice night."

The gamblers immediately scooped up their winnings and dice and headed back into the kitchen door. The one exception was the stranger, who took advantage of that distraction to slip behind a tree trunk and start to edge away. Tresado was not fooled, however, and focused on the departing Macai.

"Just a moment, please, sir."

Tresado's thoughts formed the Magic of the air into a giant invisible hand that firmly grabbed the man around his middle, stopping him in his tracks. Tresado mirrored the action with his own hand and pulled the man back.

"Going somewhere, friend?"

The Macai squirmed in the unseen grip, but remained calm.

"I believe I am looking for you, sir," he said. "I assume from your imposing demeanor that you are the person in charge."

"Looking for me, are you?" Tresado asked. "And who might you be?"

"Just a humble traveler seeking gainful employment," the man replied.

Tresado noticed how the man's speech had changed from when he was interacting with the kitchen staff. Now he was sophisticated and polished, and Tresado couldn't help thinking that maybe this had been just a misunderstanding.

"I am sure we can reach an accommodation," he said sincerely. "My name is Foxx—that's with two *exes*." The Macai crossed his fingers and held both hands to his chest. "And I am so very pleased to meet you."

Today – The Maimed Moose Inn - Ostica

The spark of life was slowly dying away in the last embers in the hearth. The same could be said of the few remaining customers of the Maimed Moose Inn. One was face down in his bowl of *gruft*, snoring quietly. There were two others, each at their own table, blearily contemplating empty glasses.

Leader had since said his goodnights and retired to his room upstairs. Tresado, Foxx, Orchid, and Serena sat staring at each other. Each one was contemplating the upcoming adventure.

"I'd be interested in hearing everybody's opinion about this," said Foxx.

"What do you want to know?" asked Serena as she grabbed another handful of salted sand pods.

"I, for one, would like to know more about our fearless Leader," replied Orchid with a hiccup. She always did drink a bit too much. "Did you notice how he avoided the question of why *he* wants to go upriver?"

"And what's with this *Group Six* crap?" Serena asked through a mouthful.

"Maybe he's tried this trip five times before and failed," offered Orchid.

"If true," wondered Foxx, "he never mentioned what became of his first companions."

"The guy likes his secrets," said Serena. "He doesn't exactly give a lot away, does he?"

"He gives away enough," said a gloating Tresado, who was a bit in his cups himself from celebrating his recent good fortune. For the seventeenth time, he perused the ownership and registry papers that Leader had bestowed upon him before retiring.

"Thanks to Leader, I'm now the free and clear owner of my very own brand new boat. Anybody who would do that can't be all bad."

"At least," Serena said with a glare at Tresado, "he doesn't piss himself every time he looks at me."

Tresado ignored her. He was just too tickled with his good fortune. "Well, anyway, I've got a new boat! I can't wait to see her tomorrow morning."

Orchid sounded skeptical, but then she always did. "Pretty generous, wasn't it? How much did he shell out for that?"

"It had to be more than four hundred tormacs," Tresado said. "I didn't think I could afford to go upriver for a year or so."

"You were going upriver?" Serena asked. "Since when?"

"I've wanted to go upriver for years," Tresado said. "Just a couple of months ago, I hired a shipwright to build a boat that I designed to do just that, but I didn't have the funds to finish it."

"Apparently Leader had it finished for you," said Orchid. "Did you know he was going to do that?"

"I wasn't aware he even *knew* about my boat." Tresado turned to his old friend, Foxx. "When it *was* finished, I was planning to hunt you up and ask you to come along."

"So Leader found out about your boat and had it finished for you," Serena said. "Maybe he really doesn't give a crap about you. Maybe he just needs your boat."

"If that were the case," said Orchid, "why wouldn't he just steal it?"

Tresado sat back with a smug look.

"Anyone who would use this boat," he said, "will need to have me along."

* * *

Macai Magic, Eryndi Magic, dragon Magic, spirit Magic . . . all have unique signatures that a skilled Magician can recognize. The different races each have a distinct resonance or tendency to their Magic because of the way their minds channel the energy. Macai, for example, invariably want to control. Their Magic tends to be obtrusive and rather vulgar.

—HIGH ELDER ALLORAN; KUERGALAN SCHOOL FOR ADVANCED COLLABORATIVE STUDIES – YEAR OF PROPHECY 13781, OLD ERYNDI CALENDAR

Today - Corsairs' Wharf - Ostica

Bunky Boatwright was just finishing painting the name on one of the pontoons.

ENCHANTER

"There she is. Oh, look at that . . ." Tresado said tearfully.

The boat was unlike any other vessel on the wharf. A small crowd could always be found loitering about, mostly old sailor-types who scoffed and chortled at the odd design. One old salt said, "Sink me if that ain't the queerest thing on the water. Nail the dining room table onto a pair of canoes, add a mast with half a sail, and down you go to Uncle Bob's Cantina."

A chorus of chuckles followed the remark. Tresado bristled but was too enthralled with his new boat to bother with the hecklers. It did, however, somewhat resemble what the sailor had said. The craft floated upon two matching pontoons, connected on top with a flat wooden deck. A steering oar was mounted on the stern. The single mast, tightly stayed to the pontoons, thrust up from the center of the deck. The furled sail was connected to a hinged boom at the bottom, which was also snug against the mast. Just astern of the mast was the peculiar thing. An upright brass cylinder was mounted on some kind of wooden tubing that disappeared down into the deck. It had a heavy hinged lid at the top with a lever mounted on the side that apparently was meant to move forward or backward.

"This is how we're getting up the river, on *that?*" Serena inquired. "It looks like a snow sledge like we had in the homeland."

"I like it," Orchid said. "It's got an organic feel to it."

Foxx studied the flimsy craft. "Not exactly an argosy, is it?"

"Ah, Mr. Tresado, you're here." Bunky put down his paintbrush and ran forward.

"What do you think of her? She won't stand up to no major storm, but she'll be hard-pressed to sink. I figure that even with half of the pontoon bladders punctured, she'll still stay afloat, unless . . ." Bunky stuck out his tongue so he could think, "that half were all on one side, maybe. But she's light as a feather and only draws ten fingers when fully loaded."

Bunky took Tresado by the arm and gave him the grand tour, pointing out little features here and there. He demonstrated the boom and triangular sail, the steering oar and the detachable oarlocks, showing how they were stowed. He explained the construction, the waterproofing methods, and finally ended with the tubing system.

"This is just like you designed, but scuttle me if I can figure out what you're gonna do with it."

"You've done a fantastic job, Bunky," Tresado said,

changing the subject. "Really first-rate and way ahead of schedule."

Bunky beamed at the compliment, "Well, that money you sent was what made all the difference. With the extra help I managed to hire, we got her done fast . . . and much obliged for the bonus too. That'll keep me and the missus in fishcakes for a while."

Tresado glanced over at Leader, who was talking with someone over on the pier.

"Yeah, uh, my pleasure."

"Well anyhow," Bunky said, "she's ready for the sea, and there's still a week's worth of dock rent paid for."

But we're not going to sea, Tresado thought to himself.

"Thanks, Bunky," Tresado said. "Thanks for everything." They shook hands, and Bunky skipped away.

By now, Leader had finished his conversation and joined the group.

"Are you satisfied?" he asked.

"She's a beauty. Just what I, *we* need to get upriver."

"I'm pleased," Leader replied, deadpan. "The arrangements are set. The supplies will be arriving within the hour. We should be able to get them loaded and set off before Midday."

"Today? We're leaving *today?"* Tresado asked, dumbfounded. "But we need to take her out for some test runs, get the feel of how she handles. I need to test . . ." Tresado glanced around and lowered his voice, "the drive system."

"All of which can be easily accomplished while traveling up the river delta. The first several days' travel will be spent in civilized waters. Ample time for training," Leader said.

Despite the lack of expression, Tresado could tell that Leader was serious. He turned toward his comrades.

"Does everybody have their toothbrush?"

CHAPTER 4

15 years ago - Foxx's high school graduation

SLAP!

The girl stomped away, gathering her flowing gown about her legs as she moved. The big, red handprint on Foxx's young cheek still stung. Nevertheless, he managed to call out to her.

"Lumperia, wait! I didn't mean that I . . . I mean, *I do*, but . . ."

By now, his fellow graduate had disappeared around a corner, leaving Foxx disgusted with himself.

"Ohhh, why can't I ever say the right thing?"

Turning back toward the school building, Foxx came face to face with six much larger classmates, who had apparently just witnessed his humiliating incident with Lumperia. The embarrassed look on his face was too much to resist. As one, the group howled with laughter.

"What's the matter, Foxxy?" asked Broog. "Having girl trouble?"

"Ahh, poor Foxxy. The girls won't play with him."

"You sure you even know what girls are, Foxxy?"

"Yeah, they're the round soft things."

Each witty *bon mot* was accompanied by a shoulder shove. The boys now surrounded Foxx and were batting him back and forth like a boingball. His first instinct was to fight, but Foxx knew he would get his butt kicked by even one of these guys. He decided to try to talk his way out of this fix like his father had advised him last week.

"Son," he had said between gulps, *"There is nothing honorable in fighting. It is far nobler to convince your enemies that violence only . . ."* It was at this point that Dad hiccupped and passed out. He never could hold his grub wine.

With nothing to lose, Foxx tried it anyway. "Look fellas, this is graduation night. We're probably never going to see each other again, so let's be friends."

Gorlik replied, "But we don't want to be no friends with no worm like you, Foxxy."

"Yeah," added Shplick. "If we wanted worm friends, we'd be worms, too."

"Yeah, c'mere, wormy!" Gorlik then spun his victim around and reached under the back of his graduation robe. A moment later, Foxx's underwear was wrapped around his tonsils. Spacklin gave him a final shove which flipped him backward over Horis's outstretched leg. Foxx went down on his back, nursing a bad wedgie and a severely bruised ego.

"So long, wormy! Have a nice day!"

The boys swaggered away, laughing and hooting. Foxx painfully stood, pulled the linen out of his buttcrack, and squeaked out a defiant retort.

"Oh, yeah?!"

Thoughts of revenge flooded Foxx's brain, but he couldn't come up with a plan that didn't end in his death or worse—a public pantsing. He headed slowly back toward the arena for the graduation ceremony, thinking how glad he was that all this school crap was about to finally end.

Here we go, here we go, here we go now;
Follow the sunrise, dead on the bow;
Come with me, come with me, come with me now;
Sailing to morning, you and me, wow!

— Ancient Eryndi nursery rhyme

Vinday, Tono 39-21876 – Day 9 on the Talus River – Tresado has finally decided that his boat is properly "tested." Apparently "max acceleration," as he calls it, is more violent than expected. As a result, he promised to install a safety rail after Foxx fell overboard during a violent lurch forward. Damned funny, though. Now that the bubble drive tests are over, we've settled down to a steady pace as we head against the slow flow of water.

Most of the time, there is a convenient westerly wind coming off the sea. Using that, we can tack back and forth on the wide river, making slow progress against the gentle current. When the wind fails, Tresado uses his motive Magic to propel us along. That does have its disadvantages, though. For one thing, it tires out Tresado, as he must constantly focus on forcing the boat upriver. The other problem is mine to bear. Being around that constant flow of Absolute Magic gives me a headache.

In its wisdom, the water deems it proper to flow downhill, and the objects that float upon it are content to do the same. It all seems so demanding of me. One of these days, Nature is going to do some demanding of Her own.

I have to admit, though, I've never seen anyone with more locomotive power to his spells than Tresado. He is able to propel a boat loaded with five people and supplies against the will of the Talus River. We make anywhere between five and fifteen leagues per day, depending on the moods of wind and water. Of course, Tresado could be putting his little coins in the bubble drive, but he says he's saving them for when they're really needed.

After a week of travel, we're finally leaving civilization behind. It's been more than a day since we passed the last farms. The terrain is more barren and sandy. Far ahead, we can see smoke from some sort of settlement, and beyond that, the canopy of what looks like a rain forest. It's restful out here, but as much as cities bother my senses, I don't like the look of that jungle ahead.

Something feels wrong . . .

—ORCHID'S JOURNAL

Today – The Talus River

The building was old but not too dilapidated. It looked like it had been built out of flat stones harvested from nearby ancient ruins that were strewn about the area. It was situated on top of a sandy rise overlooking the convergence of two tributaries. The one to the north was known as the Osagar and flowed from the mountains of the Northlands. The other was called Palantus and was born somewhere deep in the Treskan Imperium, far to the south. Here the two small rivers joined the great Talus like ducklings following their mother.

A faded sign advertised *GRANNY'S END OF THE LINE – TRADING, SUPPLIES, SPIRITS.* A variety of horses and mules were tethered outside, indicating the small amount of business that was taking place.

Enchanter was tied up to a long pier. Serena didn't want to be forced to decapitate some drooling yokel, so she had not gone into the trading post. She and Orchid were securing a few supplies that Leader had purchased while Tresado stood by at the tiller, apparently anxious to get going again. He kept his eye on Foxx, who was still ashore, talking to a crusty-looking local.

The Macai had a pinched expression, as though he smelled something terrible. His whiskered cheeks held the remains of at least three previous meals, not to mention what appeared to be several years' worth of chewing bark stains.

"My ol' pap used to haul horse grain up to the miners and bring back copper. He said that when the wind was just right, he could hear the drums way off in the distance. That mine is since played out, though. Ain't nobody been up there since I was jes' a yonker. Nowadays, nobody goes past Keffer's Bend. The river crocs get thicker every year, and the trees are full of them poison monkeys. It jes' ain't worth it."

The guy seemed to be about as dumb as a wagonload of goat turds, but Foxx believed the man's sincerity. His stories might or might not be true, but the fella believed them to be so.

" 'Preciate it," Foxx said, dropping into the same inland country accent. "Thank ya, friend . . . here, for yer hospitality."

He tossed a tormac to the man, who caught it in his

manure-stained hand. It was one of several hundred that Leader had doled out as payment for Group Six's services. The gold coin was probably a month's earnings for this guy.

"Much obliged, much obliged. If'n ya need anything on the way back, stop and see us again. What's your name, friend?"

"Name's Foxx . . . that's with two exes." He crossed the fingers on both hands and held them to his chest in his time-honored signature gesture.

"That's that readin' stuff, ain't it? 'Fraid I never was much of a hand at that," the guy said as he held out his hand.

"I'm Charley, but ever'body calls me 'Two-Poop.'"

Foxx had no desire to know why, so he didn't ask. He shook the fella's hand and wondered what diseases he had just caught.

"Still cain't believe you want to go upriver. Sure you won't change yer mind?"

Foxx hocked a loogie before answering because that's what one would do here.

"Nope," he answered. "Got some bidness to take care of. So long, friend . . . and we'll catch ya on the flip-flop."

Two-Poop Charley watched Foxx's retreating back as it headed to the end of the pier towards that funny-looking boat. He bit into the coin, not really knowing why.

"Cain't see there bein' no flip-flop . . . friend," he muttered quietly.

12,614 years from today

Good evening and welcome, this is News 16, I'm Wayne Collins. A Riveropolis man was convicted today in District

Court. Twenty-three-year-old Roger Jenson was found guilty of seven counts of unlicensed, personal use of magic in Orbin of last year. For more on this story, we go to Tiffany Lucas. Tiffany, what was the mood around the courthouse today?

Thank you, Wayne. After having been sequestered for more than two days, the jurors finally came to their decision, arriving back in court at Midday today. They found the defendant, Roger Jenson, guilty on all counts. As you know, there has been much controversy during the arguments of this trial. Proponents for the lifting of the Personal Magic Ban have been holding demonstrations outside the courthouse. Judge Clarisse Steinman had ordered the courtroom cleared of all visitors after several disturbances had erupted during the sixteen days of trial. After the verdict was read, District Attorney Ken Jackson had this to say:

'I would like to applaud our prosecution team, who have done an excellent, thorough job during a very difficult trial. There is no denying that the personal use of magic is a highly debatable subject, but the law is the law. There is also no denying what a highly dangerous practice it can be. That is why there are tight governmental controls on its proper use. Energy capable of powering a hundred reach warship is simply too potentially destructive to allow the unrestricted use of it by individuals. Laws such as this exist for the protection and safety of all.'

Tiffany, can we assume that this is not the end of the matter after two weeks of this highly charged trial?

That is a very safe assumption, Wayne. The argument of personal freedoms versus governmental safety controls is sure to continue. Mr. Jenson's attorneys have vowed to appeal this decision to Ultimate Court. In the meantime, Jenson has been returned to the Talus County Internment Center's custody to await sentencing. This is Tiffany Lucas, News 16.

Thank you, Tiffany. We'll have more on this trial on our six o'clock broadcast.

13 years ago - Foxx

"You wish to study Magic, do you?"

Sage Marison looked up from his plate of hanzel sprouts and glared at the young huckster with obvious contempt.

"I do, sir."

The grizzled old Macai took a long look at the gangly young Macai. "Why, in Nyha's name?"

"Well, let me tell you, sir," Foxx began, summoning up his recently honed oratory skills. "You simply couldn't do better than to accept me as a student."

Foxx took a step backward and adopted a wide stance. He spoke as much with his hands as with his voice. Each movement was carefully orchestrated to draw attention to himself and to accent his words. So far, the scowl on the Eryndi's face had not lessened. This was obviously going to be a tough audience of one.

"Why, there's no one in the world who will work as hard as I . . . no one in the world more dedicated to being your student, sir."

Foxx was really warming up now. He was in his element.

"I promise you, sir, if you accept me into your school, my devotion to learning will amaze and astound you! From the wilds of the Northlands to the farthest reaches of the Treskan Imperium, there is no one person, be they Macai or Eryndi, who . . ."

"You are part of that traveling *show*, are you not?"

Sage Marison's withering tone made Foxx pause for a moment. He wasn't ready to give up quite yet but now was pretty sure he had lost this sale.

"*Professor Generax and His Traveling World of Wonders,* yes sir! We have traveled the length and breadth of the known world, presenting for our audiences' consideration a variety of instructional and morally uplifting exhibits and displays which are guaranteed to . . ."

"I hear that among those exhibits is a curtained-off booth signed *Donkey Daisy's Den of Debauchery.*"

Foxx gulped but otherwise kept in character. "I'm sure there is some mix-up. Undoubtedly, what you speak of is part of some other unscrupulous group. May I ask who told you of such an outrageous thing?"

"About half of my students . . . the *male* half."

Marison turned back to his salad and waved Foxx off. "On your way, young man. I have no time for you."

Foxx held his ground for one last try. "Sir, *Master*, I assure you, I apply for entrance to your honored school with only the best and noblest of intentions."

"And I was not born last Gleeday," Sage Marison replied. "The use of Magic . . . the *proper* use of Magic is taught to only the most principled and ethical of students. It is not for cheap carnival barkers who would use it only to deceive."

With an air of finality, the sage speared the last succulent sprout, picked up his stack of books on the table, and left the café.

Foxx was disgusted. This was the fourth sage in as many towns that he had unsuccessfully petitioned for a Magical education. Apparently, all Magical adepts were of the same snooty, judgmental sort. If there was one thing he had learned in his past year and a half with the troupe, it was that no one was exactly as they seemed. All people, whether Macai or Eryndi, projected a distorted image of themselves to some extent. All Foxx wanted was the ability to use Magic to enhance and adapt his own persona. Such a skill could earn him a fortune.

Foxx sighed and turned to head back to the troupe when a thought struck him. He looked back toward the café. The stooped back of Sage Marison was just disappearing around a corner. Foxx began to follow even as a plan was forming in his head.

Today – The Talus River

Ah-rahh! Ah-rahh! Woooop, woooop!

The farther up the Talus River the *Enchanter* sailed, the darker, creepier, and noisier the jungle became. Sinuous ripples moved around the boat, hinting at something under the surface. Furtive movements in the trees rustled the canopy as the vessel slowly tacked upstream. Serena stood at the prow, her bow at the ready. She sent a shaft into the river several times, hoping to score a hit on whatever was swimming around down there. None of them apparently found a target, so she gave up before she ran out of arrows.

Orchid kept a close eye on the passing riverbanks. She could sense the presence of the trees and some of the creatures that lived in them. That much was agreeable to her Worldly psyche, but there was something more, something that didn't belong. Instead, what should have been a pleasant experience was filled with foreboding, and she did not know why. For the nine-thousandth time, Orchid wondered if an Eryndi could have sensed more. She thrust the thought from her mind and kept concentrating.

Foxx kept the sail and rigging in trim while Tresado manned the tiller. Fortunately, the slow current and westerly breeze made his Magical abilities unnecessary for now. *Enchanter* was making slow progress on her own, tacking back and forth between banks. Nevertheless, Tresado kept his "special box" nearby.

Even though there was no apparent danger at the moment, nerves were on edge. There was just something about this jungle that gave everyone the creeps; everyone but Leader, that is. He calmly sat near the stern, trailing a fishing line behind the boat.

"There's something out there," Serena whispered. "Something that won't show itself."

"I *think* you're right," said Orchid.

"You sense something?" asked Foxx in a hushed tone.

"It's what I *don't* sense that I . . . I just don't know," said Orchid with a worried look. "This cursed river! I can detect plenty of life, but it's as though there are more living things than . . . what are *alive.*"

"Whoa, what do you mean cursed?" asked Serena. "You think the river has a curse on it?"

"I didn't say *cursed.* I said *cur-sed!*" replied Orchid. "It depends on where you put the accent."

Serena persisted, "But you *did* say the river is cursed."

"How could something like a river be cursed?" said Foxx.

Orchid was already edgy. Now she was getting pissed. "Look, I never said anything about a curse on the river! There isn't even such a thing as a curse."

"You're the one who started the talk about curses," Serena countered. "If there's no such thing, how come you said . . . ?"

"I NEVER SAID THE RIVER WAS CURSED! I just said that there's something out there that bothers me!"

"You said you *can't* sense anything. Which is it?"

"Serena, I don't know, okay?" Orchid said between her teeth. "I'm just bothered, and I don't know why, okay? Okay!!?"

Tresado asked, "Are you sure you're not overreacting? We *have* heard a lot of fantastic stories lately."

Foxx shifted the boom over to go on the other tack, then said, "I don't know. Some of those stories were pretty convincing."

"Like what?" asked Tresado.

Foxx watched the water ripple behind the boat. "Like *river crocs,* five or six reaches long."

Tresado was skeptical. "Who told you that?"

"Two-Poop Charley at the trading post."

"Too-Pooped?" replied Serena. "What, was he always tired or something?"

"No, I think it . . . oh never mind," Foxx answered. "But this guy has lived on the river his whole life and swears that the water is full of these giant lizard things. And he also talked about some kind of poisonous monkeys that live in the trees. One touch and you're covered with mushrooms. He believed it, so I believe it."

At that, Serena took a firmer grip on her bow. Tresado grabbed a coin from his box and kept it at the ready. Foxx took note of the nearest land. Orchid made a ceremonial gesture, and all nervously kept swiveling their heads.

A sudden splash from astern!

Everyone gasped and jumped. Serena pivoted at the speed of thought and aimed a deadly arrow at the source of the sound. She lowered it quickly because it was only Leader's bamboo fishing pole, which was twitching. He calmly started pulling his line in. A fine-looking silver fish, at least thirty fingers long, leapt out of the water, trying to dislodge the hook in his mouth.

"I'm sorry if our forthcoming lunch has startled you, Gentlefolk." Leader bent over the stern to retrieve the fish. "Perhaps this will serve to remind you that you are simply allowing yourselves to succumb to hysterical paranoia. These stories have no basis in fact. There is absolutely nothing to fear from . . ."

The fish suddenly disappeared in an explosive frenzy of water and sharp teeth. A set of jaws the length of a man erupted from the water and snapped shut on Leader's prize, mere fingers from his fingers.

Technically, Tresado did crap his pants, but not seriously enough to impede his reflexes. He quickly dropped his Magic coin into the Bubble Drive's fuel canister and threw open the flue. The currency exploded in a Magical surge of fizzy bubble action. The open throttle released all the energy out of the exhaust tubes along the insides of the pontoons. *Enchanter* leapt forward with a furious wake of foaming water surging out her stern. This blast of bubbles erupted in the face of the croc, who was just contemplating taking a bite out of this sizable floating prey. The bubble wake blinded him momentarily, just long enough for the boat to surge forward out of reach of his jaws. Foxx, from experience, knew now to hang on. He had no desire to be pitched into the water at this particular time.

Serena again aimed and fired faster than the eye could track, despite the pitching deck beneath her feet. Her steel-tipped shaft squelched into the great beast's skull just below its right eye. The croc screamed out a hissing challenge while pawing frantically at the offending arrow.

Tresado kept the throttle open for another half-minute, then reduced speed when it was evident that the croc was not pursuing. Group Six watched the massive, writhing reptile behind them. The creature was as large as *Enchanter*. The head itself was a full reach wide and packed full of teeth as long as one's hand.

As soon as everyone released their death grips on whatever they were holding onto, Leader faced them unflappably.

"Or not."

* * *

The different ways Magic can be used by people are as varied as people themselves. Magic knows no morals and has no convictions. It takes no pride in what it can accomplish, nor does it express regret when used nefariously. Indeed, Magic does not possess intelligence or awareness of any kind. Much like a brain with no mind, Magic is simply a natural phenomenon with organizational properties . . . but it does wish to be used.

—SAGE MARISON, *CHALLENGES AND ETHICS OF BASIC MAGIC USE 101*

13 years ago - Foxx

Foxx remained hidden in the shadows behind the walls of the old collapsed temple. The rubble provided a screen from the sharp eyes of the constabulary searching the neighborhood at this very moment. It would be dark in less than an hour, and Foxx was willing to wait for it. When he was sure that the coppers had given up, he secreted his prizes in the folds of his clothing so that at first glance, it didn't look like he was carrying a sack of stolen books. Foxx then emerged from hiding and headed back toward the edge of town where his troupe was encamped, keeping to the back lanes as much as possible. He passed city guards patrolling the streets several times but managed to look innocent enough to not get challenged.

Eventually, the wagons and tents bearing the name of *Professor Generax* came into view. Foxx passed the anthropoid cages and gaming tents. Taking a shortcut through the main performance tent, he nodded greetings to a couple members of the Hanky-Pank Dancers, who were taking an opiate break. Tonight's show had ended a half-hour ago, and the various performers were winding down.

Exiting the far side of the large pavilion, Foxx headed for a line of ragged tents that housed most of the employees. Before he could reach it, he was accosted by Grumban, the manager.

"And just where were you while there was work to be done, huh?" The large, greasy Macai scratched his groin and gave Foxx the evil eye.

"Sorry, boss. It couldn't be helped. I was . . ."

"You was out not doin' your job, that's what you was doin'!" Grumban's fish and liquor breath slammed into Foxx's face like a thrown brick. "I've had it with you, Slick! Get your crap and clear out. NOW!"

Foxx had a dozen responses he could have made, but he choked them all back and just nodded. He turned away and headed for the third shelter from the end that he shared with two lice-ridden clowns and Fru-Fru the Decorated Giant. It only took a moment to gather his few possessions, all under the watchful eye of the stinky manager, who followed him in.

Probably wants to make sure I don't steal anything, Foxx thought to himself. *There's no trust left in the world these days.*

Without a word, Foxx left the home he had known for more than a year and headed toward the road out of town. He was not too disappointed in losing this job. His acquisition of Sage Marison's Magical texts was the key to his future. If no one was willing to teach him to use Magic, Foxx would just have to learn it by himself.

The tomes were a diverse lot, but they all specialized in variations of Absolute Magic. A textbook on kinetic Magic, another on transmutations, a lab manual on infusion Magic, and most important to Foxx, a volume titled *Influential Spell Use*. Each one was prefaced with a warning lecture from old Marison. There seemed to be a strong undertone of morality in all his works, but Foxx was pretty sure he could work around that. All he needed now was time and some peace and quiet to learn this stuff.

CHAPTER 5

Anthropological studies indicate that Macai, Eryndi, and the various sub-species and mutations on Lurra all share common needs and desires, such as nourishment, security, comfort, companionship, etc., despite broad physical and cultural differences. That much is not surprising. It is amazing how such disparate creatures can also share traits like sacrifice, compassion, and mercy, as well as territoriality, selfishness, and xenophobia. Apparently, you're pretty much the same animal whether you're a city-dwelling Eryndi or a flint napping Macai who worships the four winds . . .

—Starfish archival sphere 61

Today – The Talus River

There was no fresh fish, so lunch consisted of jerked bergalo and dried sand pods. That was all right with everyone, as they were still at a heightened state of alert. They passed a sandbar jutting out from the jungle and noted with interest the three giant crocs grinning at them as they basked in the sun.

The coin that Tresado had used to avoid the first croc still had some remaining energy, so *Enchanter* was running on bubble power until that ran out. He opened the throttle a notch until they got past the reptiles, which eyed them hungrily.

"Nasty big things," commented Foxx.

"I find them quite magnificent," replied Orchid. "They're no different than any other creature that's trying to survive. Whether it's lions or ants or even people . . . they just do what they do."

"If they try to do what they do to me," said Serena, "I'm gonna do what *I* do to *them* first."

"In fact," she continued, "I think it would be a good idea to do a little preemptive strike on critters like that; wipe 'em out before they can figure out a way to do the same to us. Look at 'em back there, scheming and plotting the best way to have us for lunch."

Orchid looked pityingly at Serena. "That is really an offensive attitude. These crocs are just simple life forms that exist in nature alongside everything else, including you. They do not *scheme and plot*. They simply act on instinct."

* * *

What say you, Sir Humphrey, shall we actively pursue and devour the passing bipeds who float upon Mother River?

'Tis a tempting proposition, Milady Agatha. Such creatures would indeed provide for a sumptuous repast, methinks. Lord Bertram, shall we have at them?

Would that I were not settled in comfort upon the sand. Indeed, how the sun doth warm my skin! Such exertion is beyond my desire for sustenance at this time. Apologies, Milady.

Pray, do not concern yourself, Milord. Another culinary opportunity shall present itself anon.

Today – The Talus River

Enchanter continued for another thirteen days through the dark jungle. At times the canopy closed in so tightly that the top of the mast barely cleared the low hanging branches. There was little breeze, and Group Six (including Leader) took turns at the oars to spare Tresado constant Magical stress. The sun could not penetrate the thick foliage, and perpetual darkness enveloped those portions of the river despite it being the middle of the day. When needed, Tresado created a Magical burning white light that hovered around the boat at his command and lit their way. Weird shadows danced about as it moved, increasing the creepiness of their surroundings. Mixed among the birdcalls and monkey chattering was an occasional high-pitched, throaty scream, suggesting the granddaddy of all panthers. The death bleats of victims could usually be heard after those roars.

"Not exactly the Tunnel of Love," observed Foxx.

There was movement up ahead. Something seemed to be sliding into the water from the muddy bank. At first, it looked like a large log slowly sinking below the water. A closer look revealed it to be a snake of some kind as big around as a man. It took a full minute for the whole creature to disappear below the surface.

"So Serena," said Tresado nervously, "just how well does your diamond work against snakes?"

"Not so good, I'm afraid," she said, readying her bow. "It's never had much effect on animals."

Fortunately, that didn't seem a problem this time, as the snake didn't reappear.

"You never did tell us how you got that thing," said Orchid.

"Long story," Serena replied.

"We have time."

"Fine," she sighed. "What's one more telling? It was about four years ago . . ."

About four years ago - The Northlands – Serena

Serena was particularly proud of her precious sword. Technically classed as a scimitar, it had a heavier, thicker blade, more like a falchion. It had been folded twelve times during forging, creating a beautiful, layered pattern in the steel, which she kept honed to a razor edge. The long, reverse curved hilt was capped by a heavy brass pommel, creating a perfectly balanced weapon. It was not nearly as heavy as the broadswords some of her fellow warriors carried, but she was damned fast with it. The long pommel's counterbalance allowed her to whirl the blade about faster than the eye could follow, whether on foot or from the saddle.

The fine steel must be kept clean and oiled, so Serena jumped off her horse and yanked the sash off of the barbarian whose head she had just split. She used the cloth to wipe the gore off her dripping blade. She knew that blood would corrode the metal if left on too long, and Serena was ever respectful of her equipment.

She kicked the corpse out of the way and looked around for more enemies. There were none anywhere near. The barbarians were in retreat, and her fellow Northlanders were mopping up the few remaining stragglers. The incursion into their homeland had been driven off easily and Serena looked forward to the inevitable celebration that night in the longhouse. Such parties involved a great deal of boisterous singing and drinking to excess, which was exactly what she wanted to do tonight.

The man leading today's battle, Eymon the Rank, was half a league away from Serena bellowing orders to his warriors from up on the ridge. He was a very large Macai, at the moment wearing a necklace of fourteen freshly harvested left ears, trophies from today's victories. It was a great honor for those victims who fell beneath his axe in today's skirmish. By adorning Eymon's neck, the ears (where the soul resided) were guaranteed a place in the afterlife, there to await Eymon's arrival as his servants. What more could any ignorant barbarian ask for?

During the battle, Serena had become somewhat separated from the others while chasing down that last guy. With no more enemies to fight, she sheathed her sword and started walking back to regroup with the others, leading her overheated horse. She had taken only a dozen steps when a low moan came from somewhere ahead. The charred, smoking ruins of a farmhouse lay nearby, apparently destroyed by the invaders. A still figure lay near the water well, half covered with collapsed debris.

Some poor, innocent farmer murdered by barbarians, thought Serena. *They should be slaughtered to the last man, woman, and child for invading civilized countries.*

She warily approached the figure. You never can tell when it's a barbarian trick. The dead body moaned again, and Serena could tell there was something different about this corpse; it was still alive. The man was obviously not a Northlander, nor a barbarian. He wasn't even a Macai. The man was one of those Ernies that Serena had always heard about but never seen. She noted the cone-shaped ears and the long, pointed chin and the arrow sticking out of his neck. Serena decided that the latter item was not a racial trait and moved closer.

A sudden feeling of caring and a desire to help came over her. It was a new kind of sensation for Serena and she wasn't sure exactly how to feel about it. All she knew was that this man needed help. Quickly, she pulled away the debris that was covering his legs and belly. The action roused the man slightly. He looked up at her and coughed up some blood in greeting. Serena knelt down next to him. There was no choice; she simply had to help in any way she could.

"What's your name, friend?"

"Par-Parsomal."

"Par-so-mal." Serena struggled to pronounce the unfamiliar, foreign sounding name. "Parsomal, my name is Serena. I'm going to do everything I can for you."

"We were too far away," he said weakly, "too far away . . ."

Serena ran to her horse and dug into the saddlebags, pulling out a portable tool kit and a flask of grain alcohol. She again knelt down by the Eryndi and opened the flask.

". . . there's nothing it can do when we're too far away . . ."

"I'm so sorry, Parsomal, but this is going to hurt."

Serena poured a bit of the liquid around the wound. Serena didn't know why this was helpful, but her clan's healers said that this action would prevent the wound from rotting. She then took a crude pair of nippers out of her kit and cut off the arrow shaft. The arrowhead remained buried in the man's neck, but there was little she could do about that. If she yanked it out, the man would bleed to death faster than he already was. At least now there wasn't a half-reach of shaft sticking out.

Due to the serious nature of the wound, this was all Serena or anyone could have done for the man, and she knew it. Nevertheless, she was frantic to find some way to help the poor fellow.

Parsomal seemed to know as well as Serena what was about to happen. With his last bit of strength, he reached into his tunic. A strange look flickered across his face, his hand grasping an object. Whatever it was, he thrust it towards Serena and dropped it in front of her.

"Take it," he whispered. "It wants you to take it."

"Don't talk, Parsomal, lie still," Serena said, daubing at his neck.

Parsomal spoke his last words, "Thank you for all you've done."

Maybe that was a natural enough thing to say, but Serena got the impression he wasn't talking to her. Parsomal looked up at her one last time, smiled, and nodded slightly. Then he died.

Serena laid the man down, suddenly not feeling quite so sad anymore. She searched the body in an attempt to find out more about this strange fellow. From his belongings, he was a traveler. He carried maps of the Northlands, which Serena recognized, but also those of lands with unfamiliar names. The writing on the charts was legible but in a strange, foreign-looking kind of script. There was some money, too; several gold and silver coins that seemed quite spendable, but stamped with odd, unrecognizable symbols and images.

In going through his clothing, Serena noted what she first thought was another wound on Parsomal's body. There was a good-sized depression in the middle of his breastbone, but it didn't seem like it had been caused by a weapon. There was no blood or trauma, and the skin was intact. Maybe it was normal for this Ernie. He was the first one of his kind that Serena had ever seen, after all.

A glint next to Serena's foot grabbed her attention. Whatever he dropped was glistening in the sun, scintillating with flashes of color. She found she could not take her eyes off the object. She bent down and picked it up, suddenly realizing with astonishment what it was she held in her hand.

* * *

Weekend Honor Day, Troya 16-21876 — My Homage to Mother, who taught me to understand transgressions, if not to forgive them - Day 26 on the Talus River — It's been more than a week and a half since that first croc attack. They seem to be getting fewer in number and a little less bold, although yesterday one of them took a bite out of the starboard oar. Now that I know what to sense for, I can usually keep them at bay with some simple suggestive spells. They don't attack if they don't think they're hungry . . . unless they're really pissed about something. Once I convinced Serena to quit shooting at them, it was easy enough. Anyway, we seem to be leaving their territory. The jungle is a little less thick ahead, but I still can't figure out what makes me so jittery about it. It's the same kind of claustrophobic feeling I get when I'm in a city surrounded by thousands of people, but all I can sense here are birds, crocs, fish, monkeys, a few cats, but no people. At least I don't think so . . .

—Orchid's journal

Today – The Talus River

"So what you're saying is that I'm not getting the full use out of my Magic, is that it?"

Orchid glared at Tresado for daring to suggest such a thing. It really hadn't been meant as an insult, but she was crabby. Group Six had consumed the last of the brandy yesterday, and Orchid wasn't happy about that. Actually, it had been she who had consumed most of it. It was Leader's fault. He should have packed more.

"Noooo, I didn't say that at all," Tresado replied. "I'm just saying that Absolute Magic is more efficient, more diverse, and you get more torque for your tormac."

"And that's why you decided to go against tradition?" asked Orchid snidely. "Not many Eryndi practice Absolute. That violates the ethics of most of them."

"Oh, here we go again," sighed Foxx. "Do you think maybe we could get through one day without arguing?"

Tresado ignored him. "Well, what with my lack of *ethics* and all, I decided to follow my own path. All of my cram school classmates were going on to study Worldly with plans to become shamans and healers. That just wasn't for me. Too many restrictions."

"What you call restrictions, I call conservative respect," said Orchid. She stood up straight on the deck, clutching her staff, which fumed and sparked in response to her foul mood. "You know as well as I how much potential power there is in Magic. But that power isn't unlimited. It can't be. I'm a Macai, and I can sense that even if you don't. I don't understand how you as an Eryndi can't see that."

"What I can see," Tresado snapped, "is that I'm not bound by a zillion years of tradition and dogma. I use Magic in any way that I see fit. Absolute works well for me."

"But you both do the same things," interjected Foxx.

"What?" Tresado looked at Foxx.

"Same things, what do you mean?" Orchid asked.

"You both cast the same spells," Foxx explained.

"What?"

"How do you figure our spells are the same?" Orchid's voice held an edge of irritation.

"I've heard you both talk about lightning," Foxx said. "You can both command a bolt of lightning to strike where you want it. What's the difference?"

Orchid was indignant, "When I cast a lightning spell, I don't *command* anything. The potential for lightning is already there, in the air, in the ground. What I do is to use the power of Magic to gather that potential. In essence, I *ask* Magic to use existing natural forces to cause what I wish. What *he* does," she said, indicating Tresado, "is to rip the power of a lightning bolt directly from Magic itself."

"And why go through all that mumbo-jumbo?" Tresado countered. "By coalescing Magic directly, it saves time, and you're always sure of your power. If there isn't storm weather in the area, *your* lightning bolt might wind up with no more of a zap than if you petted a cat on a goatskin rug."

Serena usually stayed quiet when the conversation turned to Magical debate but now spoke up.

"Well, *I* have a suggestion for you, if you'd like to hear it."

"What's that?" asked Tresado.

"Why don't you all just shut your fat gobs before I break your jaws?"

A gentle surge of affection for the lovely Serena swept over Tresado, Orchid, and Foxx like a warm tropical wave.

"I apologize for interrupting," said Leader. "But look up ahead."

Enchanter came around a bend in the river, and there on the right was a structure.

Four years ago - The Northlands – Serena

Serena kept the knowledge of the diamond to herself not because she thought someone might try to steal it (as someone certainly would), but because she felt *compelled* to tell no one. At first, she thought that she would hide the stone somewhere, perhaps bury it or something. That just didn't sit right with her, however. When she tried to secure it in the furs of her bed, she found she couldn't even leave the bunkhouse without having to immediately return and check on it. Serena, therefore, took to keeping it on her person at all times, eventually sleeping with the gem tightly clasped to her chest.

A week after finding the diamond, Serena was in the throes of a really weird dream. It was romantic, yet there was no one else involved. It was immensely pleasant yet terrifying. There was a sensation of intense loneliness which became one of belonging, yet in her dream, this feeling was not hers. Sometimes the dream was in first person; other times, she was an observer, experiencing a flood of images and sensations that overlapped, repeated, and contradicted. There were violence and joy; death and birth; continuation and change; all in one frustratingly convoluted nightmare (or was it a joyful fantasy?).

Serena bolted up in bed in a cold sweat, finding herself laughing hysterically. Not really sure where or who she was, the giggling warrior groped around in the darkness—for what, she did not know. The universe was empty; she was alone until voices called out to her from the void.

"Hey, shut up over there!"

"Go to sleep!"

"Knock it off, you loony!"

Awareness slowly returned as Serena finally recognized that she was in her own bed in the bunkhouse. The grumbling of the other women subsided, as did the images of the dream. She lay back down, but sleep did not come again. Dawn found her still awake, unable to remember any of the bizarre images that had stalked her in the night.

The others started to stir, and Serena forced herself to rise as well to begin the day. Her head was still in a fog as she tried to shake the disconcerting remnants of last night's dreams. She felt unrested and could easily have gone back to bed, but there was an axe-throwing competition scheduled for this morning, and she didn't want to miss it. She had placed a wager on Olaf the Thick, a sure thing.

As she headed for the bunkhouse door, Serena collided with Magda, a large shield maiden. Magda had a reputation among the Northland women as one of the strongest and most terrible in battle, not to mention a bit of a bully. There had been trouble between her and Serena in the past, mostly because Magda was a blubber-brained fool who couldn't find her boobs with both hands, but she did throw a hefty punch. Serena tensed for the inevitable fight that was now sure to commence. Magda scowled at her old enemy and started to ball her fists but stopped in her tracks. A strange look came over her face, and her features softened. She looked with adoring eyes at Serena, who had adopted a defensive stance and was ready to rumble.

"Serena, good morning! Oh, I love that jerkin! Is that new? Say, after the tournament, what do you say we go to the market and do some shopping? Or maybe we could take some ale and snacks up to the fjords and watch the ripper whales. What would *you* like to do?"

CHAPTER 6

*Well, I'm certainly not coming back to this place
again—there's no gin.*

—TRAVELOGUE OF DEMENTUS, THE MAD TRESKAN

Today – The Talus River

Enchanter sailed slowly for another whole day through
what appeared to be a drowned city. Either the buildings had
sunk or the waters had encroached into the former streets.
Collapsed stone walls draped with rotting vegetation lined
both banks of the river, which had slowed to a crawl. Empty
windows and gaping doorways ominously greeted Group Six
as they passed.

"This was an old city," observed Tresado. "Look at that
archway."

"Some of those walls are solid stone, half a reach thick,"
said Serena. "And look how the blocks are dovetailed together,
a perfect fit. Not even siege engines could penetrate them."

"That's the only reason anything is still standing,"
whispered Foxx. "Eryndi built this a long time ago."

"Quite right," Leader said.

"You know this city?" asked Orchid.

"It was once known as *Mennatu,*" said Leader impassively, "the center of an ancient empire. The Eryndi inhabitants were educated and cultured, but contrarily, known as fierce and competent warriors."

"Why is that contrary?" Serena growled. "Great warriors can be just as cultured and educated as the next bumhole, you know!"

"Indeed," Leader responded unabashedly. "These Eryndi controlled a vast area from here to what is now the eastern Treskan Imperium and all the way to the sea."

"Ostica was part of this empire?" Foxx asked.

"It did not exist in its present form, of course. The city you now know as Ostica was built upon many layers of ruins. As civilizations rise and fall, so do their accomplishments, even those of the Eryndi."

"But Ostica is mostly Macai," said Orchid.

"That is true of much of the world," replied Leader, "*today,* that is. In the distant past, it was not so. In this city of Mennatu, and throughout the empire, a few primitive Macai were retained as servants and laborers."

"You mean *slaves?*" asked Orchid and Foxx at the same time.

"Understand," answered Leader, "it was a different time, a time when the closest concentrations of Macai were savages living along the banks of the northern fjords, hunting whales with stone-tipped lances . . . your ancestors, Serena. The ancient Eryndi invaded these lands and took many of your race as prisoners, in much the same way that Macai today use horses and oxen as beasts of burden."

As Leader droned on, Foxx listened carefully to his

words, unable to garner any emotion or empathy in them. It was as though Leader were reading from a menu.

"But of course, aside from warriors," Leader continued, "the Mennatuans were also farmers, potters, metal smiths, poets, artists, scholars. One of these buildings housed a great library where centuries' worth of ancient texts from many different cultures were kept. Somewhere there was an amphitheater where actors and musicians performed. But their civilization revolved around the waters. The river was the home of their deity and the very core of their being. It was their lifeblood. It nourished them, irrigated their crops, and allowed them to travel the length of the empire."

"It seems like their lifeblood kind of hemorrhaged on them," Tresado observed. "I wonder what caused the river to jump its banks."

"You'd think a society as advanced as this could do something about a little high water," scoffed Foxx. "All it would take would be a decent system of levees. Builders this skilled should have no trouble with that."

"Cities are creepy enough when they're occupied," said Orchid. "A dead city is even worse."

"I know what you mean," said Tresado. "It's like these buildings are watching us. You know, like a painting whose eyes follow you across the room."

"What a bunch of wieners!" snorted Serena. "I never heard such a load of crap in my life! *Oooh, oooh, the buildings are watching us . . . help me, help me!* Would you take a look at what we have on this paper canoe? We've got offensive power up the butt!"

Serena pointed at Tresado. "We've got Mister Lightning Bolt and his coin-operated bubble boat . . . we've got Nature

Girl Orchid with her Super Power Staff, who can make every plant and animal sing and dance . . . *and most importantly,*" she said, drawing her scimitar with a threatening *shwink,* "we've got Serena Brimstone, the baddest-ass berserker who ever beheaded a *berg bear!* So just what is it you're all afraid of, anyway!?"

BOOGER, BOOGER, BOOGER, BOOGER . . .

The strange call echoed through the buildings like a death knell.

"WHAT THE CRAP WAS THAT??!!" a startled Serena yelled.

Orchid smiled and said, "Now it's my turn to calm *you* down. I recognize that call. It's a *booger bird*, about the size of a large turkey and twice as tasty. I'd be glad to introduce you, Serena."

The blonde warrior sheathed her sword and grabbed her bow. "Well, in that case . . . what say we all pull up for the night and pick us a booger?"

Four years ago - The Northlands – Serena

This is getting ridiculous, thought Serena. Everywhere she went this day, her fellow warriors treated her in this damned odd way. During the axe tournament, the other spectators paid more attention to her than to the throwers. There was only one thing to do.

I need a bath, Serena decided.

She made her way down the road out of town toward the fjords. The spring snows were receding, turning the ground muddy. Signs of greenery began to poke their heads out of the soil. Summer would soon be here, and the barbarian raids like the one last week would increase. The thought of battle stirred her warrior blood. Even as unsettled as she was, of this, Serena was sure.

A dull roaring sound ahead increased as Serena approached the Cliff of Springs. It was a section from which numerous small waterfalls poured out of the granite crags for more than a league. She passed the irrigation flumes and freshwater reservoirs, heading for one of the smaller springs farther along the cliff where she could get a bit of privacy. Right now, Serena was tired of being around people who all wanted to tell her how fond of her they were.

The spring water was ice cold, but fresh and invigorating. Serena stripped off her jerkin and gave it a good pounding on a rock. She hung it on a branch to dry and eased herself into the freezing pool. Lifting her face to the cascading water, she let it blast her hair clean. Using a piece of soft lava stone, she scrubbed her body vigorously, hoping to wash away this weird sensation of uncertainty and confusion that had bugged her all morning. The feeling just wouldn't go away. It was familiar, like she knew there was something she had to do but just couldn't put her finger on it.

No, that's not right, Serena thought. *It's not like there's something to do. More like, there's something I have to find, or . . .*

Her hands were still automatically scrubbing her skin while she thought. It was then that it suddenly became clear. Serena looked where her fingers had stopped. She traced a small ridge in her skin; almost like a scar. In the middle of her sternum, something was sparkling in the sunlight, creating little prisms of light in the water droplets that ran down her body.

That's it! How could I have forgotten about the diamond?

The stone that she had picked up from the dying Eryndi was now embedded flush with her skin in the middle of her chest. It had seemingly changed shape. Instead of a smooth oval, one side of it now was slightly concave, matching the contours of Serena's breastbone.

She remembered now. The cobwebs in her brain had finally blown away. That Ernie she had gotten this from—she now recalled the unfamiliar feeling of wanting, no . . . *needing* to help him.

It was this jewel, she realized. *It made me give a crap about that stranger. It called out to me for help. If the man hadn't been wounded, maybe I would have fallen in love with him the way people are doing to me!*

GROSS!

Serena shouted to the heavens, *"I can't have this happen to me! I am a shield maiden of the Northlands! A warrior! I DON'T WANT THIS!!!"*

'I DON'T WANT THIS ! I DON'T WANT THIS!' her yells echoed up and down the fjords, mocking her.

The very thought of what had happened to her chilled her to the bone. Or maybe it was because she was standing in ice water. Serena splashed out of the pool and started drying herself. A brisk nor'wester was blowing off the sea up the fjord, increasing the chill. Her clothing wasn't dry yet, but she donned it anyway and headed back to town, wondering if the shamans could do anything for her.

Today – The Drowned City

Using silent gestures, Orchid pointed out a leafy shrub, one that provided plenty of concealment and was downwind of their prey. Serena nodded, hiding behind the bush. Silently, the Northlander fitted an arrow to her bow.

Orchid moved back behind Serena about twenty reaches and posted herself on top of an ancient stone pillar that thrust itself out of the muddy ground. She closed her eyes and reached out with her mind, touching the Magic in the air. The life around her—the trees, the grass, the fish and frogs in the water, the flying creatures in the air, and the very worms in the ground—all resonated upon her psyche.

Concentrating, Orchid humbly entreated Magic to pick out the one she wanted. The booger bird's life presence was revealed to her mind's eye as an illuminated phantasm, swimming in a sea of darkness. Starting slowly, so as not to startle it, Orchid sent out a spell to the bird, filling its mind with its very own desires—in this case the promise of many tasty, easily obtainable bugs. The impression of a rich food source was gradually amped up into not only a desire, but a definite necessity in the bird's mind. At the same time she projected the Magical suggestion, Orchid also pursed her lips and twittered out a warbling kind of whistle. That was all it took. The booger bird winged its way through the trees, belting out its call as it went.

BOOGER . . . BOOGER . . . BOOGER . . . BOOGER

Serena heard her dinner approaching and drew back her bowstring. She counted to four, then sprang up out of cover, releasing her arrow in the same motion. The feathered shaft flew straight and true, piercing the meaty breast in mid-flight.

BOOGER . . . BOOGER . . . BOO-GLEEEAAAGH!

Orchid heard a rustling of leaves followed by a squishy thud and smiled to herself, knowing they would eat well this evening. The whole hunt had taken no more than twenty minutes.

A bunch of years ago - The Northlands

Dear Mrs. Torgaldson,

Thank you for watching Serena last week while me and hubby were out raiding. I'm really sorry she threw little Leif down the well. I hope the goat pot pie makes up for any trouble.

—Hulde Brimstone

Four years ago - The Northlands – Serena

The triad of town shamans had been less than helpful. Their professional services consisted of disemboweling a goat and examining the stomach contents for signs and portents. That didn't even come until after they had brought Serena tea and sweets and gotten her a softer pillow to sit on and a seal fur cloak to cut the cool breeze and on and on and on. When at last she talked them into skipping over the fawning and getting on with their business, they came up with nothing. Frankly, they were puzzled over Serena's considering this a problem. Being loved and adored was something to be sought after, not discouraged. A gift from the Gods, as this surely had to be, was not to be scorned, they said. This was getting her nowhere. Going to the shamans was a bad idea. It was up to Serena to deal with this in her own way.

Time to pick a fight . . .

Serena left the Temple and made her way to the great hall where warriors were gathering to honor the tournament winners. It was just the place to prove her prowess in front of lots of witnesses. Drinking in earnest had already begun. What did it matter that it was only two in the AfterMidday? These were Northlanders, after all.

Upon entering, Serena scanned the large, smelly hall filled with large, smelly warriors. There at a table, drunkenly trying to grab his stein, was Ibarr the Scary. His tangled orange beard was dripping with ale, and the leather patch over his right eye did nothing to hide the jagged triple scars that raced down his cheek. He had lost that eye and half his face in a hungry berg bear encounter some years before. Both Ibarr and the bear had wanted to eat the other that day. Ibarr was the one who had fed. Serena strode up to the table and glared at him. Ibarr blearily stared back at the blonde warrior before him.

"Well, what do *you* want, *shield maiden?*"

The second half of that sentence was pronounced through a long belch. Ibarr guffawed at his own crudeness.

"Just wanted to make sure you knew about your mother," Serena challenged, "what with her being a diseased old sow with whores for daughters and bog leeches for sons."

Ibarr set his drink down and thoughtfully stroked his beard as he considered the efficacy of the taunt.

"Not too bad, not too bad, shield maiden," he said. "Although the whore thing was pretty standard. That could use some spicing up. But *'bog leeches,'* that was good, I liked that. The delivery was good, the body language fair, and although I've seen better, a reasonably effective challenge."

Ibarr farted like a trumpet to finalize his judgment. Then with a joyful roar, he hurled the table out of his way and drew his *seax,* a huge, single-edged knife. To a Treskan Legionnaire, it would have been a battle sword. To a Northlander, it was an eating utensil.

"And why do you challenge me, shield maiden?" he hollered with a great open grin, spraying Serena with ale and spit.

"Just a test, nothing personal," replied Serena, drawing her own dagger. Her war cry pierced Ibarr's ears like an arrow, even as she swung her weapon at his huge belly. It had been so distracting that Ibarr almost didn't parry her blow in time to save himself from disembowelment. He had to admit this chick had one fierce war cry.

But as their weapons clanged together and their eyes locked, the murderous scowl on Ibarr's hideous face melted into a kind of mindless rapture. He shoved his opponent back with his blade, not to attack or defend, but just to get a good look.

Light a thousand times purer than that of Crodan's Keep itself shone forth from this woman. Her golden hair framed her angelic face, and armor that shone like the sun graced her perfect body. The seax dropped from Ibarr's hand as he shamefully realized he had intended harm to this divine vision of womanhood. He sank to his knees and beheld perfection.

"Shield maiden . . . Serena, is it not? I am yours to command. In war and peace, I am your man forever. Just allow me to be near you always."

Serena's test was decisive, but not at all the results she wanted. She sheathed her dagger and grabbed Ibarr by the face. She pushed him back onto his ass to the roaring laughter of the rest of the warriors who had watched the brief contest. She turned and looked back at her fellow Northlanders. About half of them were starting to get that same weird mindless stare in their eyes. The implications of this made her a bit ill. Seething at the applause and the insulting flattery and respect the crowd was showing her, Serena stomped back outside.

Today – The Drowned City

Enchanter was pulled up to what looked like a flat stone jetty but was probably a former rooftop which the water level had not quite reached. Foxx soon had a fire going, and the only thing missing was something to cook on it.

The river had widened significantly to the point where it didn't even look like a river anymore. The tops of drowned buildings stretched for as far as one could see in all directions. Sandbars and mud banks were scattered about. Drippy trees grew from them to form a thin canopy above.

To the south was a muddy area somewhat resembling more solid land. It was here that Orchid and Serena had headed out in search of dinner. In a very short time they returned, bearing their quarry. Serena flopped the dead bird onto the surface and pulled out her arrow.

"I gotta admit, you're a handy wench to have along on a hunting trip," she said to Orchid.

"And you're a pretty fine shot with that bow," replied Orchid, "although you could have waited even longer to fire. That bird was coming fast. You probably could have just tackled him."

"Why go for the easy shots when you can fire from a hundred paces?" Serena quipped. "Makes the bragging that much sweeter."

The two laughed, lightly punching each other in the arm.

"It looks like you two are finally learning to play nice," Foxx said, tending the campfire.

"Well, after all, who couldn't get along with Serena?" Tresado added. "You know I've never met anyone more fun to be around than Serena." It was a bit of a jibe at first, but now his eyes started to mist over.

"Doooon't go there," Serena warned. "You'll just break me out of this good mood."

"Sorry, sorry." Tresado choked it back. Now that he was more familiar with the gem in Serena's chest and its effect on him, it was easier for him to control.

Still a struggle, though . . .

"So, who gets to do the plucking and cooking?" Orchid asked. "We brought it in. Somebody else can be camp mommy tonight."

"I will prepare the bird," volunteered Leader, "if Foxx will do the roasting. He is the gourmet among us, after all." He pulled the bird onto a flat log and started plucking.

For a guy who likes to be called 'Leader,' Foxx admitted to himself, *he is never shy about pulling his share of the load. Unusual.*

"Agreed," said Foxx. "Tresado, what are you going to do to contribute, have us wait on you?"

"Funny," Tresado said, taking a sideways look at the peculiar bird the hunters had brought in. It had a long neck like a goose but with a copper-colored spherical head and a thin pointed beak. Its body was mostly a dull green to match the surrounding trees, and its bright blue tail feathers could fan out like a turkey's. Leader was expertly pulling them all out.

"Are you sure this . . . *creature* . . . is edible?" Tresado asked hesitantly. "I'm not sure I'd like to eat something called a *booger bird.*"

"Don't be such a puss," said Serena.

"You'll like it, don't worry," said Orchid, "and if you don't, then just do as Serena says and not be such a puss."

"You'll like it the way I intend to spice it," bragged Foxx, who took over when Leader was done plucking and gutting. "Trust me. Way back when I was known as 'Chef Foxx.' That's with two exes." He flashed Serena his cross-fingered gesture and winked at her. "So, is your last name really *Brimstone?*"

Serena responded with a quick flip of her wrist. A long, needle-sharp stiletto thudded into the cutting board, a hand's breadth from Foxx's groin.

"You can use that for a roasting spit, *can't you?*" Serena asked coyly.

Foxx gulped and pulled the still vibrating blade out of the wood.

"Perfect."

Tresado snickered at his best friend's near vasectomy. "I'm going to take a look around the neighborhood and make sure we're okay."

"Good idea," said Orchid. "I'm still getting that weird feeling that we're not alone, even though I can't sense anything other than what swims, flies, or crawls."

Tresado looked around to pick out his post. A crumbling old bell tower stood about a hundred paces to the east of the camp. "Call me when dinner is ready . . . *Chef,*" he said to Foxx.

Gathering the Magic surrounding him, he formed it into a comfy, invisible harness and lifted himself through the air. To the untrained eye, it appeared that he was flying, but bipeds can't fly. This was just a simple levitation of matter from one point to another using the power of Magic. Moments later, Tresado was on top of the tower, scanning the jungle in all directions. Yet his alertness failed to detect the many sets of eyes intently watching both him and the camp.

Four years ago - The Northlands – Serena

A warm, summer wind danced upon the crags high above the fjords. Upon this lofty lookout Northlanders were constantly stationed, ever watchful for danger. The outlook from this post allowed a panoramic view of both the fjord and the whole of Luftar Valley. Nothing could approach by land or sea without being seen leagues away.

On this day, Ginnia Axebeard had taken up her pre-dawn shift only an hour before. Having only twelve summers beneath her belt, she was not yet an adult. This coming Inxa, Ginnia would take the Trials of Snow and Ice, elevating her to the status of apprentice shield maiden. Until then, it was a great honor to be trusted with lookout duty on the cliffs, and she took her responsibilities seriously. A hint of movement to the southeast caught her attention. She shaded her grey eyes against the rising sun, watching the distant line of moving figures approaching the town of Grannugh from the hills beyond.

Barbarians!

Ginnia took a long look to count their numbers, then ran for the warning tower. A few steps carried her to the top, where hung the horn of an adult *grilk*. It was a great spiral cone over two reaches long. After three blasts to indicate trouble, Ginnia used the signal mirror to report her findings to the town below.

Eymon Skagsgard, known as the Rank, Chieftain of Grannugh and Belzar Fjord Environs, was deploying his warriors to form a defensive perimeter at Kroeger's Pass. The very old and very young were busy in the town, building an inner defense barrier with wagons, meat racks, furniture— anything they could find to keep out the invaders in the event the warriors could not stop them. According to Ginnia's report, this was no minor barbarian raid. It was a full-scale incursion that included heavy siege weaponry.

"Ibarr!" he hollered, "Take three squads to Frigga's Rock and reinforce the garrison! Get those grain wagons into town!

If these barbarian pukes burn the fields, we'll need something to eat other than our horses! Serena! Your cavalry will deploy along the . . ."

Eymon's voice trailed off. His great Northlands broadsword, weighing over two stone, slipped from his hand and thudded to the ground at his feet as he beheld his one true love. He saw a halo of the purest light surrounding the shield maiden as though she were the daughter of Crodan himself.

"S-Serena . . ." he stammered. "Serena, my precious. No harm must come to you. Go back to the town and barricade yourself! Better yet, retreat to the fjords and take shelter amongst the rocks. They must not find you!"

"What?" exclaimed Serena. "My Lord, the enemy has come in force! We need every warrior to defend . . ."

"Serena!" Eymon shouted almost desperately. "You must retreat!"

Eymon took a quick look at the advancing horde. Their cavalry was rapidly approaching, spreading out in a great, sweeping arc of destruction.

"Serena . . . now! . . . I BEG YOU!!!"

"Beg all you want," Serena yelled back, "I FIGHT."

Ignoring Eymon's orders, she leapt aboard her horse, wheeled it around, and, with a fierce war cry, galloped off toward the approaching barbarians.

The line of riders ahead was forced to split at one point due to a large rock outcropping. Serena headed for a group of four of them on the right. She was now close enough to see them more clearly. What the barbarians were riding could not be called anything close to horses. Maybe they were huge running birds, maybe giant two-legged greyhounds. Serena just couldn't tell. She drew her sword on the gallop, ready to take the head off the closest one. But before she could close, a swarm of arrows from the barbarians' archers in the rear rained down from the sky. Two of them thudded into her horse, which went down immediately. Serena pitched forward over its neck but managed to hit the ground rolling. The wind was knocked out of her, and she lay stunned for a minute.

Struggling to her feet, Serena realized she was surrounded by fearsome barbarians. Shaking off the weakness caused by her fall, she picked up her sword and waited for the inevitable charge from all sides. She knew she could not prevail against all twenty or so of them, but Serena was more than willing to take as many with her to Crodan's Keep as she could. They would make fine servants in the afterlife.

The barbarians' hideously deformed faces leered and grimaced at her. Their bodies all had that weird disproportionate business to them. Most of them had one arm longer than the other or huge swollen legs. One fellow's right earlobe hung down below his chin and flapped in the summer breeze. Every one of them had some kind of crazy-looking nose. It was as though each barbarian was his own species. The only thing they had in common was that they all smelled like corpses.

Serena waited and waited. The barbarians just stared at her. She feinted with her sword at them, but all they did was to back out of her way. She whirled around, trying to provoke them into attacking.

"FINE!" she shouted. "I'LL GO FIRST!!"

Shrieking her war cry, Serena charged the barbarian directly in front of her and swung her scimitar for all she was worth. The barbarian tried to duck but, other than that, did nothing to counter Serena's attack. Her sword bit deep into the creature's collarbone and continued on through, leaving a clean diagonal slash across his chest. The man went to his knees and pitched onto his face wearing a strange, euphoric look. It was as though he considered being killed by Serena as the greatest (and last) gift of his wretched life.

One down, Serena thought, *but that was just too easy.*

She leapt on top of the corpse, ready to deal with the next one, but they all had that same stupid, vacuous look on their horrible faces. Serena realized she could probably kill them all one at a time, like mowing down cornstalks, but the thought gave her no pleasure. The sound of many running feet turned her head. Coming up fast was Eymon and his main body of infantry. The barbarian line broke at this point as more and more of them ran up to behold this vision of loveliness instead of charging the Northlanders. Four beats later, the wall of Eymon's warriors crashed into the throng of enraptured barbarians, which had now grown to almost a hundred love-sick mutants. The carnage was terrible even by Northlanders' standards. The old expression about 'heads will roll' literally came true as the enemy just let themselves be slaughtered.

Eymon was quick to see the advantage of the situation.

"Duro! Give Serena your horse. MOVE IT!"

The young warrior looked resentful but obeyed orders. He jumped out of the saddle and tossed the reins to Serena.

"Serena, my glorious one," said Eymon, "you have just saved us all! Do us the honor of leading the charge into their center. Go! We will follow . . . but *don't engage them!* Keep yourself clear of danger at all costs, but just head into them!"

The bloodlust was still upon her, so Serena had not yet had time to think about it. She shrieked out her war cry and galloped forward, waving her bloody sword above her head. The throng of barbarians was freezing en masse as she flew through them. There were hundreds of the enemy all around her, but none were threatening her. It seemed like the 'rapture' effect was getting stronger, as if when any danger to her increased, so did this weird phenomenon. As she headed into the horde, Eymon and his army followed behind, slaying mutants right and left. This was not battle; it was an outright slaughter. The enemy was not striking back at all. The only thing they were interested in doing was staring stupidly at the blonde goddess riding through their midst.

The Northlanders laid waste to an entire battalion of barbarians without taking a single casualty. Serena soon broke through the line and kept going. The slow-moving siege engines were just ahead. They were like enormous bows mounted on heavy wheels. These cumbersome, house-sized machines were being dragged along by teams of foul-looking giant beasts—like mangy, whale-sized bergalos. There were dozens of barbarian support troops with every machine, some to operate it, some to guard it. As soon as Serena was within their sight, they all just stopped what they were doing and gaped with open mouths. The beasts kept plodding on, continuing to pull the machines along without their masters. Serena reined in her horse and stopped.

Maybe they need to be provoked . . .

"Come on, you bastards!" she cried out. "You came all this way from that turd pile you live on. Come on, attack! Are you cowards? Are you afraid of one woman? I piss on all of you and your filthy mothers! You're nothing but scum. You're not warriors, you're not . . ."

Serena's challenges trailed off. Her taunts were obviously falling on deaf, mutated ears. Many of the barbarians were falling to their knees in worship. So much drool dripped from their gaping mouths it turned the soil under their feet to mud. More were approaching. The ranks of mutant archers dropped their bows, trying to shove their way to the front of the pack to worship at the feet of their new goddess.

It would have been so easy. Nothing was standing in Serena's way. The mutants were lining up to be slaughtered like a herd of cattle. Duro's horse was giddy to begin the attack. It trembled and pawed the ground in anticipation of a battle charge.

But the order never came. Despite her hating the guts of these mutated scumbags, Serena just couldn't bring herself to kill these things. Not that she had any compassion or anything for them, but because there was zero honor in defeating an enemy that wouldn't fight back. Imagine how Crodan would look upon an offering of ear trophies that had come at no charge. He would look down His all-powerful nose and kick her ass out of the afterlife for such a cheap trick.

Eymon's warriors had caught up with her and began to systematically execute the invaders, who went to their deaths happily and with no resistance. There was no reason to take prisoners. Mutant barbarians were of no use to anyone. Their bodies were to be loaded on carts and hauled to the fjords as gifts to the ripper whales. They would eat well this year.

A group of Northlanders was examining the siege crossbows and the wagonloads of ammunition. The giant arrows were tipped with clay warheads filled with some kind of poisonous, flammable oil. If these had been loosed on the town, the devastation would have been horrible. These barbarians had come not merely to raid and loot but to destroy utterly.

Serena continued to just sit unmoving on her horse and watch the mop-up. Eymon and his captains gathered around her.

"WARRIORS!" he announced. "My Lady Serena, Shield Maiden of Grannugh, is a hero to the Northlands! Her bravery on this day will be recorded in the Sagas for all time!"

Cheers erupted from her fellow fighters. Ibarr, Magda, Olaf, and a hundred others surrounded her. They roughly (but in a nice way) pulled Serena from her horse and threw her to their shoulders, carrying her in triumph back toward the town. They sang praises of her bravery and fortitude. They called her things like 'savior' and 'hero' and promised a huge feast and drinking bout in her honor.

But Serena did not feel very brave. This had been a major invasion, and she had scarcely struck a blow. The invaders had to be stopped, to be sure. There was no denying that. Also, had it not been for Serena's effect on them, the overwhelming horde of barbarians would have destroyed Grannugh and killed everyone in it. That didn't make her feel any better about herself, however. To Serena, there was no honor in winning the way she did.

The celebration continued well into the night. Serena eventually managed with difficulty to escape back to the confines of her bed. There was no privacy in the bunkhouse, but she hung a couple of blankets from the rafters, so she could at least be out of sight. She threw off her clothes and flopped down on her back, trying to keep the room from spinning. She had had more ale poured down her throat this night than she had drunk in her entire life.

As sleep approached and her blood cooled, Serena began to know . . . something. There was someone with her, close to her, closer than anyone had ever been before. Her fingers reached under the blanket covering her and sought the diamond embedded in her chest. For the first time, Serena became aware of the spirit. She could feel its presence within her. And she knew something else. The spirit was grateful to her, thankful for a place to call home. It would always protect her from enemies, would always create love and adoration in others. The spirit needed that, somehow. It craved it, thrived on it, even fed on it. But right now, Serena was aware of one other emotion within. It felt confusion at her resentment.

CHAPTER 7

Magic naturally exists everywhere, in the air, the water, the soil, even in living creatures, but most people are completely unaware of it. Even a heavily enchanted transmutation oven is just a fireplace to the untrained. The average person knows of the presence of Magic but has no sense of it, so he cannot understand.

—Sage Marison – Permanent Infusion Techniques, 3rd Printing, 21872

11 years ago - Foxx

There was much that Foxx didn't understand in the books that he had *acquired* from Sage Marison. For one thing, these texts were written for a student who had already gone through rigorous conditioning and mental training—a *boot camp*, as it were. It wasn't like the books were filled with incantations that would allow the casting of spells. It doesn't work that way. To manipulate Magic, you first have to be able to sense its presence. Even this small act typically requires a full year of training and discipline. Depending on the teacher, there is a series of meditation techniques and mental exercises that have to be mastered before a student is allowed to go on to the next level. The student's progress is monitored very carefully by the instructor and about two-thirds of the novices wash out the first year, never to be readmitted. You're either right for Magic, or you're not.

None of this was covered in the texts that Foxx possessed. Most were designed for third or fourth-year students. This was all very frustrating to him. Foxx just wanted to learn to influence and manipulate people. He wasn't interested in turning them into newts. Despite this, Foxx persevered and eventually gained a rudimentary insight into what makes Magic work, if not how to use it efficiently.

In all his books, Marison continued to stress the need for ethics and discretion in the use of Magic. Every chapter had a preachy introduction warning about the dangers of misusing this incredible power. Foxx pretty much ignored this.

It's just a legal disclaimer, he thought.

The text on influential Magic use that Foxx studied the most was actually the most advanced of the bunch, written at the grad-student level for prospective teachers. It focused on the reading of peoples' psyches and personalities. The advanced forms of these spells created a Magical bond between teacher and student, used as a monitoring tool to evaluate student progress (and to ensure a continuing sense of ethics, of course).

Do-gooder! sneered Foxx to himself.

Because of his relative ignorance of established training methods, Foxx's attempt to duplicate the disciplines involved sort of worked, but not really. He never managed to fully read someone, that is, to sense thoughts or subconscious desires in a particular person. At best, he could read surface emotions that a mark was feeling at the moment. The problem was that it didn't always work reliably. Foxx would secretly practice on people. He could usually tell when a merchant was trying to overcharge him or when a woman was not being honest with him. But every now and then, he would get a false impression. The first time he tried reading Benny Butcher, his spell told him that Benny was about to split Foxx's skull with his cleaver. Of course, it turned out not to be true, yet it scared the crap out of him anyway. Benny got a good laugh out of Foxx's girly scream and backward fall over a stool.

The first practical application of his rudimentary skills was using it to win at cards. This was how he supported himself during his study period. There was actually little Magic use involved (good thing, since he still pretty much sucked at it). But Foxx was naturally intelligent and perceptive. He had picked up and developed these skills during his time with Professor Generax. The old bastard was a con man and damned good at it. He taught Foxx how to read a crowd's mood and to steer that mood in whatever direction he desired. Generax could sell anything to anybody, whether they wanted to buy it or not. While certainly not the norm taught to regular Magic students, this training was just close enough to allow Foxx to follow along, if not fully grasp the basics. But these were the beginning skills that got him started. As a result, after two years of self-study, Foxx developed his own style of Magical persuasion.

Oh Mother of Waters; Oh Bearer of Fruit;
Shall Children of Woe Come Unbidden to Sup;
When Bindings of Friendship Be Loos'd . . .

—Trianna of Sylvas; Poetess to the Glades

Today – The Drowned City

The sun had gone down, and Group Six was sitting around the fire enjoying a damned good meal. The booger bird meat was juicy and flavorful. Tresado humbly offered his apologies to the creature as he devoured it.

"Damn, some brown ale to wash this down would be perfect," sighed Orchid.

"We have plenty of water," said Leader pragmatically.

Tresado and Foxx had refined their sarcastic 'oh brother' looks between each other to mere flicks of the eyelids. It was all that was needed.

"So," said Serena, not bothering to swallow her food first, "Nature Girl . . . when we first met, weren't you working as a game warden or something, that you protected birdies and bunnies for some lord?"

"Chief Land Steward and Wildlife Guardian for the Forest of Ulan in the Manors of Duke Armigan of Jasperia," Orchid replied.

"Big title."

"Small pay."

"So if you're a friend to all the woodland critters," Serena asked, "how is it you can wolf down that meat? As a matter of fact, you lured the bird in for me. You used your powers to make that weird-ass Magical birdcall thing that you do and pulled that booger right in where I could shoot it."

"Following Worldly ways doesn't mean I'm a vegetarian," said Orchid. "Just like the booger bird. He eats bugs; those bugs eat other bugs, which eat even smaller things. None of them begrudge the other. I have no problem with the river crocs trying to eat me. I just try to not let that happen, like every other living thing does."

"I get that, all right," said Serena, "but isn't using your powers to bring in this bird kind of cheating?"

"Yeah, I lured it in with a suggestive spell. But as far as using my 'powers,' as you call them, that's common in nature. Plenty of animals and plants use dirty, underhanded tricks to get what they want. Lots of things emit scents or tastes or blink lights or imitate distress calls to lure in victims. A dragon hypnotizes its prey with Magical happy thoughts so that you're never so content as when it eats you. And also I was getting damned tired of ration cakes . . . *drumstick?*"

Serena snorted out a chuckle through her nose and helped herself to more booger.

The day jungle noises yielded to the night noises, who now started their shift. The orb had risen in the east and cast its bluish light on the bleak landscape around them. Nyha was a brilliant blue and brown disc as large as the palm of one's hand held at arm's length. When it was full like this, the land was lit for leagues in all directions. The full moon had a definite effect on the world. Certain flowers bloomed only once a month. Certain animals could be seen only once a month. Every forty days there was a special kind of Magic in Nyha's fullness.

"Full moon tonight," observed Tresado.

"Boy, nothing gets past you, does it, detective?" answered Serena.

Tresado stuck his tongue out at Serena. It was the fiercest response he could come up with.

"You know why it's called a full moon, don't you?" Tresado asked after a couple of beats.

"It ate too much?" burped Foxx, patting his belly.

"Because it's full of our ancestors," replied Tresado. "Let's see, my great-great-*great*-grandmother told me that story. It's an old Eryndi fairy tale. I can't quite remember the details. It was about Nyha being the destination of the ancient ones, I forget if it was ancient Gods or ancient Eryndi, but some ancient somebody-or-other went there. It was . . . I remember now. There was an exodus to Nyha to escape something, the wrath of the Gods, maybe. And some old-timers think that's where you go when you die. But this is the 219th century. We don't believe in that sort of mumbo-jumbo anymore. At any rate, all the stories I heard have something to do with somebody running away."

"Sounds like an Eryndi story, all right," scoffed Serena. "Now *my* people have stories, too. The shamans say that the Orb is alive. It's supposed to be the face of Daeria, the wife of Crodan. She watches over the world from the sky to make sure we are living honorable lives. She can't watch the whole world at once, so She turns her head back and forth. And She makes different faces, too. Sometimes She's frowning, sometimes pleased. In the Northlands, fewer crimes are committed when the Orb is full because Daeria is looking right at you. That's what mothers tell their kids, anyway, to try to get them to behave. Afraid it never worked with me."

"No, no, no, that can't be," said Orchid, joining in the fun. "My teachers said that Nyha has nothing to do with the Gods. It's a little round ball in the sky, just like Lurra, except tiny."

Orchid held out her hand at arm's length and spread her thumb and index finger apart.

"See, it's only about that big."

Serena snorted at that.

"Well, it's obviously a lot bigger because it's a couple of leagues away," said Orchid, smirking. "And of course, you know *Sensang* is even smaller."

"So the Orb is *this* big . . ." Serena held up her fingers, "and the sun is *this* big," she said, narrowing her fingers. "Boy, you eggheads will believe anything."

Orchid kept a straight face and continued the joke, "But you know, they also say that there are living things coating the outside surface of Nyha. Not much life, though. Nothing bigger than ants or mites."

"Leeeeetle tiny people?" teased Serena, holding her thumb and forefinger barely apart.

"No, not people at all," said Orchid, "not even intelligent . . . more like an infestation."

She pointed at Nyha. "You see those patches of green on the upper right side? That's probably mold. But this is the 219th century. We don't believe in that sort of mumbo-jumbo anymore."

The group all chuckled at that, except Leader, who had never been known to chuckle. Foxx had always been frustrated by this. Leader was one of the few people he had met who was a total mystery to him.

"What do *your* people think the Orb is, Leader?" he asked, testing the water.

"Where I come from, no one is known as a theorist or storyteller. When we find out, that's when we'll know. What does Foxx with two exes believe?" replied Leader.

Foxx inwardly sighed. Once again, Leader had smoothly avoided a direct answer.

"Well, for every opinion you guys have," said Foxx, "there

are scores of others from all over. There's like thirty provinces in the Treskan Imperium, and each one of those ex-countries has their own collection of beliefs and theories . . . some of them pretty outlandish. But they all make just as much or as little sense as anything I've heard here tonight. I guess I'm pretty open-minded when it comes to creation myths and such."

"Put Mister Foxx down for one wishy-washy vote, if you please," said Orchid.

"I like to keep my options open, in this life or the next," philosophized Foxx. "Besides, when you're dealing with a hostile somebody, it doesn't hurt to respect their beliefs, maybe even devoutly follow them, if it means saving your ass."

"So when we get to the end of the river," said Tresado, "and we find this super Magician, and it turns out that he worships circus clowns, you'll go right along with it?"

"Hey, I used to live with circus clowns."

"Now we know where you got your fashion sense."

Laughter echoed amongst the dead buildings. It didn't last, though. It was just too inappropriate in these creepy surroundings. Orchid shivered as she had several times since entering this jungle.

"Still have the *jigglies* about this place?" asked Serena.

"Yeah," answered Orchid. "I just can't figure why an entire city is empty."

"You mean, aside from the fact that everyone has water in their basement?" inquired Foxx.

"I don't think that was the cause," commented Orchid soberly. "It could be that the water rose *after* everyone abandoned the place."

Serena suddenly sat bolt upright and said stiffly, "I don't think it's all the way abandoned just yet."

Her mouth opened as if to say more, but instead, Serena suddenly tipped over face first into her dinner plate and stayed there.

A bizarre trilling sound erupted on all sides. From out of the trees and from out of the dead buildings and from out of the fetid river water itself came small dark forms that screamed and chittered. The creatures were completely naked and no bigger than small children. They carried tiny blowguns that shot darts just like the one sticking out of Serena's back. Scores of them swarmed onto the platform, overwhelming Group Six.

Honor is All – Glory to the Brave!

—Hrolvad the Berserker – Year 178
- Old Macai calendar

Four years ago - The Northlands – Serena

Glory to the brave, my cousin Eggbert's pink ass, thought Serena as she took another of many, many swigs of ale.

Fine words though, ones she had grown up with and lived her life by. The Credos of Hrolvad were taught to all Northlanders at a young age. They were the tenets of life for an entire culture.

But now they don't apply to me . . .

As a Northlands warrior, you can earn no glory if you can't be brave . . . and you can't be brave if your enemies just stand there drooling like idiots and let you slaughter them.

Many of her fellow Northlanders had told Serena what a wonderful gift she had and how marvelous it would be to have this power of domination over all enemies. Of course they also said how much they admired her clothing or hair. A lot of them seemed to have just plain fallen in love with her. Thorvald Bonesnapper even wanted a child. Serena kicked him in the nuts.

This whole thing with the diamond, the spirit within her, the ridiculous behavior of everyone around her, the seeming lack of any future enemies to fight, and now the fact that *she had just spilled her drink was . . . !*

"CRAP!" The heavy table went to the floor with a crash as Serena leapt to her feet, scimitar in hand. Several patrons of the ale house did the same in a reflex action. The sound of a sword being drawn in a bar never fails to get noticed.

"COME ON, FIGHT ME, YOU WHORESONS!" Serena hollered in a drunken roar.

She spun in a full circle, sword extended in a two-handed grip, glaring at the other patrons. To anyone with any sense, this would have been a tense situation. There were a dozen razor-sharp blades out and ready for mayhem. Bloodshed seemed inevitable. Then Serena felt it. The air of danger triggered something deep inside her. She knew the spirit within was reacting to the situation and doing something about it.

To the warriors who had drawn their weapons, it felt like a gentle breeze caressing their stout hearts. The blonde woman before them, Serena—Serena *the Beautiful*, Serena *the Glorious*, Serena *the Precious*—was a treasure beyond value. Swords were sheathed, and steins were raised in salute and praise.

Chieftain Eymon the Rank picked this moment to enter the ale house. He had a retinue of followers who were carrying several items. He pushed his way through the throng of love-struck brutes and addressed the crowd.

"Northlanders! Today we honor the Hero of Grannugh. Serena Brimstone, Shield Maiden, has saved us all from certain destruction by the hordes of barbarians that descended from the escarpment. No amount of thanks is sufficient. No praise could ever do justice to the glory that . . ."

Eymon turned from the crowd to Serena and quickly lost his train of thought. He gulped and collected himself.

"Serena, oh glorious one . . . there can be no higher distinction for we of the Northlands than to have you among us. And we have humble gifts to honor the Gods' gift of *you* to us."

He clapped his hands and motioned for the women following him to come forward. They placed their loads at Serena's feet. There were magnificent furs and feminine gowns of fine cloth, silver jewelry, and delicate strands of pearls and coral made to adorn the necks and arms of gracious ladies. This was all booty taken in past raids of other lands, of course, but it was the finest of booty from the collections of Grannugh's best warriors.

As the pile grew, Eymon finished up with, "I, Eymon Skagsgard, bestow upon you the title of Queen of Honor and Love and humbly ask you to reign in that capacity."

Queen of Honor and Love. There was no greater position among Northlands culture. It was a title implying almost divine stature. A Queen of Honor and Love was said to be a paragon of perfection in deportment, wisdom, and of course, beauty. A town or region graced with a Queen held mystical importance among the peoples of the North. Pilgrims would come from across the land to worship at Her feet and to seek Her grace. There had not been a queen in generations, ever since the time of Leticia Silverlocks. Cheers and claps resounded through the greasy bar. Still, the solemnness of the occasion was no less than if it were being held in the Imperial Palace of Tresk itself.

The object of everyone's love and worship stood, sword drawn, smelling of beer and swaying drunkenly with murder in her eyes. However, to all in the room, it was as though a daughter of Crodan Himself had descended to Lurra in all Her glory.

Serena had never felt less like a queen in her life. What she really wanted to do was fight someone. She really *needed* to fight someone. She needed to feel the strength of the warrior coursing through her veins. She needed the personal satisfaction she got from defeating a strong opponent in a fair fight. Dressing in silks and waving to worshippers from a throne didn't quite fill that need. Sadly, she lowered her sword and pushed her way out of the bar and onto the street. The 'Queen of Love and Honor' leaned against a wall, puked on her feet, and made the decision to leave.

Today – The Drowned City

The initial attack literally buried all the Group Six members under a pile of chattering little naked people. A hundred little hands were grabbing and poking from all sides. Some of them carried lengths of braided plant stems and tried to wrap them around whatever Eryndi ankle or Macai wrist presented itself.

Tresado and Orchid and everyone else on the platform did essentially the same thing, the purely instinctive move of throwing up their hands to ward off the attackers. But to the two skilled Magicians, that reflex action had more potential than just a solid punch. It took a couple of beats for Tresado's Magic to coalesce. Orchid's followed in a couple more. With hers, it always took just a bit longer, but the results were just as good.

Twenty of the little guys exploded outward, violently thrust away by an invisible force. Kindergarten-kid-sized warriors were hurled twenty paces away into the water or onto the bank. A few of them collided with low tree limbs. Whether a branch or a spine broke, there was a similar cracking sound. One of them bulls-eyed butt first into the window of a drowned building. His body could be heard crashing through rubble inside.

That was Tresado's spell. Orchid's had a little more to see. Thick tendrils of swamp reeds snaked out of the water, their asparagus-like heads peering around. A half-beat later, they lashed out and wrapped around the remaining attackers. A quick jerk by the reeds tore loose the weak grips they had on Foxx and Leader. The reeds quickly retreated back into the water, dragging a dozen more squirming little guys with them. Orchid continued to direct the plant vs. pygmy battle, communing with her swamp reed pals in steady concentration.

"Get on the boat, quick!" Tresado shouted. "Foxx, give me a hand with . . ." Before he could finish, Leader grabbed Serena under the armpits and dragged the shield maiden to the edge of the stone platform, where *Enchanter* was moored.

For the moment, the way was clear. The tiny attackers had backed off when they saw the power of their potential captives. But now they changed their tactics. They may have been naked, but they weren't stupid. Out came the blowguns, and soon the air was filled with the soft whispers of flying darts. They didn't have much power to them, though. Several little darts struck Leader as he struggled to pull Serena's limp form onto the boat. They didn't appear to penetrate his clothing enough to take effect.

Foxx produced a knife from somewhere and quickly severed the mooring line. He leapt aboard just as a flurry of darts caught him in the belly and legs. His eyes rolled up in his head, and Foxx went limp in mid-leap. His body hitting *Enchanter*'s deck sounded like a dropped gunny sack full of cantaloupes.

"Foxx!" Tresado yelled but got no response. Foxx's face was plastered against the deck as he lay there unmoving. Tresado could do nothing for his friend except to keep scattering the attackers as best he could. There were just so many of them, though. Darts were whizzing by him from all directions. Some of the little buggers were hidden from view up in trees or in the ruined buildings. Tresado changed focus and gathered Magic into a pinpoint, which flew towards the bank and exploded in a burst of light and burning energy. Half of the attackers were blinded or scorched.

Tresado even used some of the little guys as projectiles. He Magically grabbed a group of three who were launching darts from the muddy bank and twirled them around his head like an invisible lasso. He flung them one at a time at groups of the enemy, scattering them like twelve-pins. One of them violently collided face-to-face with another pygmy who had just raised his weapon to his lips. Both bloody ends of the blowgun protruded from the backs of their necks as they slowly dropped to the ground in an eternal kiss.

There were still swarms of pygmies popping out of the water and launching darts. Orchid continued to use her Worldly Magic to deal with them. The water around the boat churned with the turbulence of struggling pygmies being strangled and drowned by reeds.

Orchid seemed to have the battle under control for the moment, so Tresado took his attention from the pygmies to give *Enchanter* a Magical push away from the platform. He flung open the box next to the steering oar and grabbed a Magic coin, dropped it into the fuel canister, and threw open the throttle. *Enchanter* roared to life in a torrent of bubbles and fled upstream. Tresado kept a careful eye out for obstructions and dizzily steered the boat around mud banks and rubble. *Enchanter*'s wake raced across the sluggish waters and slapped the ruined buildings with unaccustomed whitecaps. The inertia of those fast turns had everyone hanging on for dear life. Leader had lain completely across Serena's body, trying to shield her from danger as well as keep her from rolling into the water. Foxx's inert limbs were wrapped around the mast like an old shirt blown against a fence post.

"Are you sure you want to go this way?" yelled Orchid as she released her plant grip on several pygmies, their strangled bodies bobbing to the surface. "You don't want to go back?"

"We've got to get past these little bastards!" Tresado yelled while steering the speeding boat around broken buildings and mud banks. "Besides," he said confidently, "there's probably more of them behind us now than ahead."

Orchid was crouched at the bow as *Enchanter* flew around a bend. She peered upriver and discovered the awful truth.

"I'm gonna write that down in my journal if we live through this. Look ahead!"

Tresado did so and wished he hadn't. The riverbanks and trees were overflowing with little naked chattering guys. Hundreds of little blowguns were lifted to hundreds of little lips, all ready to blow when in range. Tresado threw the tiller hard over, trying to turn *Enchanter* away in time. It was too late. A swarm of darts swept over the deck from all sides. He felt a couple of slight stings on the leg and chest. There was a splash of water, and then . . .

CHAPTER 8

Twelve years ago - Orchid

The smell of juniper and the morning song of the moonlarks that nested in it were all Jennick needed to wake up. It was a glorious day. The sunbeam filtering through the trees highlighted the sleeping face of his young love. He carefully slipped out from beneath the giant *banda* leaf so as not to disturb her. Quietly, he pulled on his tunic and gathered his few belongings. The quicker this was over with, the better. It would be so very easy to just slip away into the forest. Jennick was on the verge of doing just that when the far-off cry of a hawk halted him.

That wouldn't be very nice, the bird insinuated.

Or ethical, Jennick thought. *This whole crazy affair was unethical. But I can't just leave without telling her.*

Jennick made the decision and turned around, only to look directly into the face of Orchid.

"Good morning," she cooed affectionately, throwing her arms around his neck. Her tender kiss had the delicacy of morning dew.

He allowed himself the indulgence just long enough

until guilt and practicality took over. Holding Orchid at arm's length, he gazed into her green eyes.

"You're going, aren't you?" said Orchid, reading his expression.

"You've always known this would have to happen," Jennick said.

"I've always known it *could* happen. I never thought it would."

"I . . ." Jennick started to say.

"I thought we decided," Orchid challenged, "that you being an Eryndi didn't matter . . . that you being *my mentor* didn't matter!"

Jennick steeled himself for what he had to say. "*Orchid* . . . Orchid, by all rational thought it doesn't matter. We could come up with countless logical reasons why we could be together. But life isn't logical."

Orchid absolutely refused to let her eyes tear up. It wasn't easy.

"Is it the Elders? Is it because I'm your student? I just don't understand," she said.

"And that is precisely the problem," Jennick replied. "You've been a remarkable pupil. You've worked hard to learn everything I've taught you. For a Macai to accomplish what you have is, well, unprecedented."

"*But?*" Orchid demanded.

Jennick paused while the hawk spoke to him again. He heard it plainly. She didn't.

"But the fact is, you're right. *You just don't understand.*"

Jennick gently pulled away and slung his satchel over his shoulder.

"Goodbye, Orchid," he said. "Have an amazing life."

And like a dandelion seed in the wind, he was gone.

Tresado - "There's probably more behind us than ahead of us."

—ORCHID'S 'LIST OF STUPID THINGS
PEOPLE HAVE SAID'

Today – The Drowned City

Orchid had started her spell as soon as she saw the danger. There were hundreds of hostile pygmies shooting darts at them, and Group Six needed protection. She reached out to the river with her mind, imploring it for help. The wake from the fleeing boat agreed and began to rise in a roar of spray. She looked back toward the stern just in time to see Tresado stiffen and slump over the tiller, jamming it all the way over. The boat gave a lurch as she turned for all she was worth. There was nothing Orchid could do about it at the moment. *Enchanter* was locked in a high-speed turn with nothing but a dead-weight Eryndi at the helm. The boat roared in a tight circle, spewing a rooster tail of bubbles from her stern. Orchid held on for dear life, fighting the forces that threatened to hurl her from the boat while simultaneously concentrating on her spell. Pygmy darts whistled past her nose, and she knew it would be mere beats before one hit her.

A whirlwind of spray rose from the river as Orchid's spell took full effect. The rushing water matched the wild spinning of the out-of-control bubble boat. The drizzle thickened until *Enchanter* was completely surrounded by a swirling water spout.

It worked! Orchid thought. The darts were being deflected by the water, but another problem presented itself. The Magic bubble drive was still at full throttle. The boat was still wildly spinning, and now its waterspout cocoon was rapidly filling with bubbles.

Fighting the G-forces, Leader released his grip on Serena and clawed his way to the stern. He was immersed in bubbles as he blindly pulled Tresado's limp body off the tiller and dropped him to the deck. He then grabbed the throttle handle and shut down the drive. The boat stabilized immediately, and Leader stood up, adjusting the lapel of his tunic back to perfection.

"Well done, Orchid," he said stoically. He leaned down and checked Serena for injuries. He plucked the small dart from her back and held it up. "Everyone appears to be relatively undamaged except for these."

"I may be able to do something," Orchid said, not taking her eyes from the swirling water she was controlling, "but I need to . . . just a minute . . ."

Orchid concentrated and asked more simple favors of Nature. The swirling water slowed and turned a frosty white. What had been a waterspout was now a teardrop-shaped twisted cone of floating ice that enveloped and protected *Enchanter* and her passengers. Now that she no longer needed to maintain concentration on keeping the waterspout going, she would be able to get to her herb kit and help the others.

"Ah," Orchid said smugly, "damn, I'm good! Now let me . . ." Her smile faded as the deck started to tilt at an alarming rate, faster and faster until the bubble of ice surrounding the boat upended. The teardrop-shaped, hollow ice cube had decided on its own that it would rather float point-down in the water. Cargo and people, conscious or otherwise, all fell at once into the narrow end of their ice-shelter.

Leader, his face smashed against the tip of the mast, was upside down at the bottom of the pile. A mixture of supplies and comrades was heaped on top of him. The bright moonlight from the outside world filtered through weakly with a dirty green color. They were underwater!

"Orchid," he mumbled, his words distorted by the varnished pole across his lips, "I am quite incapacitated. Is there anything you can do?"

Orchid was only half-buried. Foxx's left leg was draped across her throat, and there were a couple of boxes pinning her feet, but she was able to function.

"Yeah, hang on. Don't move."

She concentrated again, this time with more deliberation. Water flowed up and over the wide patch of ice covering *Enchanter*'s twin keels, which bobbed upside-down. Orchid now persuaded the temperature to drop. She was not using Magic directly to lower the temperature, as someone using Absolute Magic would do. Her Worldly spell politely edged the existing heat away, allowing the cold to naturally move in and, just like that, the water froze, adding to the mass of ice. Over and over Orchid directed this action, gradually thickening the layers above the upside-down keel. At last, the weight became enough that the ship in a bottle slowly began to right itself.

Enchanter swung up onto her port side, then began a slow rising to fully upright. Barrels, boxes, and bodies tumbled back down to the deck. A small food cask rolled free and smacked into Foxx's lifeless face.

That's gonna leave a mark, thought Orchid. *Twigs, I need a drink!*

* * *

Beans and the blood of life for lunch. Lurra's vein dissuaded from home to suckle the ones without. The last of the dwellers have fled into its arms. Never to count the stars again, poor buggers.

—Travelogue of Dementus, the Mad Treskan

Four years ago - The Northlands' southern border – Serena

The Axenon Escarpment loomed in the east, like a great stone vulture waiting for something to die. The imposing mesa thrust obscenely above the surrounding plain, blocking out the rising sun, obviously with evil intent. Serena let her horse pick its own path through the inhospitable terrain. These foothills were barren and rocky, and most respectable life had decided to exist elsewhere. A few scraggly bushes poked up from between sharp boulders, but that was it for flora. A malignant-looking lizard with contempt in his eyes scurried away as Serena searched the rocky slope. She ignored it and moved on, wanting to get this mission out of the way as soon as possible.

It had been three hard weeks since she left Grannugh to seek the southern countries. Normally, anyone traveling to those far-off lands would make a wide detour around the escarpment. This was barbarian territory. Everyone knew that hordes of mutants lived on the summit and slopes of that forbidding, evil place. It was from up there somewhere that last month's attack on her home had originated. It was said the barbarians practiced all manner of foul rites and committed any number of unspeakable acts. Serena wasn't sure just how much of this was correct since no one she knew had ever been here. The only contact Northlanders had with these people had been fighting off their raids.

But Serena did not wish to avoid this area. There was someone here she was determined to see. Supposedly there was a woman who lived on these dark slopes that might be able to help her. In every village and farmhouse that she passed, people spoke of the Prophet. In some places, she was called a seer or an oracle. Some folks spoke of this woman as a witch or some kind of evil spirit. Others said she was a great Magician who could grant wishes, but only for some horrendous price not worth paying.

At least that was one good thing about possessing the diamond. People were willing to tell Serena everything they knew. It didn't matter if they didn't know what they were talking about; they told her anyway. The only thing everyone agreed upon was that the woman was called Bata and that she lived on the western slope of the Axenon Escarpment.

Of course, as big as the escarpment was, the western slope covered hundreds of square leagues. Serena tried to pick out as many commonalities as she could from all the different stories, but finally it just came down to searching every canyon and draw.

Serena was on the verge of giving up and continuing south when she spotted a thin line of smoke far up the slope. She dug into her saddlebags and pulled out her *looker*. It was a wonderful device; three tubes with lenses in them that slid into one another, allowing one to bring the horizon many times closer. This particular toy had been part of the booty taken in a Northlanders' raid on a foreign merchant vessel a few years ago. It was one of the few items of tribute given to her as the *Queen of Honor and Love* that she kept. It was far more useful than the fancy dresses and jewelry.

The smoke seemed to come from beneath the ground. It curled out from amongst the rocks themselves. Whatever the source, it didn't seem to be natural. The way up was too steep for her warhorse (another gift from her admirers), so Serena dismounted and let the animal fend for himself. He took a nibble of some of the scrub brush and snorted at the bitter taste.

Serena's hackles stood up in this place and she wasn't sure why. She made sure her sword was loose in its scabbard and started to climb. The way was difficult. The loose rocks slipped beneath her feet and skittered down the slope in her wake. She lost two steps for every three she took, but struggled on. The source of the smoke was on a ledge just ahead. Now Serena could see there was some kind of shelter fashioned from the rocks. A large slab formed the roof, and the place couldn't be distinguished from the natural hillside unless you were right in front of it. The smoke was the only thing that had given it away from a distance. Now that Serena was near, she could smell an aroma coming from the place. Something was cooking. Her stomach growled in response. Serena instinctively checked her surroundings and found nothing. She slowly approached the dwelling.

"You have come."

The wispy voice came from behind. Serena spun, drawing her sword in the same lightning move. The figure was just standing there, no more than a reach away. It was a small, crooked form, clad in some kind of loosely draped, thin leather poncho. Its head was completely wrapped in a long scarf of the same material. The tip of Serena's scimitar hovered in front of the creature's yellowish eyes, which peered from beneath the scarf.

"Who the crap are you?"

The figure just stood there, its papery clothing fluttering in the dry wind.

"I said, who are you? Tell me!" Serena demanded again.

"I am Bata." The voice seemed unattached to the creature, as if its words came via the wind.

The scimitar lowered slightly.

"I have been looking for you," said Serena, warily, "to ask you for your help."

A thin arm gestured toward the shelter.

"There is food."

If this was Bata's way of reacting to the love bead in Serena's chest, it was certainly a different approach.

At least she's not fawning over me.

Serena sheathed her sword and carefully moved several steps toward the door, keeping an eye on the creature the whole time. Bata remained unmoving. Serena took a quick glance inside. There was lots of stuff, but no other living things. She turned back to Bata . . . and almost peed her pants. Serena's host was standing nearly face to face with her!

"You may enter."

Serena did just that, if for no other reason than to put some distance between them. There was a fire burning in the crude rock hearth on one side of the shelter, a pot of delicious smelling stew simmering over it. A dim oil lamp illuminated shelves containing pots of herbs and seasonings, all neatly labeled. There was nothing fancy about the furnishings, but all seemed sturdy and functional. There was a comfortable looking bed, a chair, a table . . . the whole place screamed *one, simple, tidy occupant.*

Serena could have sworn that Bata was behind her in the doorway, but now the creature stood by the fire, holding out a bowl and spoon.

"Eat your fill."

Serena's tummy rumbled again and, despite any better judgment, she accepted the food. It was mutton and potato stew, one of her favorites. She sat at the table and dug in.

Delicious, Serena thought, *just like Mom used to make.*

The bowl of stew was gone quickly. Serena burped and smacked her lips.

"Thank you, Bata," she said, "I didn't realize how hungry I was."

The figure regarded Serena for a moment with its yellow eyes, then reached up and started to unwind the leathery scarf covering its head. The face that emerged was very old, very wrinkled, and very Eryndi. This was only the second Ernie Serena had ever seen, but there was no mistaking the cone-shaped ears and long, pointed face. The thin lips parted.

"You bring another."

There was something immediately apparent to Serena. Bata was aware of everything. She knew who Serena was, about the diamond, where she had come from, and why she was here. Bata knew all these things. And inexplicably, Serena knew that she knew, but she asked anyway.

"How do you know?"

"I see much," Bata replied.

"Can you take this thing out of me?" Serena asked, cutting to the chase.

"Cannot be taken."

"Can I give it to someone else?"

"Cannot be given."

"There must be some way to get rid of it!" Frustrated, Serena lashed out and knocked her empty bowl across the room.

"Only one way."

Serena perked up. "What is it? Please tell me!"

"You must die."

Just like before, she knew that Bata was telling the truth. Serena thought back to the day she had acquired the diamond. She put her face in her hands, thoroughly dejected, not knowing what to do or where to go.

"You are thirsty."

"Bata, you have been kind to me," Serena said. "Thank you for your hospitality, but I . . ."

"There is drink."

Serena looked up slowly and reached for the cup in front of her. There was just no denying anything this old woman said. She took a long swig of the old-fashioned cider and felt any remaining care about life starting to drift away. Through nearly closed eyes, she saw Bata just heading out the door.

"Where are you going?" Serena asked sluggishly.

Bata turned and looked at Serena for a long moment.

"I must hunt."

Serena watched the brown liquid as it swirled in her cup.

She peered down into a deep dark place . . . infinitely large . . . familiar . . . everything was familiar . . . but long gone. The myriad scenes that danced in the liquid flowed as one, but were as

*separate as the years. Serena felt intensely tired as she took the tour
of her life . . . from her birth to her death to her birth . . . There
was sea and land . . . horses and boats . . . mountains and deserts
. . . a tower of blue and a prison of glass . . . There was fondness
and pain . . . she played with her little cousins in the fjord and
dueled with the sword master on the main t'gallant yardarm . . .
the iron fish . . . a seal hunt with Dad . . . the brothers . . . the
Enchanter . . . the trial . . . the sword . . . Avarice and Greed . . .
the Imperium . . . Parsomal . . . fighting and killing . . . dying
dragons . . . the lost tooth . . . the endless wait . . . best friends . . .
life and death and life . . . the roar of the crowd . . .*

Serena forced herself to wakefulness, trying to remember
what had just been revealed to her, but it had fled. Visions of
the past as seen from the future . . . all questions had been
answered, but the answers were not allowed to stay. She had
not been asleep . . . she didn't think so, anyway. She still sat at
the table, clutching the skull that she had just drunk out of.

THE SKULL?

Realizing what she held in her hand, Serena jumped to
her feet, pushing over the chair in the process. It fell backward
with a loud bang, cracking one of the rib bones that made
up the back. Rattled, Serena gripped the hilt of her sword
and quickly backed toward the door as she checked out the
alarming changes around her.

The shelves, table, cot, chair, even the oil lamp were
made of *bones* . . . barbarian bones. The legs of the cot
were a crisscrossing of misshapen femurs. They all had that
characteristic distorted shape that marked them as coming
from dead barbarians. The single oil lamp that glowed with
a flickering yellow light was made from an upside-down
barbarian skull. The burning wick protruded from the nose

hole. Even the spoon that she had eaten the stew with was carved from an arm bone. The empty bowl she had flung onto the floor was also fashioned from a skull. It and the iron pot reeked with an evil, sickly-sweet smell that was definitely not mutton stew.

In the corner was something else she recognized. It was a stack of weapons. There were arrows, spears, axes, some of them broken or missing parts. All of them appeared to be of barbarian origin. Serena noticed that the frame holding the stewpot above the fire was fashioned from iron pike heads.

The rest of the place was filled with the oddest bunch of junk Serena had ever seen. Pots and baskets overflowed with bits of metal, dried weeds, colored dirt clods and some unidentifiable stuff. Several glass jars contained what looked like nothing more than gravel. They seemed identical but were labeled with different titles, all of which were unreadable to Serena.

"Bata?" Serena called, getting no response. Backing quickly out the door, she saw no trace of the old Eryndi woman.

Something rustled and grabbed Serena by the legs. She jumped away, startled. The dry wind had blown Bata's thin, leathery clothing and scarf to wrap around Serena's feet. She bent to examine it. The dry, papery material was not leather . . . not exactly. On one corner of the poncho was a grayish stain. Serena spread it out and examined it more closely. The pattern was familiar. She had seen it before adorning the bodies of dead barbarians. It was a tribal marking of some kind . . . a tattoo! Bata's poncho and scarf were made from *barbarian skins!*

Serena's palms and butt got pretty badly scraped in her haste to scramble down the face of the mountain. Her horse was still there waiting for her. He looked impatient to go as well.

"Let's get out of here, Lucky," she said as she swung into the saddle.

The horse agreed, and after a twenty-minute gallop, the Axenon Escarpment finally began to pass behind them. This adventure had been a bust. Serena's trek to the southern countries to seek help for herself was apparently not over.

"That was really freaky," she said to her horse, easing him back to a walk. She looked down the slope ahead of them. Leagues in the distance, Serena could see green valleys.

"I tell you, Lucky, if every Eryndi turns out to be that weird, this is gonna be one wild journey."

CHAPTER 9

Today

Tresado waited on the bench for his turn to play. There was a cold draft blowing, and he hugged his bare knees for warmth. Boingball was not his sport. Tresado didn't really have a sport. He sucked at athletics. He had always sucked at athletics. But right now, he felt a swelling of pride. This was Tournament, a yearly event when all schools in the area competed physically. As he and his fellow junior cram school players headed for the prep room to suit up, they passed the bleachers filled with spectators watching the earlier games. Two young girls were excited to be let out of school to watch the Tournament games. Overhearing this bit of childish excitement made Tresado feel very important.

Tresado disliked sports and really disliked sports players, but he had to admit to being jealous of them. They got all the girls. They got special treatment in classes taught by coaches. They were popular. And now, here he was, ready to play boingball in front of everyone in town; ready to get out there and give a hundred and ten percent; ready to prove himself to be a manly Eryndi. It was really a shame that he was naked. He had tried and tried to find his locker where his gym stuff was, searching up and down unfamiliar corridors of the school looking for it, but time ran out, and the next thing he knew, he was freezing his ass off on the bench, waiting to play . . . why was it so cold in the gym?

"Tresado! You're up," shouted Mr. Beeblebum. "Take, uh, the back court flank spot!"

There was no other choice. Maybe the crowd wouldn't notice that he was naked. Tresado ran out onto the court to replace Fermie Marstigon, whom Coach called back in. As luck would have it, the ball boinged right in front of him. He tried to make a dash for it, but his feet just wouldn't get him there. It was as though his legs were weighed down with lead. Every step took an eternity. The other players moved effortlessly, running circles around Tresado. He then realized his next problem. Being naked, he was not wearing a uniform or even a jockstrap. What team was he on? At last, with great effort, Tresado managed to get possession of the ball. But what were the rules? He didn't know. He felt he should throw the ball, but where? The guys in the red jerseys were yelling, "Tresado! Here! Here!" The guys in the blue jerseys were yelling, "Tresado! Here! Here!" Everybody on the court was yelling, "Tresado! Here! Here!" Even the spectators in the stands had their arms in the air and were yelling, "Here! Here!" His entire hometown was looking at the naked Tresado and yelling, "Here! Here! Tresado! Tresado! Here! Here! Tresado! Tresado!"

Slap, slap, slap.

"Tresado? Tresado!"

Slap, slap, slap.

"Tresado. Are you with us? Wake up!"

His Eryndi eyes opened and immediately looked down at himself. He was no longer naked. That was a relief, since it was colder than a berg bear's ass. There was a strange bitter taste in Tresado's mouth, and his breath fogged in the icy cold.

He looked up at the faces above him. Orchid's was closest. "You okay now?"

"Yeah, I think so," said Tresado, shaking the cobwebs out of his head.

"Didja catch her?" asked a vision of purity, internally lit with the soft light of dawn.

"Serena!" sputtered Tresado, struggling to his feet. "You're all right! . . . Did I catch who?"

"Well, while you were laid out," she replied, "your legs were twitching, and you had your hand on your crotch. I figured you were after some poor farm animal."

Any rebuke for her insult was rinsed away in a sparkling shower of pure liquid adoration. Tresado now had most of his wits back and looked around at the smiling faces (except Leader's, of course) of Group Six on *Enchanter*'s crowded deck. Foxx was leaning against the mast and nursing a whale of a shiner with a cold pack.

"Where did you get ice?" Tresado asked, looking around. "Oh . . . I see. So that's why it's so cold in here."

Enchanter was encased inside a translucent, swirled cone of ice. The twisted teardrop came to a point at the top of the mast and widened out to disappear below the pontoons. Apparently, it was daytime now. Mottled sunlight filtered through the ice.

"Not bad," Tresado said, rapping his knuckles on the frigid wall. "Did you do this?"

Orchid almost blushed. "Well, yeah," she said, "those darts were flying pretty thick. But I'm afraid I was a little late. You got hit just as it went up."

"We're not going to suffocate in here, are we?" asked Foxx.

"Don't worry, I thought of that," said Orchid. "I put air holes in the top."

"Great," Foxx replied, "makes me feel like a pet hamster. Just throw in a piece of lettuce and some shavings."

"Har-de-har," said Orchid. "Next time, I won't bring you around. It's quieter if I let you sleep."

"And did you bring me around as well?" asked Tresado.

"Nature Girl brought all of us around," said Serena. "You and Foxx and I got hit with these things."

Serena reached up and plucked a dart from the sail. It looked like a thick cactus needle with a leaf cone wrapped around the base.

"It's a thorn from a *sleeper bush,*" explained Orchid. "It's actually a vine. The spikes are coated with a strong anesthetic. If an animal scratches itself on one, it falls asleep where it stands. The vines then eventually entwine the animal. A hundred more spikes drill into it and inject more of the poison. The body is then slowly broken down into plant food. It took me a few hours, but I managed to counteract the effect, although it would have worn off by itself eventually."

"Thanks for the nature lecture," said Serena, "but we've still got problems."

Furtive dark shadows flitted about the outside of their ice shelter, silhouetted by the sunlight. Something was crawling around out there.

Tresado quickly checked his precious boat. The deck was a mess. The supply crates were strewn about, some broken open.

"What happened here?" he asked.

"Oh that," said Orchid. "We, uh, had some unexpected turbulence and . . . well, you know."

"But it's all right now, though," she added quickly, glancing at the ever stoic Leader.

Tresado was only half paying attention because he had spotted his little box of Magic coins amongst the clutter. Like many other supply crates, it had come open and spilled its contents on the deck. He quickly went to his knees and started gathering them up. There were several missing.

"Only six left," he muttered as he carefully replaced the coins in the specially made container.

Foxx was still fussing with his blackened eye, gingerly poking it and whispering '*ow.*'

"Don't worry about it, pretty boy," said Serena. "Where I come from, scars and bruises are considered marks of distinction."

"I'm not a Northlander. I would just as soon *not* get my face bashed in," replied Foxx.

"I might be able to help with that, too," Orchid said. "I'll just have to find the right variety of bog leech."

"Great," winced Foxx, "I can hardly wait."

There was a small jolt of the deck, just enough to make everyone grab whatever was closest. Tresado peered through the frosty cone of ice that enveloped the boat. The shadows were still scurrying around out there.

"I can't quite tell what's going on."

"Maybe I can clear things up," said Orchid, gathering her thoughts.

The ice surrounding them melted and flowed about, smoothed itself, ejected bubbles, and finally refroze. The hollow teardrop had turned completely transparent, and now Group Six could clearly see the trouble they were in.

1,347 years ago – City of Mennatu

Elder Jarayan stepped onto her balcony and looked out at the construction site for the . . .

Let's see, it's been seventeen years and about two months, so that's roughly the six thousand eight hundred eightieth-some time, she cyphered to herself. The Elder had made a point of personally inspecting the progress every day since the beginning.

And also, for the six thousandth-some time, Jarayan felt a stab of sympathy for the Macai workers.

Poor things.

She knew perfectly well, of course, that their lives here in the city were infinitely better than in their predator-infested wilderness origins. Here in civilized lands, the Macai were kept safe and fed. But still, dragging those heavy loads of stone and sand in the hot sun had to be taxing. Much of the major lifting, such as raising the Central Obelisk, had been done through combined levitation, but there was still a tremendous amount of digging and earth-moving to be done, hence the need for the Macai.

They are *built for it, though,* Jarayan rationalized.

Those large, stocky bodies are made to order for heavy work, and they don't really know any different—no more than the Militia's horses or my own pet cat, for that matter.

It was coming down to the end finally. The giant transformation furnace and the stone edifice to house it were complete. There was but a week's worth of final touches and cleanup work, and then it would be ready to receive the Creation Matrix.

Jarayan had done a lot of soul searching these past few months. What was she to do when the project was complete? Much of her life since achieving Elder status had been spent on the design and construction of the Hearth. The project had consumed her soul as nothing ever had, including, regrettably, her family. Her younger two children scarcely knew their mother. Little Zarosen just had his fourth birthday celebration. It was the third one Jarayan had missed.

Perhaps that was the answer to her question. The idea hit her like one of the stone building blocks.

Spend time with my family again? Now why didn't I think of that earlier?

Once the Hearth was complete and functioning, she could do just that. Of course, when the Hearth was finished, all the people could do just that.

That was the very point Jarayan wished to stress to the Assembly members, who were coming from all across the Domain to witness Commencement. This project had been such a vast undertaking: endless delays, supply problems, labor shortages, Magical reallocations. The Assembly needed to be reassured that it had all been worth it.

A disturbance in the work pit snapped Jarayan out of her reverie. A small group of Macai had set down their loads and gathered around another that had apparently collapsed. Their Eryndi wranglers quickly shooed them away, getting them back to work. Water was brought, and the worker was revived—a simple case of heat exhaustion. Once it was able to stand, the worker was led away to its stable to recover. There were no whips used on the Macai any more than they were used on any of their other domesticated beasts. That sort of cruelty was almost unknown among the Eryndi. Their wise nature long ago realized that plenty of food, water, and shelter made for healthier and more productive livestock.

Fortunately, there had always been plenty of food and water to spare. The River had remained faithful for eons and never failed to produce enough water for the people and their farms. Over the centuries, the farmers acquired more land as the surrounding forest was harvested for its hardwood to build homes and infrastructure. The soil was fertile, and the crops flourished through sophisticated irrigation techniques. The city had public baths, and most houses had running water. It was not surprising that ages ago, the worship of the Waters of the River guided many Eryndi lives.

Hopefully, Quiseran, the water god, will still bless the faithful even after the Hearth is functioning, Jarayan snickered to herself.

Few people still prayed to the old deity. Most Eryndi eyes were on the bright and promising future that the Hearth would bring. The old ways of gods and demons were bowing to the age of reason and self-reliance. The Hearth would ensure that.

Today – The Drowned City of Mennatu

The protective coating of ice surrounding *Enchanter* cleared, and Group Six peered out at what was crawling around on the outside. And what crawled around on the outside peered right back at them. They were the same little naked figures that had attacked the boat with anesthetizing blowgun darts. The little savages, both male and female, scurried about using twisted vine ropes stretched around the ice as footholds. When the ice cleared, the pygmies studied their frozen captives. About forty of the little gray buggers pressed their naked bodies hard against the ice in their chattering enthusiasm. Tresado screamed in disgust for a full minute and a half.

"If you would get a hold of yourself," Orchid said to him, "take a close look at them . . . their *faces,* I mean."

Tresado gulped and tried to put on a clinical expression. He steeled himself and moved closer to the transparent wall separating him from the . . . *Eryndi! These creatures were Eryndi!*

They were tiny, with mottled gray skin. But there was no mistaking the little pointed chins and the conical ears. They were definitely Eryndi—or used to be. These creatures were drained, shrunken, used up. They seemed to have no language and just chattered and giggled like monkeys.

However, monkeys aren't smart enough to tow a floating ice cube full of captives with woven vines pulled along by gangs of pygmies on the shore. And that's just what was happening. A dozen primitive ropes were fastened around the ice protecting *Enchanter.* She was being towed along the base of a stone wall. The pygmies struggled along on top of the ruin, pulling on the vine ropes for all they were worth. There were still more swimming in the water, working as a team to push their prize along.

Foxx coolly regarded the little fellows and tried to put his unique skills to work. Over the years, his talents had evolved to the point where some simple concentration and subtle Magical inducement was all he needed to size up most anyone.

This should be no problem, he thought. *I've talked my way out of a lot worse situations.*

The first step in Foxx's process was to survey the scene around him: body language, voice tones, accent, local customs, even the weather, and any other observable variables were gathered by his senses and fed into the ether that was the Magic in the air. Foxx then used the Magic to process and organize all this information, which then was fed back into his psyche. Of course, he wasn't aware of every detail of all these things; he had developed his skills to the point where it was all automatic. The result was a very reliable sizing-up and understanding of the recipient. Years ago, he had coined the process *The Knowing Spell*.

Unfortunately, Foxx got very little from these fellows. It was like trying to read an animal. There was no spark of personality there at all. All he could read were basic emotions, mostly glee and expectation.

"Orchid, I'm not getting a thing," he said. "What do you make of these guys?"

"If I didn't know better," she replied, "I'd swear I was sensing a troop of pine lemurs for all the intelligence that's there."

"But pine lemurs don't weave ropes or use blowguns," commented Tresado. He took another hard look at his distant cousins. His Eryndi psyche could sense it. Even if he wasn't a tree-hugging Worldly Magician like Orchid, he could still feel a bond with the poor little buggers.

"Something happened to these guys," Tresado said sadly. "Something did this to them."

"Not to them," said Orchid, "to their ancestors. Look there."

She pointed to a mud bank that protruded from the water. On it was a small group of females, who were joining in with the hooting and chattering. Clinging to their backs and legs were several small children. The tiny forms had the same gray coloring and shrunken appearance as the adults.

"These people were born like this," said Orchid. "Whatever caused it happened a long time ago."

"Is there anything you can do to help them?" asked Tresado.

"We need to worry about helping ourselves," growled Serena. "I, for one, am not gonna end up in a cooking pot without one hell of a fight."

"Serena is quite right," said Leader. "Our priority is to escape these creatures and continue on our way."

"At whatever cost," Leader added, looking at Tresado.

The sunlight shining through the ice got brighter as *Enchanter* in her frozen shell emerged from under the tree canopy to an open expanse of water.

"I'm not sure where we're going," said Foxx, peering ahead through the ice, "but I think we're about there."

What looked to be a small lake lay ahead. As they got closer, it became clearer. The pygmy-Eryndi were pulling them into the flooded remains of a great, circular auditorium. Stone bleacher seats climbed out of the water on three sides. The large, open side they were headed for had broken, jagged edges as though from erosion. The structure must have been massive at one time. The seats protruded more than thirty rows above the surface of the water. How much was underwater was impossible to tell, but the *lake,* as it were, was more than two-hundred reaches across.

"This arena must have seated tens of thousands," estimated Foxx, "and it looks like the floor could have held everything from a chess match to dragon fights."

"I'd say they're getting ready for the main event now," observed Serena.

There was some kind of large ruin protruding from the water at the center of the former arena. A large stone base covered in heaps of rubble thrust up from the water. Hundreds of pygmies were gathering on this island. *Enchanter* was being towed right toward it.

"That's where we're going, I'd say," said Tresado, pointing. "Anybody have a plan?"

"Fight till we die," said Serena immediately.

"Good plan," said Orchid, "simple and direct."

"Except for the dying part. I'm afraid I'm not going to be of much use," said Foxx, drawing a dagger, "but I'll do my best."

"I'd rather have you ready at the helm," said Tresado. "Serena, Orchid, and I will do the fighting.

"Here," he continued, handing Foxx his precious box of Magical bubble coins, "take these and be ready to haul ass out of here."

"Unfortunately, I am also ill-equipped to fight off these creatures," said Leader. "I will assist Foxx, if I can."

"How fast can you get us out of this ice cube?" asked Tresado of Orchid.

"I can create an unequal heat in the ice from the inside," she replied. "It should explode the shell outward."

"And then we come out shooting," said Serena, hefting her bow and loosening her sword in its scabbard.

"Right," said Tresado, "as soon as we have clear water, drop in a coin and get us out of here fast."

"We'll be ready," replied Foxx, glancing at Leader.

1,347 years ago – City of Mennatu

Citizens. On this glorious day of new beginnings, I greet you. This project is the result of many hard years filled with sacrifice and effort. The finest minds and the greatest Magicians of the Domain have labored to produce this unprecedented merging of Absolute and Worldly Magic, the full potential of which can only be imagined. Today we are witness to Commencement. The Creation Matrix is complete and ready for activation. Starting today, we begin to eliminate hunger and want. No more must our sustenance depend on the toil of farmers or the slaughter of animals. No more must we decimate the great forest to build our homes. No more must the face of Lurra be scarred and violated with the extraction of ores. Gentlefolk, I give you the ultimate creation . . . creation itself. The Great Hearth.

—Elder Jarayan - Address to the Assembly
– Opening Remarks

* * *

Today – The Drowned City of Mennatu

The deck of *Enchanter* lurched slightly as the frozen teardrop bumped against solid ground. The pygmies quickly tied off the tow ropes to several huge chunks of broken stone that littered the beach of this apparently artificial island. That was not all that littered the beach. Amongst the rubble lay countless thousands of gnawed bones of all kinds.

"Kind of obvious now what they intend to do with us," observed Serena.

As soon as their prize was secure, the pygmies picked up several fist-sized (for them) sharp rocks and began to hack at the thick ice, sending out showers of slush.

"Well, that gives them a hobby for a while," said Foxx. "See that opening ahead?"

Foxx pointed with a slight nod of his head. Beyond the stone island lay the far side of the arena. There was a huge stone gateway leading back out onto the river. Giant square stone pillars flanked the opening on both sides, while a solid stone arch towered twenty reaches above. The water under this gateway churned and fussed violently, throwing up showers of spray. The river was apparently under some sort of violent influence. It definitely did not look boat-friendly.

"I don't think we want to go that way," warned Foxx.

"Agreed," replied Tresado. "Somehow we need to get back out of this arena the way we came and sail around it."

"When I explode the ice," said Orchid, "it should take out enough of them that we can get away."

"What about their stupid little darts?" asked Serena. To her, any weapon that did not draw massive amounts of blood was unworthy.

"The antidote that brought you around should continue to protect against the darts' drug," Orchid reassured her, "for a while, anyway."

She looked out at the pygmies. Their weak little blows were making slow but steady progress hacking through the ice.

"Everybody ready?"

Orchid started to gather her thoughts to cast her spell when a hand grasped her shoulder.

"Wait," said Foxx calmly. "Before you do that, I think we need to talk about some things."

"Yeah, one or two," replied Tresado.

"Or even three or four," agreed Serena.

Four heads turned as one and looked at Leader.

"Did I miss something?" he asked stoically.

"I did," replied Tresado. "Eleven of my special fuel coins."

"That is unfortunate," answered Leader. "They may have fallen overboard when the boat upended."

"The boat was encased in ice at the time," said Orchid. "Nothing could have gone over."

"It has been an eventful trip," said Leader. "It is equally likely that they are in the stomach of a croc or taken by pygmies when they attacked the boat."

"Notice how he always manages to avoid giving a direct answer?" said Foxx to the others, talking as if Leader were not standing right there.

"And how calm and emotionless he is, even when the pressure's on?" added Orchid. "You should have heard him when the boat tipped over and he was trapped upside down. You'd think he was standing on a street corner for all the concern he showed."

"Wait a minute, the boat tipped over!?" demanded Tresado.

"Oh . . . I was gonna tell you," said Orchid.

"When?"

"When I thought you were ready to hear it."

"Later, guys," said Foxx, stepping in. "Let's get back to

our fearless leader. Have you noticed how his hand is slowly moving down? I wonder if he's looking for *these*."

Foxx pulled a small pouch out from his sleeve and tossed it to Tresado, who opened it up.

"My Magic coins!"

"Yeah," said Foxx, "I lifted that pouch off him while the pygmies were towing us . . . well, look at that! I do believe that was the briefest glimmer of surprise that just flicked across his face."

"I wonder just where he was planning on taking *Enchanter* once he'd stolen her," said Tresado, glaring at Leader.

"One of several questions I'd like answered," said Foxx.

"Oh, like why the pygmy darts had no effect on him?" offered Orchid.

"And what about that weird-ass smooth skin of his?" said Serena. "He looks like he's carved out of ivory."

"And you ought to see the way he writes," added Foxx. "I've never seen such perfect printing."

"There certainly is something *different* about him, isn't there?" said Orchid.

"All people are different, in some way," replied Leader, as though commenting about the weather.

"There he goes again," said Foxx. "You see? He never *lies* about anything, but like a sleight-of-hand artist, he just changes the subject to distract you from the trick he's playing."

"Being extremely overpaid for this job was a big distraction," said Tresado. "It kept us from asking too many questions. I have to admit I was mighty grateful to him for paying for the boat. Damned nice of him."

"A little too nice," answered Foxx. "When Leader first approached me with this expedition and sent me to recruit the rest of you, he emphasized several times that money was no object. Naturally, I was suspicious, but *hey*, who am I to argue with money? I looked for some motivation, but it seemed that I couldn't Magically read him for some reason. But I learned a thing or two about dealing with people from old Professor Generax. Even without Magic, it was clear that Leader had some hidden agenda."

"I'm a pretty trusting soul most of the time," added Orchid, "and even I could tell something was up when he seemed to know so much about all of us and our needs."

"Especially about my diamond," said Serena through narrowed eyes. "I don't exactly take out ads about that."

"Good point," said Tresado.

"I have another *point* I'd like to bring up," said Serena, drawing her scimitar in a meaningful way.

Leader backed up a step at the sight of the razor-sharp blade hovering under his perfect nose. Other than that, not a glimmer of reaction crossed his face.

"I think we'd all like to hear your *point*, Serena," said Orchid. "Do tell."

"Gladly," Serena said. "For one thing, anyone who names himself *Leader* needs to act the part. I have no respect for a man who says he's in charge but offers to pluck feathers and help with housework. As much as he paid us, you'd think he'd have us waiting on him hand and foot."

"Maybe he was trying to lull us into trusting him," offered Foxx.

Serena advanced on Leader and spoke to him directly.

"You never did really need my *mighty sword arm,* like you called it," Serena said. "Yeah, I'm a badass. I'll be the first to crow about that. But there are plenty of other badasses out there for hire."

"And for what you paid," added Tresado, "you could have hired a small army of badasses to escort you to this super Magician at the end of the river, if there even is such a person."

"Yeah, you could have had all the badasses you want," said Serena, "but there's only *one* badass with *this.*"

Once again, Serena pulled the lapels of her jerkin apart and the brilliant colors of the diamond burst forth like fireworks. Tresado and Foxx probably would have fallen overboard were it not for the protective ice. Leader remained impassive.

"Doesn't affect you at all, does it?" asked Serena. "Just what are you, anyway?"

"As interesting as this all is," said Leader, "I must point out that the pygmies are almost through the ice."

Tresado looked out at his withered little cousins. "Well, what do you know? He's right. What say we get on with things?"

"The sooner, the better. I'll keep an eye on Mister Perfect here," said Serena, ominously keeping the tip of her sword in Leader's face. He did not react except to calmly close his eyes as though waiting to be beheaded.

"Good," replied Foxx, "I was starting to get cold. Orchid, you want to do the honors?"

"With pleasure," she lilted. A moment's thought and the protective cocoon surrounding their boat immediately filled with a great web of cracks. The ice then exploded violently outward, filling the air in all directions with deadly shards of destruction. The shrunken Eryndi took the full brunt of the explosion, their tiny bodies hurled away, pierced and bloodied.

"NOW!" shouted Tresado.

Foxx was ready with the Magical coin, but a half-beat before his hand could drop it in the fuel slot, he and everyone else on board were violently heaved upward. The deck rose beneath their feet as a great wave of water surged up, swamping the boat and hurling everyone and everything into the river. *Enchanter* came down hard, bow first, her mast snapping off as it collided with the edge of the stone island. The boat's hull plunged underwater from the fall and painfully refloated itself to emerge wounded and broken. Several bladders in the pontoons were ruptured from the impact, and the ship listed badly.

Tresado was the first one to bob to the surface, sputtering and coughing. Foxx and Orchid followed a moment later. The three of them managed to struggle to the floating hull and hang on to a pontoon.

"You okay? Orchid? Foxx?"

"Yeah," sputtered Orchid, spitting out what felt like half the river.

Foxx painfully nodded as he hung on to the wreckage, blood streaming down the side of his face from a gash on his skull.

Tresado looked around for the rest of the group. "Serena? . . . Where's Serena? . . . SERENA!!"

Orchid took a deep breath and dove beneath the water. A minute later she emerged, clutching the shield maiden's scimitar.

"I found this on the bottom," wheezed Orchid, gasping for breath, "but there was no sign of *her!*"

"SERENA! *SERENA!*" Tresado called desperately.

But it was no use. Both Serena and Leader were gone.

CHAPTER 10

1,335 years ago – City of Mennatu – Twelve years after Commencement

"You think you can boss me around just because you're an Elder?"

"No," replied Jarayan angrily, "I think I can boss you around because I'm your *mother!*"

"But it's not *fair!*" answered Zarosen in a whine. "What about my gaming? My team is in the final five. I just got named to the first squad. And you know *The Gargoyles* concert is next month, and the water festival is this Vinday and the new cloak styles are coming out any day. And what about my friends? How do you expect me to keep in touch with my friends if I'm off on some shitty river barge?"

"I'm beginning to think I can't expect much of anything from you," sighed Jarayan, "and you watch your language, young man."

"Yeah, well, that's what I am now, you know, *a man!*"

Jarayan took a breath and tried to calm herself down.

"Son, I know you're an adult now," she said. "I know you can make your own decisions, but this is *important*. It's for your own good *and* the good of the Domain."

"It's important to you, not to me," Zarosen said. "This was your project in the first place. Besides, the city is rebuilt now. It's time to take it easy and enjoy. Wasn't that what you wanted? Wasn't that the whole idea of the Hearth?"

"*Mennatu* is rebuilt," Jarayan answered, "but how about Samose and Prennit and all the other cities? Everybody else in the Domain wants to *take it easy and enjoy*, too, just like you and your friends. To do that, goods from the Hearth need to be shipped."

"But why me?" he demanded. "Let those goons down at the piers do it. They've got plenty of Macai workers and plenty of barges and wagons. That's their job."

Jarayan tried once more. "Yes, there are plenty of workers, but what is needed is people who are willing to *crew* those barges and *drive* those wagons. There is a *huge* demand on the Hearth and not enough personnel to keep up with distribution. People all across the Domain want their goods. Do you think that you can just train the *Macai* to do it?"

"Why can't the other cities come and get their own supplies from the Hearth themselves?" asked Zarosen. "Why do we have to deliver everything?"

"Because it's easier to simply conjure a fleet of barges with loads of food or bricks or whatever already on them than it is to send those transports here from hundreds of leagues away."

And that's part of the problem, Jarayan thought silently to herself. Zarosen's point of view was hardly unique. More and more people every day were pouring into the city from across the Domain. They all wanted to take advantage of the Hearth's bounty and simply kick back because they *could*. She didn't want to admit that to her son, though. It would weaken her argument.

Zarosen folded his arms and rolled his eyes in a way that only a young Eryndi can do.

"Son, I'm not trying to nag you into taking this job," she said. "I just want you to experience the satisfaction of doing what's right."

"Let me guess," he replied with a sneer. "Getting a job builds character?"

"I know you don't understand now," Jarayan said almost sadly, "but trust me, it would be really good for you in the long run. You may be technically an adult now, but you still have a couple of hundred years of life ahead of you. You're going to need to find a career with some meaning, and shipping is a good place to start."

"Well, I guess that means I've got plenty of time," Zarosen said haughtily, "and right now, I'm going down to the dispersal center with my friends. I need some new clothes. These are almost a month old."

Jarayan sadly watched her son's retreating back as he strutted out of the house.

If only he would realize that, even though everything in life is now provided, people still have responsibilities.

The water clock in the sitting room chimed ten times, reminding her of her own responsibilities. The Hearth was being overtaxed; the planning for the new upriver Magic infusers was being discussed at the Midday meeting and she was late.

Today – The Drowned City of Mennatu

The battle against the pygmies was a short one. Tresado kept them at bay with flaming Magical projectiles that exploded in their shrunken little faces, while Orchid helped the injured Foxx out of the water and onto the stone island. She also retrieved her precious staff, one of the few things from *Enchanter* that floated to the surface.

Foxx recovered quickly and did his part defending the group, clumsily swinging Serena's scimitar. He connected with a couple of pygmies, but mostly he was more of a danger to himself and his friends than he was to the enemy. Once he missed wildly, and the blade pranged off a piece of stone rubble, sending sparks flying.

Occasionally one of the group was hit with a blowgun dart, but thanks to Orchid's antidote, they did no damage other than annoying pinpricks. Eventually, all the pygmies dove into the water and retreated in the face of the Magical attacks, leaving the three soggy survivors alone on the island.

Tresado ceased fire and looked all around.

"What could have happened to Serena?" he whimpered. "If she were hurt or . . . *she should be here somewhere!*"

"There's hardly any current in this arena," said Foxx, "so there's no way she could have been washed downstream."

"There's no sign of Leader either," said Orchid. "That can't be a coincidence."

Still worried and utterly depressed, Tresado looked over his broken, half-sunken boat.

"Orchid, keep an eye out for a minute."

"Right," she replied.

Gathering sufficient power, Tresado reached out Magically, gently lifted *Enchanter* from the water, and levitated her onto the stone surface. He set her down and bent to examine the damage.

"Can it be fixed?" asked Foxx, painfully holding a bit of rag against his scalp.

"I think so, but it will take a while," Tresado said. "I'll have to take some of the bladders from the left pontoon and transfer them to the right one to balance them out. Then seal the skin back up somehow. She'll ride low in the water, but level. The mast is another matter. Maybe I can salvage what's left of the old one, but it would be only half as tall. The sail would have to be recut. If we can get back into the forest, maybe I can find some wood to make a whole new mast . . . but that's not our biggest problem."

"What is?" asked Foxx.

"All our supplies and tools went overboard. Before I can start on anything, we'll have to go diving for them, and I'm a terrible swimmer," Tresado said.

"I wouldn't recommend that," said Orchid, watching the river.

"Oh?"

"I think we have another problem," she said. "When I was down there before, I sensed something . . . big."

"Something big?" asked Foxx. "You mean like more crocs?"

"No, nothing like that," Orchid replied. "I don't mean an animal or anything. There's something here, in the river, and it has more power over the water than I could ever muster."

"If it's not an animal," asked Tresado, "then . . . what?"

Orchid hesitated, "It's almost, I don't know, like it was the *water itself.*"

"Was?"

"I'm not sure, but I think it's gone now," she replied. "Look." Orchid pointed to the archway above the now calm water. "We better not worry about fixing the boat just yet. We should get off this island and up to higher ground right away."

"And find Serena," said Tresado emphatically.

Foxx was examining the arena surrounding them. "If we can get to those seats, we can climb to the top and get a good view of . . . *whoa! Aaahhh!*"

He found himself lifted off his feet by an invisible force and floating over the water toward the tiers of the ancient stone arena. Foxx twisted about and saw Orchid and Tresado floating behind him on the same course.

"Just hang on," Tresado called, "we'll be there in a minute."

Tresado's levitation spell deposited the three of them onto the top of the massive ruin. He had to take a few beats to catch his breath, Magically speaking. Transporting three people that distance was taxing. From that height, they could see the entire arena and what was left of the ancient city spread out before them. Tiny moving figures scurried in and out of the ruined buildings like ants. Downstream lay the dense forest that they had traversed on their way here.

"Look at that," said Orchid, pointing upriver.

Beyond the arena, the water was back to being a definable river with two banks. About half a league away, they could see a high cliff overlooking the city. From its heights, a huge waterfall cascaded over the edge. Two immense boulders at the top of the ridge divided the water into three separate falls, creating a cloud of mist cut by a rainbow shining in the bright sunlight. Even at this distance, a dull roaring could be heard.

"If this weren't such a sinister place, that would be quite beautiful," Orchid said.

Tresado closed his eyes and focused on the ever-present Magic in the air.

"Can you feel it?" he asked.

"I do," Orchid said after a few beats.

"Wow," added Foxx, "even I can."

The three companions turned to face the stone island below.

Being on top of the arena allowed a larger perspective of just what was Magically going on around here. In their minds' eyes, they were able to perceive what could be described as *lines of force* spiraling down out of the sky, converging at a single point, the stone island they had just quitted. The Magical strands were somewhat disrupted by the open, eroded section they had entered through. Even so, the invisible spectacle was a wonder to behold.

"An incredible amount of Magic is being directed into the center of the arena," said Tresado.

"It's not being directed, more like *gathered*," Orchid said. She then turned around and concentrated upriver.

"And even more is coming from the water itself," she added, "upstream from the falls."

"Is that what you sensed earlier?" asked Foxx.

"I don't think so," she said. "That was more of a *presence*. What we're seeing here is raw Magical energy all being directed to a central point in the middle of the arena."

"I'm beginning to think this wasn't even meant to be an *arena*," theorized Tresado. "Maybe it was used as one, but I bet ten tormacs that this whole structure was designed as the world's biggest Magic gatherer. Whatever used to be on that island in the middle was the focal point."

"I once saw a transmutation oven in Tresk," said Foxx. "One of the Imperial Magicians had created it to refine the metal in the armored cuirasses for the Legionnaires. It had a kind of copper antenna on the top. Somehow the Magician used it to gather Magic and enhance his own power, but it was nothing on the scale of this."

"It's unbelievable, the amount of energy this thing gathers. Yet there's no drain. I don't think it's being used by anyone," said Tresado.

"What's unbelievable," said Orchid, "is that, however much Magic it's gathering from the air, there's still more flowing in from the river."

She turned and pointed at the distant waterfall.

"It's coming from there."

1,332 years ago – City of Mennatu – Fifteen years after Commencement

"We are ready, Elder," said Bralick, Chief of Absolute Operations, nervously. He had to almost shout. The roar of Trebalian Falls below thundered in their sensitive ears.

Jarayan was no less nervous but did not show it.

"Proceed."

Bralick nodded to his assistant, who was standing by with a collection of different colored pennants. The man picked up the blue and yellow one and waved it above his head. Upriver of them, twenty Magicians were standing by on both banks. Each of them stood next to an intricately molded metallic cone known as a Gatherer. They were smaller versions of the one that capped the Central Obelisk. These cones were mounted on stone pedestals that had been placed on top of newly constructed levees that lined both banks of the river here at the top of the falls.

At the signal, the waiting Magicians each began to cast a special infusion spell upon their respective Gatherers.

Developed years ago, the spell created an invisible conduit permanently connecting the Gatherers with the omnipresent envelope of Magical energy in the air. A negative Magical state was initiated at the tip of each cone. The difference in potential caused a natural siphoning of Magical energy onto each Gatherer, which transferred its power to the flowing river water. It was a sophisticated spell, one that took several minutes to complete.

The double row of Gatherers stretched upriver for half a league. Bralick and Jarayan watched the procedure from an observation tower. At each station, a signaler stood by. Simultaneously, twenty red and white pennants rose into the air.

"Infusion underway, Elder," said Bralick, beaming with relief. "No sign of problems."

"Excellent," replied Jarayan. She wasn't sure what Bralick had been apprehensive about, but she made sure her tone projected confidence. That was the last thing she felt. The Elder had no doubt that the addition of Magic infusers would be successful, but she still couldn't shake the feeling that what they were doing was somehow horribly wrong. While waiting for the spells to be cast, Jarayan drifted into a reverie, as was her wont.

Yes, the activation of the Great Hearth fifteen years earlier had been a tremendous achievement . . . so much so that additional Magical power was required to keep up with the demand upon its abilities. The Hearth provided anything and everything that the people could possibly ask for. The richest, most exotic foods, gold, gems, clothing . . . anything could be provided in unlimited quantities just as easily as it could produce building stones.

Even though items such as cereals, fruit, and even fresh meat could be Magically conjured, the only thing that seemed to be impossible was the creation of animate life. Grains and fruits were perfectly edible, of course, but their seeds were sterile. Many attempts had been made to conjure live animals, but whether horses, oxen, or Macai, all that ever appeared in the Matrix was a dead body.

This was hardly a problem, however. With all else in life free to be had, there was little need for animals to provide food or wool. The Militia was disappointed that their warhorse herds could not be increased, but they and anyone else who needed live animals simply bred them the old-fashioned way. Still, this was no problem, as nutritious feed for the animals was as abundant as anything else. The Macai, being the most useful of livestock, were bred in great numbers until their herds actually began to outnumber the Eryndi. Their stables were located up in the hills on the outskirts of the city to stem the odor, which most Eryndi found distasteful.

What bothered Jarayan was the continued atrophying of the populace. The people were becoming fat and lazy. Creativity and ambition were dying arts. There were fewer poems being written, sculptures created, songs composed. Anything that took a bit of effort was simply not worth it. The days of her youth may have been a bit more strenuous, but . . .

Jarayan's thoughts were brought back to the present by a voice.

"Green pennant," the assistant stated.

"Infusion complete, Elder."

"Thank you, Bralick, well done," she said. "I would say that . . ."

Jarayan paused as the hackles came up on her neck. Something was wrong.

* * *

It was not a he and not a she. Such a concept simply didn't apply. It was ancient, but one could not say aged because it did not even perceive the passage of time. It had been born of the great ring around which all moved and which had always been. Formless, it had no idea of purpose or even self but found contentment in cool, flowing water, finally adapting itself to become that which pleased it. It wandered the young world absorbing sensations until eventually becoming enamored with a place . . . a place of renewal. New sensations flowed in from elsewhere and continually rained down upon it, rejuvenating and invigorating it. Here it stayed, constantly maintaining and adapting its home and itself. Finally, it and its home were as one to the point where it could no more leave its home than its home could leave it. It became aware of others from without. It knew of their desires and heard them calling to it. Their pleas were easily granted. They asked for water, and it could understand. It now had purpose and meaning, but wanted to know the others that it provided for. But they were too different, lesser than it in many ways, but so much more in others. They had incomprehensible qualities. To understand them, it would have to adapt itself to become them. Try as it might, it had not the strength . . . until suddenly it did.

1,332 years ago – Mennatu stables

The man was strong. The bosses chose him for that reason. They used repetitious words and gestures to tell the man to raise the heavy log which had fallen, and place it back into the hole. The man held the pole steady while the other Macai were directed to kick in the dirt and tamp it down. Other poles were lashed onto it, and the fence was restored. The bosses tossed the Macai dried berry treats and released them back into the enclosure.

The workday ended, and it was evening feeding time. The troughs were filled with kibble, and the bosses went back to their building. Several women and children had already gathered at the troughs, but one had not. She stood staring down into the valley at the city. Making sure he was out of sight of the building, the man made some gestures with his palms.

"Mate . . . come . . . eat," he signed.

The man signed again, but the woman remained. She shook her head and signed for him to come to her. The man sighed and rose from the trough to join his mate. He affectionately stroked her hair and turned his gaze to the city to see what she found so fascinating. Strange sounds were starting to filter up from the city. It began with a long, low rushing. Soon, faint cries joined it. More Macai joined the man and the woman to see this curious thing. The dark ribbon of water that flowed through the heart of the city was slowly widening. The new stone buildings of the bosses were starting to disappear as the river crept over their thresholds. The sounds of distress increased. Many bosses below were crying out in terror. The bosses that had fed them came out of their building. They ran to the crowd of livestock to see why they had gathered. The Macai were soon forgotten when the bosses looked down at the city. They said words filled with fear and quickly headed down into the valley. The Macai were left without bosses for the first time that any of them could remember. Their instincts told them that their lives were about to change. The woman turned to her mate.

"We must go," she said aloud.

Today – The Drowned City of Mennatu

The remaining three-fifths of Group Six made a thorough search of the arena's interior (if that's what it was), but there was still no sign of Serena or Leader. It was starting to get dark, and they decided they would rather spend the night on dry land. They made their way across the water to the northern shore on the upstream side, again with the help of Tresado's levitation powers. There was no sign of pygmies or any other danger, and the ground seemed stable. The area of the flooded river that had inundated the city appeared to end here. Some driftwood was gathered and a fire started, but dinner was a problem. All of their supplies had gone to the bottom when the wave swamped their boat. Here, the sandy shore supported only a few stunted trees, and there was no game or edible plants anywhere near. Foxx produced a small pouch of dried sand pods that he happened to have in a pocket, but it didn't go very far among three people.

The dancing firelight reflected on the nearby river, making for weird shadows amongst the sparse trees. The waning orb soon rose and added its bluish light to the landscape. Downriver in the distance, the chattering of pygmies and the occasional animal sound could be heard from the forest.

"At first light, I suggest we head for the waterfall," said Orchid.

"Any particular reason?" asked Foxx.

"Not really," she replied, "only because I know of no better place to look. Besides, something fishy is going on there."

"It looks like this northern bank is the best route," said Tresado, staring into the fire, "but I sure hate to leave *Enchanter* behind."

"It would just take too long to fix it," replied Orchid, "but we'll come back for it."

"Her. *Enchanter* is a *her*."

"Right," said Foxx, "once we've found Serena, we'll come back for our other girl."

"You guys are hopeless romantics," said Orchid.

"*Enchanter*'s been a lot kinder to me than any other woman," said Tresado.

"Serena treats you like pig crap," she countered, "but you still want to go after her."

"Serena is worth a hundred *Enchanters*," answered Foxx.

"A thousand," added Tresado.

"We'll find her," stated Foxx.

"And Leader," added Orchid, "he's got the answers to a lot of questions."

In the morning, it took less than half an hour to walk along the bank to the waterfall. Along the way, they kept a sharp eye out for danger as well as their missing companions. Neither greeted them. This section of the river had well-established banks with grasses and trees and looked as though it had not flooded. The towering cliff lay just ahead. The roar of the plunging triple falls was deafening. Orchid called a quick halt to peruse the area. She got on her hands and knees and peered into the water.

"There's life here," she shouted. "I can sense fish and

crawdads. There's also a kind of wild rice growing along the bank. We won't starve."

"We can't take the time," said Tresado, chafing at the slight delay. "We've got to keep looking for Serena."

Orchid stood and brushed off her hands. "Then let's get moving."

"Any sign of your *presence?*" asked Foxx.

"It's somewhere up ahead," Orchid said immediately, pointing to the waterfall.

The spray thrown up by the cascade made it impossible to see much of anything. Tresado, Orchid, and Foxx made their way as close to the cliffs as they could. They stood on the bank, getting soaked by spray and staring up at the amazing triple falls that towered over sixty reaches above their heads. The huge twin boulders at the top looked uncomfortably like a pair of canine teeth thrust up between the rushing waters. Tresado held out his palms to the spray.

"This water is highly charged with raw Magic," he said, looking up. "Feels good."

"Yeah," agreed Orchid, pointing to the top of the falls, "something up there is causing it."

"You think Serena is here?" shouted Foxx.

"I don't know about Serena . . ." Orchid started to say.

A rogue wave surged out of the river, catching the friends right in their faces and knocking all three on their butts.

". . . but the entity is *definitely* here," she finished.

* * *

It had always been sustained by the great ring from which it was born. Now the power of that sustenance had increased a hundred-fold. It found the strength to extend itself out from its home under the falling waters. Its newfound vigor enabled it to find and contact the others that had asked for water. It granted their requests to a degree far beyond what it had ever been capable of giving them. Yet, when it embraced the others, it discovered that it still could not become them. There were too many impurities amongst their water, though it did its best to understand them. Their minds were easily incorporated. The memories and knowledge it gained from them taught it much of the world beyond home. Much had changed since its first wanderings. There were other mortal creatures everywhere, as well as the ones that it now embraced. It learned of their history and abilities. It learned about what they considered their greatest feat, the Matrix. But all that was only half of what the others were. They were also made up of incomprehensible concepts that their minds held titles for. It knew of but had no method of absorbing these things that the others called *love, hate,* and *fear.* The others scorned the latter two, but actively sought the first. It decided . . . that is also what it must search for. It could not leave home to find love. It needed a way to bring love to home. If only it knew where to look . . .

1,332 years ago – City of Mennatu – Fifteen years after Commencement

The pinnacle of Jarayan's career was widely considered to be the Hearth, but to her, it had been achieving Elder status at the young age of seventy-nine. She was, as contradictory as it sounds, the youngest person to ever become an Elder. Her sensible, cut-through-the-horse-crap way of doing things was legendary amongst her peers.

It was not Jarayan who had originally conceived the idea of the Hearth. That thought was born in the minds of a pair of opiate-blasted, failed Magical students who had lost their seats at the Academy for abuse of meditation-enhancing herbs. Their theories, wild and unrealistic as they were, held a promise that only Jarayan recognized. She had been the only member of the Academy Board not to recommend dismissal for them, but she had been outvoted. Nevertheless, using her own resources, she took those two nutballs in hand and made introductions and proposals to several of the more prominent Magicians in the Domain. Her ability to herd the cats of the academic world like no other eventually brought enough brilliant minds together that the Hearth became a reality. This had been the greatest collaboration of Magicians ever attempted. Only with Jarayan's diplomatic skills had this coalition been able to hang together. It was ironic that the greatest Magical creation in history was credited to Jarayan. She had only barely dabbled in Magic during her long life; she was an administrator, not a Magician.

Even so, only moments after the new upriver Magic gatherers were activated, she became aware of something disastrous happening. Jarayan and her aides hurried to the bridge, crossed to the center of the river and ascended the ladder to the top of Nurian Pinnacle. From above Trebalian Falls, she gazed down at Mennatu. Her Eryndi senses told her that the water of the river below, now highly infused with Magic, had somehow acquired a life of its own. It had become a presence . . . an entity.

No, that's not right. 'Become' is not the right word. Whatever is here now, has always been here . . .

Hundred-year-old childhood memories came to the surface . . .

She was with her family at the Temple, but her thoughts were with her new kitten. Little Jarayan would much rather be at home playing with Maisie than be here in this boring place. In a seven-year-old girl, such thoughts translated to fidgeting.

Quiseron will not be happy with you, Jarayan, her mother quietly chided her. *Now sit still and pay attention.*

The Celebrants were droning on with their appeals, beseeching the River God to continue blessing the people with the gift of water. Jarayan did her best to obey Mother, but she never fully bought into the whole religious thing, even as a young child. There had always been water. There would always *be* water. Singing hymns and reciting prayers had squat to do with how the river flowed.

As she grew into an adult, one with potential and promise, her personal confidence in herself and her abilities molded her into a modern, far-seeing visionary who looked to the future . . . a future of independence and resourcefulness. She was proud of herself for that.

Jarayan's thoughts snapped back to the present as she beheld the tragedy unfolding below. She watched in horror as the waters rose. The buildings were inundated, the people foundering helplessly. The Central Obelisk, still lit by the setting sun, wavered hesitantly. Then painfully, Jarayan watched as the stone spire slowly collapsed in the center of the Collector, now reaches deep in water.

All Eryndi are connected—to the world around them and to each other. What one Eryndi feels strongly, another feels with him. From her lofty perch atop the falls, Jarayan saw her kind far below, tiny squirming figures struggling within the grip of the river. She felt their life forces being consumed by the water, and it tore at her heart. She knew their pain . . . she knew their world was ending . . . and she knew something else.

This is my fault . . .

CHAPTER 11

Today – Trebalian Falls

"We better back off."

"Really, you think?" Foxx replied to Orchid's recommendation as he picked himself up. He was the only one who landed in a sticker bush after being knocked down by the water-thing beneath the waterfall. Foxx painfully plucked a cockle burr out of his butt and moved away from the water with his friends.

Tresado sympathized with his friend's troubles and said so.

"Man, you are really taking it in the shorts this trip," he said, noting the black eye and the lacerated scalp and now the sticker problem. "But as much fun as that was to watch, I think we should figure out our next move."

"Thanks, I live to entertain," Foxx said.

"That thing in the water," Orchid said, "it seems stronger."

"*Stronger?*" Tresado exclaimed. "When it threw *Enchanter* out of the water, it already seemed pretty damned strong."

"I think it's this place," said Orchid. "When that water made contact with us, it *was* the entity. I could tell . . . it was *home*."

"It said that?" asked Foxx skeptically.

"Not in so many words," she answered. "I just sensed something secure and familiar about this pool. That says home to me . . . and home means *strongest*."

"What do you think this thing is, Orchid?" Tresado asked.

"Mind," she said in a hushed voice, "nothing but *mind*."

"For being nothing but mind," Foxx said to Orchid, "it's pretty handy with the water. You even said that it *was* the water."

"The mind is what controls Magic," observed Tresado. "If it is all mind, there's no telling what kind of powers it has."

Foxx furrowed his brow. "Do you remember what Leader said when Serena showed us her diamond for the first time?"

Tresado got a dreamy look on his face and sighed, "Mostly, I remember Serena showing us the diamond."

"Yeah, that was rough on me, too," said Foxx, grinning, "but Leader said that some kind of *spirit* lived in the diamond, and that was what gave Serena her . . . charm."

"What are you getting at?" asked Orchid.

"You're wondering if the thing in the water is something similar," said Tresado to Foxx.

"I learned a little about spirits in school," said Orchid.

"So did I," said Tresado, "but only a little. I think a little is all *anybody* knows about spirits."

"So what *do* we know?" asked Foxx.

"Not much," said Orchid, thinking. "They don't have anything like a body, but rather are said to be creatures of pure Magic."

"A teacher of mine said that too, that they're nothing but energy," said Tresado. "But maybe being all mind isn't enough. Maybe they have to have some kind of physical body, whether it's a diamond, or . . ."

"Or water," said Orchid.

"But if that pool is home, its water is changing every second from the falls," Tresado said.

"Maybe," Orchid mused, "it just hangs in the water like a fish in a current."

"But it attacked us in the arena. That's half a league away," Tresado countered, his voice rising.

"It lives in water. Maybe it can swim."

"Maybe, maybe, maybe!" exclaimed Foxx over Tresado's and Orchid's debate. "Maybe it's my Aunt Winnie in that pool! *Maybe* what we should do is to stop theorizing and find this stuff out for sure!"

"Well, who peed in your porridge today?" inquired Orchid.

"Foxx is just crabby and needs to be put down for a nap," said Tresado, "but he is right."

Tresado craned his neck upward and looked toward the top of the falls towering above them. "We need to find out where this Magic is coming from."

"Think you can make it?" asked Orchid, following his gaze.

"It's a long way up," Tresado replied, "but I think I can get myself up there."

"We'll take a look around down here," Foxx said.

"Okay, back in a beat," said Tresado, preparing himself.

After less than a quarter-minute, Tresado's diminishing form disappeared over the top of the falls. Watching his progress from below, Orchid quietly whistled in admiration at the Eryndi's Absolute powers. She didn't care for it, but she had to admit Tresado was damned good at it. He shot up the face of that waterfall like a cork from a green beer flagon.

"I'm gonna take a walk and see what I can find," said Orchid to Foxx.

"Yeah, okay," he replied, staring into the pool.

Foxx didn't move away from the shore. His attention was focused on the waterfall.

"Everything all right?" asked Orchid after a couple of beats.

Foxx seemed very distracted.

"Find anything?" he asked, not taking his eyes off the base of the falls.

"I haven't left yet," she said, waving her hand in front of his face. "Hello . . . anybody in there?"

"Oh, sorry," he said, shaking his head, "I'm just . . . looking."

"Don't get too close to the water," she warned. "Our spirit friend is definitely in there. It's big. I can sense its presence both in the pool and behind the waterfall. There must be a cave back there. I also got the impression that it's guarding something. I felt its defensiveness . . . but no sign of Serena."

"Maybe that's negotiable," Foxx said.

"How do you mean?" Orchid asked.

"I'm gonna talk to it."

Today – Trebalian Falls

After a moment's concentration, Tresado was hoisting his pudgy Eryndi body up the face of the triple falls in an invisible harness. The enchanted liquid that was the water rushed downward in front of his face. Childlike, he opened his mouth wide to catch the drops of spray on his tongue. To the Magic-obsessed Tresado, it tasted as good as the finest bubble wine. It was even helping with his levitation spell. There was so much concentrated Magical energy in the water that this difficult lift was as child's play. He soared upward at twice what would be normal speed. The feeling was as intoxicating as the finest brandy. Never had Tresado felt this much potential power to his Magic.

The giant twin boulders came into view before him as he reached the top. As he rose above the water's level and out of the spray, Tresado felt his new strength ebbing back to normal. He kept near the north bank and circled around behind the great rocks. He saw the remains of ancient, rusted iron works that had at one time been built around the back side of them. The metal was highly degraded, but he could still see what was left of stairs and railings ascending the boulders on the upstream side. There was also what looked like a former bridge that had crossed the river just above the falls. The stone foundations and some decayed ironwork on each bank were the only artificial remains. The bridge itself was long gone.

This section of the river above the falls was contained on both sides for half a league by strong stone levees constructed with the familiar dove-tail blocks Tresado had seen in the city ruins. Ten pedestals lined each bank about a hundred and fifty paces apart. The stone bases were pockmarked with time and covered with clinging vines. The coppery, intricate cones capping them were another story. The metal alloy was spotless and polished and looked like it had been forged last week. Tresado could almost physically feel the vast amount of raw Magical energy that was being drawn into them and then fed into the water.

Tresado got a little altitude and followed the river upstream from the pedestals. The water was running fast here.

Beyond the rows of collectors was the mouth of a narrow rock canyon where white water hurtled down from the distant mountains. There was no sign of civilization, either past or present.

Tresado felt Magically fatigued. He knew he had to take a break soon from all this levitation. He was about to turn and make for the bank when he did a double-take at the narrow canyon. The colored striations of rock layers in the cliffs were mostly variations of browns and reds. A thin band of silvery-gray caught his eye. Tresado concentrated harder and squeezed a little more endurance out of himself to take a closer look. A couple more minutes of flight time took him to the canyon, where he alighted on a narrow ledge about twenty reaches above the rapids.

Now Tresado was really tired. This layer of ore that he took a sample of confirmed just why that was.

* * *

To My Lady of the Emerald Eyes: Give my journal and my shell collection to my kid brother Cyrus. The little creep always did envy my Junonia.

—Travelogue of Dementus, the Mad Treskan
– Final Entry

Today – Trebalian Falls

Orchid turned her attention to her surroundings. She left Foxx and walked the shore as close to the water as she dared. Opening her mind to the environment around her, Orchid looked for anything useful. There was much life in this pool. Fish and crustaceans abounded. Wading birds patrolled the shore, picking at delicacies. Orchid even sensed a family of water weasels living on the opposite bank. Above all, though, the presence of the spirit registered heavily on her psyche. She ranged a bit further from the shore, away from its influence.

Orchid took a walk to check out a small grove of silly billy trees a quarter-league to the north. It was a quiet place, no sign of pygmies, spirits, or anything else harmful to one's health. But something was a bit out of sorts from a plant's perspective. Orchid could sense an uncomfortable feeling from somewhere amongst the trees. That was nothing unusual. Probably a beetle infestation or something. Normally she would have ignored a tree's discomfort, as there were other priorities at the moment. Still, Group Six had lost all their supplies in the river. The medicinal billy bark had many uses, so she quickly gathered some to start replenishing her herb kit. She entered the grove and looked for a good source of the bark. Now that she was closer, the *voice* of the troubled tree rang loudly on her psyche. A tree doesn't actually use words, of course, but if it did, they would be something like, *ouch, ouch, my left root aches!*

Orchid could see why. There was some kind of long spike sticking out of the ground next to the tree. It was clearly artificial, a lathe-turned, hardwood staff with a carved handgrip on the top end. It had been driven into a patch of bare earth. Orchid pulled it out with some difficulty. The bottom of the staff ended with an iron spike that had penetrated the root below. She felt the tree go *aaahhh* as the spike was removed. It was a walking staff of fine quality. There was some kind of engraved symbol on the grip. Orchid wasn't familiar with it, but the design might be Treskan. Having never visited the distant Imperium, she wasn't sure.

The ground looked like it had been disturbed, so she used the iron tip to loosen up the soil the staff had been stuck in. Something else was buried here. Being careful not to damage the tree, she dug with her hands and eventually pulled out a well-worn backpack. It also was of good quality, despite the family of earwigs that had made it their home. Orchid gently shooed them back into the hole and examined the pack. Some kind of family crest was inked on the closed flap. She opened it up and dumped the contents.

Beans . . . lots of beans . . .

Except for the several sacks of dried beans and some basic camping gear, the only thing in the pack was a thick, hardbound book with a single title: TRAVELOGUE.

The pages were made of the finest calfskin Orchid had ever seen. They were thin, durable, and covered with tiny handwriting. A quick glance told her it was a diary or something. There were thousands of entries going back a long, long way.

Orchid didn't have time to read it thoroughly, so she quickly perused the last couple of pages, her eyebrows going up as she read. Putting the book and the other items back in the pack, she picked up the walking stick and headed back to where she had left Foxx.

* * *

It always comes down to someone who wants something you have. And when they want it bad enough, a deal can always be made. If not, they'll just take it from you . . .

— Professor Abadiah Generax, 21862

Today – Trebalian Falls

Let's make a deal, Foxx thought.

It was obvious that Serena had been abducted. She had been right. The only thing truly remarkable about her was the love-inducing diamond. With both Serena and Leader missing at the same time and the spirit in that pool possibly in cahoots, it was just too big of a coincidence. Someone, or *something* maybe, wanted that diamond.

Foxx stood by the pool and reached out with his *Knowing Spell.* But in this case, he was not trying to *read.* Actually, he made a concerted effort to project his own personality. It was his way of introducing himself to something that didn't have a hand to shake. There were also no eyes to look into, so Foxx closed his. He searched and searched, looking for a response. His spell gathered and filtered every scrap of input but came up with nothing. He just couldn't seem to sense the thing the way Orchid could. He was about to give up when there was a faint touch. It felt like a feather tickling the back of his head. There was someone there, all right.

Foxx relaxed and allowed the spell to draw images on the insides of his eyelids. A shape coalesced.

It's Leader.

Foxx wasn't sure whether it was his mind or someone else's that had just said that.

Mister Foxx with two exes . . .

Hello, Leader.

Leader is me, but I am not Leader . . .

Foxx felt a moment of confusion. *Who are you?*

I have no name of my own . . . only those others have given me . . .

Serena is here.

You know that, Mr. Foxx, because I know it . . .
Yes, we are both aware of much.
Of course . . . you and your friends should depart . . .
Serena must accompany us.
Your mission is complete . . . you have fulfilled your obligation . . .
Our mission was not to bring you Serena.
Your mission was to get Leader safely upriver . . .
I stand corrected. Nevertheless, Serena must come with us.

The image of Leader continued to project itself into Foxx's mind. But it was more than just a talking image; Foxx could *read* this presence. His *Knowing Spell* had never had a stronger link. Never had he been so absolutely connected to another mind. And he could tell that it worked both ways. Foxx was sure his own psyche was being laid bare. There would be no untruths spoken here.

But as strong as the connection was, this was only half a person. There was great intelligence, knowledge, capability, and experience, but not a hint of any kind of feeling. It was like talking to an abacus.

I am aware that you wish to bargain . . .
There must be something we can offer. Knowledge? A service?
I have knowledge of the world and you have provided the service required . . . You possess nothing more I want . . .
And that service was delivering Serena and her diamond to you. Is she safe? Foxx's heart beat faster.
She is safe . . .
Will she remain so?
Why must you ask if you already know . . . ?
Yes, I know. I see it in your thoughts, removing the diamond is dangerous.

I will not be harmed . . .

Serena will be. The diamond cannot be taken or given.

That is why she must know . . . she must understand . . .

I fear it is you who do not understand, Leader. Foxx felt Leader slipping away.

You are quite correct . . . that is why I must proceed . . .

A heavy door slammed on Foxx's brain as the spirit abruptly ended the contact. He staggered back a few steps from the shock. An out-of-tune voice from above added to his headache.

"Yo! Foxx!"

Tresado was descending the face of the falls a little faster than one would think prudent. In fact, at the last beat, his maneuver turned into an uncontrolled crash. Fortunately, he landed on his ample ass in soft sand, creating a small crater. A small object wrapped in a cloth jumped out of his hands and plopped down in front of Foxx, who picked it up.

"Gee, a rock," Foxx said as he unfolded the loose cloth. "You shouldn't have."

"I'm fine, thanks," said Tresado, brushing sand off himself. "I have a lot to tell you."

"I have a lot to tell *you*," replied Foxx.

Soft footsteps sounded behind them as Orchid approached in her non-intrusive way. She always picked her way carefully through any environment, avoiding stepping on fragile plants or insects whenever she could help it. That usually meant she was the last to arrive anywhere.

"Hyah, fellas," she said. "Boy, have I got a lot to tell *you*."

CHAPTER 12

I am as the eagle in its egg,
The oak in its acorn,
I am the unrealized dream,
Striving for release . . .

—TRIANNA OF SYLVAS; POETESS TO THE GLADES

Today

Serena came fully awake in the dark, but she didn't feel as though she had been asleep. The first thing she wanted to do was scratch her nose. Unfortunately, she couldn't raise her hands from her sides. Her feet seemed to be restrained somehow, as well. Her back was up against something hard and rough; all she could do was to sit on whatever she was sitting on and try to peer into the darkness. To her left was a slight glow coming from the same direction as that roaring sound. What little she could see over there showed her that there was not much to see, anyway. If there was anything else in here, wherever she was, it was too dark. All that she could tell was that it was damp and cold. Something skittered over her foot but didn't seem to bother with anything more.

For anyone else, the first reaction might be to call out something stupid like 'hello' or 'is anybody there?' Serena was a warrior, however. A warrior knew when to be silent and gather as much information as she could first. Serena thought back. The last thing she remembered was being on *Enchanter*. Orchid had just broken the boat out of its ice shell.

I was guarding Leader, ready to split him if he tried a false move. Then that freaky wave heaved up the boat, and I got pitched into the water. And now I'm here . . .

Serena's hands and feet were restrained, but they didn't feel anything like ropes or chains. She simply couldn't move them. Her inner senses told her that some time had passed, but there were a few odd things. For one, she had needed to pee while on the boat. She still did, but it wasn't any worse than before. That would mean she had only been here for a few minutes. Also, even though it was cold and damp in this place, she could tell that her clothing was not wet. Maybe she had been here long enough for them to dry . . . she just wasn't sure.

Her warrior's sense told her she was being observed. It felt like that time the berg bear had stalked her across the base of Strondheim glacier. She had not seen it yet; she just knew it was there.

There was a sound in the darkness. Quiet, measured footsteps were approaching. A light appeared from around a corner and came nearer. Serena could now see that she was in a natural cavern. Walls, wet with condensation, dripped moisture onto a floor pocked with dark, shallow puddles. Small rodents and large insects scurried away at the approaching light.

Leader walked up to Serena, carrying a lantern that glowed with a Magical luminance.

"Hello, Serena," he said in his usual emotionless voice, "welcome to my home."

"Your home, huh?" Serena answered calmly. "Needs a woman's touch."

"I should clarify," Leader said. "I have actually spent little time here. I don't think of it so much as my home, but my birthplace. Come, let me show you."

Serena felt the restrictions lift on her hands and feet. She looked down, but again there was no indication of anything that had been holding her there. Leader turned his back on her and started strolling away. Serena reacted with her lightning reflexes, aiming a vicious fan kick at the back of Leader's head. Such an attack would probably have snapped Leader's neck and/or fractured his skull. That was her intention, anyway. However, her foot had not even left the ground when it suddenly felt as though it weighed a hundred stone. She recovered her balance and found she could take a calm step forward, but that was all. Any quick, violent movement was apparently impossible, and Leader seemed aware of it.

"As you can see," he said, continuing his walk, "violence is not permitted. Nor is it necessary. In fact, I believe you will be quite amenable to what I have to propose."

"Okay, so I can't just kill you like you deserve," Serena said menacingly, "but that doesn't mean I have to follow you and listen to whatever crap you have to say."

"Actually, I believe it does," he said.

With that, Serena felt the invisible grip tighten on her ankles and forcibly move her feet forward, causing her to lurch unsteadily like a drunken mule driver. Leader turned and faced her.

"I assure you, it will be much easier if you simply cooperate," he said. "Come, all will become clear soon."

Serena was not one for giving up, but she also had a good sense of practicality.

"Fine, if you insist," she said with a sneer. "Lead on, *Leader.*"

"Excellent. This way."

Holding his lantern above his head, Leader moved a few steps farther away from the wall that Serena had been restrained against. He opened his hand, and the lantern floated free by itself and positioned itself above their heads.

"That's a neat trick," said Serena. "You can't even see the strings."

"Simple Magical levitation," Leader said.

"Funny you never mentioned you had Magic powers," Serena said.

"I do not," Leader replied simply.

The overhead light intensified, illuminating the entire cavern. They were in a simple rock cave. There was a tunnel leading further into the interior of the cliff. In the other direction, the roaring sound and the smell of water. It appeared they were behind a great waterfall.

That's the way out, Serena noted to herself.

"So this is your birthplace, is it?" she asked sarcastically, looking around at the bare rock walls. "Where did the midwife live?"

"I admit it does not have the comfort and charms that you may be accustomed to," Leader said, "but, as you now see, *it can.*"

Leader then closed his eyes for a moment, and the air shimmered in front of him. There was a flash of Magical light, and a small building appeared as if from nowhere. Serena recognized the style immediately. It was a cozy little cabin of the Northlands style. Sturdy logs formed the walls, and thick grass covered the steeply sloping roof. A trickle of smoke issued from the chimney, and a pleasant smell of cooking food wafted out of the open window.

"This is for you," Leader said, extending his palm toward the cabin. "There are amenities within. Feel free to refresh yourself. We will talk afterward."

Serena eyed both Leader and the cabin suspiciously but entered anyway and closed the door behind her. Inside were a stove, bed, furs, casks of ale, stores of food, even a head equipped with a water pump —everything a Northlands shield maiden could possibly need. The only thing it lacked was weapons hanging on the wall. Except for that omission, it felt just like home. She made use of the facilities to freshen up but didn't touch the food or drink. She'd been down *that* road before.

Still not believing her eyes, Serena sat down in the large, fur-draped chair in the corner. She knocked on the wooden armrests, smelled the furs, and looked around. Everything seemed to be quite real. The logs that made up the walls of the cabin had characteristic axe marks on the joints. If she didn't know better, she'd swear they had been hewn by some Northlands artisan. Serena grew tired and walked over to the bed. It was comfortable and inviting. Was it only last night that she had been knocked out by a pygmy dart? Serena still had that odd taste in her mouth, the result of Orchid's antidote.

But that all seems so long ago . . .

Serena stretched out on the bed intending to just try to think her way out of this situation. Before long, she was lightly snoring. She was in the middle of a dream about Dad taking her out for her first boat ride in the fjords when she awoke with a start. It was a bit chilly in here. The fireplace held only cooling ashes. Serena took another tour around the inside of the cabin, checking out everything. It all seemed quite real.

Serena opened the door and peered out. She was still in the wet cave. The Magical lantern still hovered above, but there was no sign of Leader or anything else. She stepped out onto the rock floor and wandered back toward the roaring sound, seeking a way out. She came to a powerful wall of falling water with a glow of daylight beyond it. Serena took a few steps back and was about to try a running leap through the falls when the aggravating weights reappeared on her ankles, pinning her to the spot.

"FINE!" she shouted to the ceiling.

Serena turned and walked back to the cabin. Apparently, *that* was allowed. She wasn't sure how long she had been asleep earlier, but her stomach growled, telling her that she hadn't eaten in some time. She was still hesitant to try the food, though. Serena remembered the weird incident with Bata a few years back. This seemed different, somehow. Bata's friendly cave had apparently been some kind of hallucination. This Northlands cabin that Leader had provided and its contents appeared very real. Even so, she didn't want to get drugged or poisoned or something, so she went back inside and just plopped down in the chair, trying to think.

A polite knock startled her. She cautiously went to the door, tensing herself for anything. Immediately she felt the still present, invisible force starting to tighten on her hands and feet again. Snorting with frustration, Serena willed herself to calm down and opened the door. Leader stood there, impassive as ever.

"I trust you have rested well," he said. "Shall we have our talk now?"

"You talk, I'll listen," said Serena. "All I ask is that you get to the point and just tell me what it is you want."

"Unfortunately, that will accomplish nothing," he said. "It is important you hear the whole story and understand fully."

"Oh fine, let me just settle in, then," she sighed, heading for the comfy chair.

"No," said Leader, "this way."

He stepped off the porch and indicated for Serena to precede him. She glared at him but went along with it. Leader escorted her deeper into the tunnel. It quickly widened into a larger cavern. Another floating lantern illuminated the place.

The circular chamber was at least fifty reaches across. The walls and roof all seemed to be made up of naturally formed rock. But there was something just a little *manipulated* about this place. Serena saw no signs of excavation or tool marks, but the cavern was a nearly perfect dome above her head. In the center of the floor was a large pit. An eerie, shifting glow came from it, causing Leader's and Serena's shadows to dance on the wall behind them.

She peered down at a very strange sight. The pit was filled with water which sloshed about, bubbling and shimmering with reflected colors. In the center of the hole was a platform protruding just above the surface, upon which sat the weirdest object Serena had ever seen. It was a kind of spherical cage about three reaches in diameter. It seemed to be made of some sort of shiny, tubular metal bars, joined together at the poles, reminding her of a peeled orange. Inside the cage was another *object*, if one could call it that. A glowing, orange pyramidal shape that seemed to be made up of nothing but colored lights spun freely. The pyramid shifted to a bluish-purple color and then morphed into a spinning cube shape. It seemed to have no solid form, but as Serena watched, the thing continued to shift colors and shapes, becoming a polyhedron, a sphere, a plane, and on and on.

"What is it?" asked Serena, the shifting colors reflecting off her pink cheeks.

"It was called *The Creation Matrix,*" he replied, "named such by the people who created it long ago."

"And who was that?" Serena asked.

"You have met their descendants," said Leader. "You and your companions have assigned them the appellation of *pygmies.*"

"You do like your big words, don't you?" scoffed Serena. "You know, if you would just learn to talk normally, people wouldn't think of you as such a dork."

Leader remained unfazed.

"Okay, I'll bite," she sighed. "How did those little creeps manage to create something like this? They don't look like they can wipe their own butts."

"Not now, perhaps," said Leader, "but long ago, those creatures were quite different. As I said, it is important for you to know this object's history and the meaning it has for all of us. Prepare yourself."

Serena didn't know what he meant by that, but she prided herself on always being prepared for anything. Leader closed his eyes for a moment. A rushing sound filled the pit below them as a forceful wall of water came roaring out as though a dam had burst somewhere. Serena threw up her arms and prepared to be swept away. Normally, walls of rushing water don't just stop in mid-rush and hang in mid-air. But this one did, right in front of Serena's face. Coming out of the pit, it retained a tubular shape. It was as though a great night crawler had emerged from the ground. It was made of liquid river water, all right. There were bits of moss and other plant matter swirling around in there. Serena even saw a minnow briefly approach the edge and swim back farther inside. The watery worm hovered about Serena, apparently perusing her from all angles. She defiantly held her ground while the thing 'sniffed' her.

With a speed that one would think impossible of a floating mass of water, the thing split its cylindrical shape and clapped around Serena from both sides like two giant hands. There was a moment's disorientation, but Serena was fine. Her body was enveloped in water, but she was not aware of it at all. Her mind was now elsewhere and seemingly . . . *else-when.*

Serena saw a bird's eye view of a large city built downstream of a mighty waterfall. Her perspective seemed to change as though she were descending from the skies to soar just above the wooden rooftops. Serena suddenly became aware that this was no ordinary vision in her mind. She found she could hear and feel the wind whistle through her ears and smell the bubbling river as it flowed past.

The view shifted from scene to scene as if she witnessed this city's history in a series of glimpses. She watched the inhabitants, who were all Eryndi, going about their daily business. The people wore strange-looking clothing such as she had never seen. There was a marketplace where goods were being bought and sold. She saw farmers farming and loggers logging. Everywhere Eryndi were living their lives.

Then she saw the Macai. About thirty of them were

being brought into the city on a large wagon with wooden bars. A group of armed, uniformed Eryndi horsemen escorted the wagon into a fortified, fenced enclosure. The Macai, dressed in simple hide wraps, were released from the locked wagon and herded into an interior, separately fenced area. A group of well-dressed Eryndi perused the new arrivals, feeling their muscles and peering into their open mouths. Serena was reminded of what she had done in the past, checking out horseflesh.

Her visions shifted back to views of Eryndi. Large groups of them were gathering at what appeared to be a temple on the riverbank. They chanted a strange, heavily accented hymn of some sort, most of which Serena could not understand. The object of their worship appeared to be the river itself. Serena had attended enough prayer sessions for Crodan to recognize pleas when she saw them. It was all very ritualized and dogmatic, but these Eryndi were obviously entreating the river for favors or gifts of some kind.

Superstitious louts, she thought to herself.

The Magical tour continued. Serena watched with concern as more and more Macai were brought into the city via wagon and barge. Hundreds and thousands of them were being shipped in from somewhere. Some of them had dark skin and black hair, but most of them reminded her of her own people ... large, blonde, square-headed folk with pink skin that sunburned quickly in the hot sun. She saw them toiling in quarries, cutting large stone blocks out of a cliffside. Others were organized in large groups pulling these blocks along on rollers. The huge blocks were lifted into place using machines with complicated pulley arrangements. Occasionally, Magicians were employed to help levitate a particularly large or delicate object. But mostly, the labor was performed by Macai.

Time accelerated, and as Serena watched, an enormous stone structure was erected along a natural bend in the river. What must have taken decades to build rose in seconds. She recognized it. It was the circular flooded arena that *Enchanter* had been pulled into by the pygmies. After the tiered sides were complete, a large stone platform was constructed dead center on the arena floor. Serena recognized it as well. It was the rubble-covered stone island. A circular well was sunk into the center of the platform, and thick pillars were placed around the pit's edges. As a final touch, gangs of hundreds of Macai were tethered to a one-piece, pointed obelisk over thirty reaches long. It had been carved out of the same type of light gray stone that the arena blocks were formed from. The stone spur was shaped more like a long, thin tapered cone than a four-sided structure. Its needle-sharp point was tipped with a metallic cap made of a special copper and gold alloy. The obelisk was transported to the platform. In a well-choreographed maneuver by gangs of Macai with ropes and several levitating Eryndi Magicians, it was carefully raised to a vertical angle and placed atop the pillars surrounding the pit.

Then Serena saw the object that Leader called the Creation Matrix. It was brought in with much pomp and ceremony aboard a kind of giant sedan chair carried by two dozen Eryndi elite in glorious robes. There were no Macai to be seen anywhere in this vision. Apparently, the installation of the object was to be an all Eryndi show. The metallic cage was carefully levitated off its platform and floated into the pillar structure beneath the obelisk. Spells were cast upon the obelisk, the pillars, and the arena itself. The entire complex shone with power. Dazzling streams of light and showers of colored Magical sparks cascaded off the obelisk to fall on the arena below. Countless Eryndi gathered about, entranced by the spectacle. Cheers were raised, and the people danced and hugged each other in jubilation. Congratulations were traded, and toasts were drunk. There was a woman, resplendently dressed, who was the center of much attention. The people cheered her and offered their thanks.

The vision altered again, and Serena saw the object being put to full use. A group of Eryndi Magicians stood round the pillars, concentrating their minds. With every spell they cast, something Magically appeared on the floor of the arena. Tons of food, clothing, and other essentials were conjured. Whatever the Magicians asked of it was provided. The obelisk glowed slightly with each creation. After basic needs were met, the most common items conjured were building stones. They were not just cubes but identical, dove-tailed blocks designed to fit within each other, providing great structural strength. Now the Macai were back. With each block produced, gangs of workers stood by to transport these blocks outside the arena to the city beyond. The wooden structures were replaced with ultra-strong, sophisticated stone buildings. Great libraries and magnificent halls of learning and music were built. Eventually, the entire city was reborn. Serena remembered seeing one of the archways on their trip through the forest. It was now a drowned ruin.

The city, which Leader had called Mennatu, was magnificent. The people were ridiculously happy. They lived like royalty. Even the simplest of former laborers had fully furnished houses of stone. There was food for all, wealth for all. This city must have been the most blessed place on the face of Lurra, until the tragedy.

Suddenly, inexplicably, the waters of what was today called the Talus rose at an impossible rate. The river jumped its banks and kept rising, barging into every building like an unwanted salesman. There was panic in the streets, for as long as there *were* streets. Within minutes the water was above the lower rooftops and still climbing. The rising waters climbed the steps of the arena and roared into the center depression, crashing against the support pillars. The Central Obelisk trembled and wavered and finally collapsed onto the platform, which had now become an island. People trapped in the taller buildings cried out in terror as the river approached their level. Some of them jumped into the water and tried to swim in the swirling eddies. The real horror, however, was that no one was drowned.

Those Eryndi in the river found themselves completely *embraced* by it. Despite every effort, water entered their mouths, noses, ears, and every other orifice. It did not just flow; the water quite literally *forced* its way into their bodies. They tried to scream but could not. Their lungs filled with liquid, their eyes and ears were invaded, their bones became soft and pliable from the interior soaking. Their skin shriveled and turned a grayish color. Their brains, their minds, their very souls were utterly consumed by the waters of the river that they had worshipped for centuries. Their bodies began a horrid transformation, shrinking as their essence was sucked right out of them. Their morals and values, as well as their separate identities, were absorbed. Everything these people had been, their civilization, their history, was . . . digested.

Serena hadn't cried since she was eight years old but now sobbed uncontrollably as grief claimed her. She bore all these terrors through the Magic of the visions. Although it was not happening to her, she vicariously felt every excruciating moment as the victims' bodies were invaded. She understood the horror of those few survivors who witnessed the spectacle from the land. She saw Eryndi on horseback and on foot fleeing from the devouring river. She became the well-dressed woman from before, perched on one of the massive boulders at the top of the falls. Guilt and regret filled her soul as she gazed down at her doomed home. Serena knew and felt every moment of the woman's anguish as she blamed herself for what had happened. She felt the need to atone as the woman plunged her body off the edge to smash into the rocks and churning foam at the base of the triple falls.

And somehow, Serena became aware that the invading water had done all this simply because it wanted to *know* something. By entering the bodies of these Eryndi and consuming them from within, the water was trying to discover something, to understand something. And Serena also knew that it never found out.

CHAPTER 13

Today – Trebalian Falls

"You go first." "You go first." "You go first."

A better three-part harmony had not been heard since *Gunther and the Graybeards* had performed at Dragonstar Palladium.

Tresado, Orchid, and Foxx snickered at each other. Foxx broke it up.

"Okay, *I'll* go first," he said. "The water spirit is behind the falls. It's got Serena."

"You know this for sure?!" asked Tresado excitedly.

"Yeah, I do. She's all right for now, but she won't stay that way. We've got to do something fast."

"What about Leader?" asked Orchid. "Does the spirit have him, too?"

"Leader *is* the spirit, or some kind of servant of it, maybe. It wants Serena's diamond. That was the whole point of this trip, to get her here and take it."

"So that whole story about a super Magician at the end of the river was just malarkey?" asked Tresado angrily.

"It would seem so. What we need is a rescue plan.

Somehow we've got to get past the falls, but the water spirit is guarding it." Foxx turned to Tresado. "I hope *you* have some good news."

"Maybe. That rock that you're holding there," he said, indicating the gray pebble in Foxx's hands. "Do you know what that is?"

"This?" Foxx asked, holding it out. Tresado backed up a step.

"You keep it. I'd rather not handle it anymore. It's called *korvanite*. We learned about it in Magic cram school."

"I've heard of it," said Orchid. "It's supposed to be the Gods' way of punishing Absolute users like you. That'll teach you to rape the natural world."

"No, it won't," he replied, "but I gotta admit, my opinion of korvanite is no better than your opinion of me. The ore contains some kind of energetic force that interferes with the direct use of Magic. It blocks it, dampens it . . . nasty stuff. It doesn't much bother Worldly wimps like you, who are too a-scared to burn their fingers.

"Anyway," Tresado continued before Orchid could reply with a comeback, "there's a whole vein of it upriver a little way. Maybe there's a way to use it against our spirit friend."

"I don't know how helpful this is, but . . . I take it you guys have heard of *Dementus the Mad Treskan?*"

They both nodded, but Orchid's question was a bit rhetorical. *Everyone* had heard of Dementus the Mad Treskan. He was a semi-mythical traveler whom every culture in this part of the world had legends about. It was said that Dementus had been beyond every known sea, crossed every mountain range, and seen wonders beyond imagination. Certain Treskan essays talked of a special sight the man possessed that allowed him to read thoughts. Melosian Canticles sang of his limitless ability to predict the future. In many countries, Dementus was considered the physical form of one god or another, sent to Lurra in Eryndi form to judge mankind. The one common story was that he was nuttier than a drunken harbor loon and probably didn't exist. Every place that had claimed a visit from him said that it had happened decades ago.

"Well, you're not going to believe this," Orchid said with wide eyes, "but I just found his journal!"

The resulting pause indicated that Tresado and Foxx were in a *Who can keep from giggling the longest* competition. Foxx lost.

"Did *Heroic Hare* pull it out of his *Bottomless Bag of Wonders?*" he snickered.

"No, I'd say the *Turd Pixie* left it under her pillow," Tresado snorted through his nose. Both of them were now blatantly cracking up.

"Funny. I'm telling you, I found it buried over there under a silly billy tree," she said, pointing with her head.

"Oh, silly billy, huh?"

"Is it good shit?"

"You gonna share it?"

As Orchid glared at them, her oaken staff thundered and flashed with power, reflecting her anger. "What did I say not ten beats ago? That you wouldn't believe it? Didn't I say that? THAT YOU WOULDN'T BELIEVE IT?"

"Well, you were right," smirked Tresado. "We *don't* believe it."

Orchid threw down the walking stick at Tresado's feet and slapped him in the stomach with the pack.

"Here, genius, look for yourself!"

With that, Orchid retreated over to a large flat rock and

occupied herself preparing the billy bark she had gathered. It was either that or kick in a pair of groins.

Tresado brushed the dirt off his tunic that had come from the filthy backpack. He and Foxx looked at each other with confusion.

"Where did you get this?" he called over to Orchid, who was busy pounding something with a rock and muttering under her breath.

"The Turd Pixie left it!" she hollered back. *"Choke on it!"*

The two jokesters grimaced at each other and left Orchid to her fury. Foxx picked up the stick and checked it over.

"This is old," he said. He spat on the handle and rubbed away a bit of dried bird guano. "Look at this emblem. Do you know whose symbol this is? Tresado, I said, do you recognize this?"

But Tresado was busy. He was picking items out of the backpack, which smelled of dirt and bugs. There was a fire starter, a small iron pot, some utensils, and lots of canvas sacks.

"Moldy beans, more beans, and this . . ." Tresado pulled out the last item, a thick book. The embossed leather cover was decorated with a gaudy grapevine motif. "This is Treskan, isn't it?"

"Yeah," Foxx said, "and so is this." He showed the stick's handle to Tresado. "See this star pattern? That's the old Treskan Imperial seal. It's not used anymore. The number of points and their positions represent different members of the royal family. An inverted pip in this position means the eldest daughter of the House of Darius. This is the symbol of Imperatrix Alythya!"

"Imperatrix *who*?" asked Tresado. "I never heard of her."

"Alythya," answered Foxx, "and I'm not surprised you haven't heard of her. She died like a hundred years ago, ruled the Imperium for decades. They used to call her *The Virgin Empress* until she married Merak."

Tresado frowned. "Merak? He's been in charge since long before I was born, for . . ."

"About a hundred years or so," said Foxx. "Not long after he married Alythya, it's said she died of a wasting disease, and he immediately assumed the title of Imperator. Right after that, he had her name stricken from all the records and replaced with his own. He proclaimed that it was to honor the name of the woman he loved. But, like I said, that was a hundred years ago. Today, it's a criminal act in Tresk to state that Merak is anything but of the royal line or even to mention Alythya's name."

"So how come you're mentioning it?"

"We're not in Tresk," answered Foxx.

"And you are kind of a criminal," said Tresado. "How do you know this stuff, anyway?"

"Criminals know everything. What's in that book?"

Tresado glanced at a few pages and whistled through his teeth. "I guess we owe Orchid an apology."

Foxx's eyebrows went up. "No way! Dementus's log is part of the legend. There are stories about it containing all the secrets of the world! That can't be REAL!"

"Well, if it isn't, it's a hell of a forgery," said Tresado, "but we don't have time to worry about it now. We've got to get behind that waterfall and find Serena."

"I agree." said Orchid, who had quietly joined them again. "Now about that apology . . ."

Foxx bowed low and elegantly kissed Orchid's hand. "Consider yourself apologized to."

Orchid found she couldn't resist Foxx's smooth manner. He was forgiven immediately. Of course, one of his strengths was that the people he charmed never knew that he was anything but sincere.

"Accepted. Now let's think of a plan."

Tresado was still thumbing through the journal. "Most of this is gibberish, but there's something here on the last page that gives me an idea. This bit about *cut him off and send him home* . . . maybe we should do just that!"

Believe it or not, an actual plan was concocted without too much bickering. Tresado again used his levitation powers, assisted by the Magically enhanced waterfall, to ascend the cliff. This time he had Orchid hitching a ride close behind him. The invisible harnesses that he created securely supported both of them. Nevertheless, Orchid squeezed her eyes shut and dug a few holes in her palms with her fingernails as they made the ascent.

The extra weight made the trip a bit more difficult, but fortunately, Orchid was a small woman. As soon as they crested the falls, Tresado headed over to the north bank and kept their altitude low, pointing out the strange Magic collectors on each bank to Orchid. He kept going upstream for as long as he could. When his spell pooped out just shy of the rapids, he deposited Orchid on the shore.

"There are the cliffs I told you about," said Tresado, panting for breath. "See that layer of korvanite?"

"Yeah," Orchid replied, squinting at the canyon wall above them, "there's quite a lot of it, but getting it where we want it won't be easy."

"That's your miracle. Foxx and I have our own to worry about," said Tresado, glancing up at the sun.

"We'll stick to the plan and go at Midday. I'll send up a signal. Good luck."

"You too."

After a few minutes of rest and meditation, Tresado was levitating himself back downriver. He stayed just above the water, absorbing the concentrated Magic in the air and water. He would need all the power he could muster. He passed over the falls, and the arena came into sight.

* * *

Graduates, you are preparing to take your places in the world as teachers and advisors, healers and protectors, and who knows . . . perhaps I am addressing a future Imperatrix. But always remember that the knowledge you have learned here will be all for nought if not tempered by the wisdom already within you. Your abilities have made you more than Eryndi, but still Eryndi . . . more than mortal, but still mortal. For all the skills you have learned, your bodies and souls are still governed by the three basic emotions that make up a sentient mind. From Love you are granted the gifts of joy, wonder, and courage . . . yet also cursed with unfulfilled desire and morbid curiosity. Hate provides you with anger against injustice yet degrades you with jealousy and contempt. Fear protects you from danger and allows you to grieve for a loved one, yet smothers you with shame and guilt. A truly civilized being or culture is a constant balance of many forces which could not exist without each other. It shall be your task to recognize and wisely administer this balance for the betterment of all.

—IMPERATRIX ALYTHYA OF TRESK
– BELATONIUS ADVANCED SCHOOL OF WORLDLY ARTS
- LECTURE TO THE GRADUATING CLASS OF 21724

When Serena looked up again, she and Leader were alone in the cave. The water thing was gone. Good. She didn't want to see any more. She slowly stood, not sure how she had ended up on her knees.

"Is your little show over now?" she asked, giving a sideways glance at Leader.

"May I ask, did what you see stir your emotions?" Leader sounded like he was asking about the price of cabbage.

"What do you want from me?" Serena demanded, in no mood to play seventeen questions.

"An answer," replied Leader directly.

"All right, YES!" she barked. "What I saw *stirred my emotions!*"

"That is your right," said Leader, "the right of all mortal, sentient creatures to be able to experience what you call *feelings*. That is what I seek."

"Are we talking about you or your wet friend?" asked Serena.

"We are as one," he said. "This form that you are addressing is but a tool, a bodily extension for the spirit that inhabits this place."

"Not that I believe a word of this goat crap, but what does this *spirit* need with a bodily extension?" asked Serena. "Sounds a little perverted to me."

"The spirit is bound to this small area of the river," explained Leader patiently. "This is its home, and it cannot venture more than a league away from this cave."

"And why should it want to?"

Leader turned his gaze toward the glowing matrix in the pit. "The spirit has knowledge that spans this part of Lurra, obtained from the minds of the original inhabitants and the travelers that have passed this way over the centuries. From them, it has learned about the outside world of mortals and their passions. It wishes to know more and to understand."

Serena's steely glare didn't soften at all. "And how's it going so far?"

"It knows of the existence of emotions," said Leader, "but for all its great intellect, it simply cannot fathom what mortals take for granted. This condition has persisted unchanged for many thousands of years, which for a timeless being is immaterial. All it knew was that the mortal beings requested water. It gave them what they asked for. When the Mennatuans activated collectors above the falls to Magically charge the water, the spirit suddenly found its power increased by a hundred-fold. It tried to use this power to seek its answers, but failed. You saw the results of that experiment."

"Yeah, I saw," said Serena bitterly. "And thank you so much for that pleasure."

"Unfortunately, it was necessary for you to witness it."

"Why?" asked Serena.

"Have you ever heard of a famed traveler named Dementus, also known as *The Mad Treskan?*"

"Sure, I've heard of him," Serena replied, "but I've also heard of *Bugsy the Butcher* and *The Snow Silkie.*"

"The Eryndi named Dementus was quite real, although there are many inaccurate tales told of him. As you know, this man was on a lifetime journey that spanned many decades and uncounted thousands of leagues. His mind contained a great deal of knowledge of the world."

A chill went up Serena's spine. "And just how would you know what his mind contained?"

"I perceive you have already deduced that," said Leader.

"Yes, the mortal known as Dementus did indeed encounter the spirit of the water and his essence was incorporated. Among his memories was an encounter he had years earlier with another Eryndi. His mind spoke of a strange power this man had, the power to make others love him unconditionally. That condition was caused by a fellow spirit that inhabited the body of this man. His name was *Parsomal;* perhaps you recall the person."

"Perhaps *you* recall that I told you that story on the boat," said Serena.

"I have known your story for years, Serena," Leader said, "nearly as long as you. When this knowledge was assimilated, it became necessary to find this person, who was also a traveler. What you have come to know as *Leader* was created using the Matrix and imparted with all available knowledge. My creation allowed the water spirit to travel vicariously beyond this cave. After years of searching, I tracked Parsomal to the distant Northlands but found nothing but his buried corpse. Shortly after that, I learned of your name and encounter with him."

"Let me guess," Serena interrupted, "you wanted to find this guy and rip out his diamond with a pry bar, so your spirit buddy could know love. And now that's what you want to do to me, is that what this is all about?"

"Oversimplified and rather lurid, but those are essentially the facts," replied Leader.

"I was just trying to keep you from talking for another twenty minutes," said Serena. "You are the windiest son-of-a-grilk I've ever seen."

"I do apologize for my pedantic proclivities," said Leader. "If you wish me to summarize, the facts are these:

after you were taken off your boat, your life functions were suspended for a time while the spirit within you was contacted and evaluated. It was hoped that it could be convinced to cooperate and leave your body. Unfortunately, it has become quite enamored with its current home and will not relinquish its hold on you. The spirit of the diamond is an entity of pure emotion. It cannot understand how it is to NOT feel. The spirit of the water does not know what it is TO feel. Water wishes to join with diamond. I have no desire to harm you. In fact, it is to all our advantage for you to cooperate."

Serena fought her basic instinct and kept silent.

"As I am sure you are aware," continued Leader, "the spirit of the diamond is entwined with your own life force, drawing sustenance from the love you engender. The diamond is its physical home, but your *soul*, if you will, is its existence. I am quite determined to possess the spirit within the diamond, but if it is removed from you without its full cooperation, it will cling to your own essence, drawing it out of your body with it, leaving nought but an empty shell. My primary concern is possibly damaging the spirit if it is forced to leave its current receptacle unwillingly. So, as you can see, it is most important for all concerned that you convince your spirit to accept the inevitable."

Serena took a few beats and just stared back at Leader. He seemed to be waiting for a response on her part. She gave him one.

"I think you know that I would like nothing more than to be rid of the rock. Even if that were possible," said Serena, defiantly narrowing her eyes, *"I wouldn't give it to you!"*

"Denying my request simply out of contrariness will not serve you well here," said Leader. "The diamond will be removed in any case. For your own safety, you must convince your spirit to part with you of its own accord."

"You really think I give a rodent's rectum about dying?" snickered Serena, genuinely amused. "I am a Northlands warrior who's unable to fight her enemies. Dying in a noble cause is my only honorable way out."

"Your death would be senseless," countered Leader. "How would that be honorable?"

"Not that you could understand such things, but I think your soggy spirit buddy is powerful enough already. If it starts learning new tricks like ambition and power-seeking, it might just decide to use that matrix thingy to create more of you . . . dozens maybe, or even armies. Just think of it, entire *legions* of dorks sweeping across the face of Lurra! Preventing that might just get me a ticket into Crodan's Keep after all."

Serena's defiant eyes bored into the expressionless ones of Leader.

"So you just go ahead and do your worst," said Serena with finality. "You're about to talk me to death anyway, so just get your pry bar and get on with things!"

If this had been anyone else, Serena would have hocked a loogie into her opponent's face at this point, just to piss him off. That wouldn't do any good here, though, so she saved her spit and just glared.

"So be it," said Leader, closing his eyes.

Serena felt the invisible bonds once again clamp down on her feet. Her hands were also thrust to her sides, leaving her standing stiffly on the cave floor, unable to move. Leader approached and drew a knife. He methodically began slicing through the leather lacings on the front of her jerkin.

"Enjoying yourself?" Serena growled.

"Not at all. That is precisely the issue."

The sound of rushing water returned as the spirit re-emerged from the pit. She and Leader were once again enveloped by the watery entity. Serena surprised herself at her own calmness as she prepared to stand before Crodan for judgment. The last thing she was aware of was the spirit within her, crying out in desperation.

CHAPTER 14

Nine years ago – Trebalian Falls

"Labored sixteen year on one bag o' beans . . . tra-leee and follee me boys . . ."

He was a freckle-faced stork of a man. The old but wiry Eryndi nearly died five times scrambling his way down the cliff face. That certainly didn't stop him from singing at the top of his lungs. In his one hundred eighty-two years of travel, Dementus of Tresk had not stopped singing the same song. The original version of *Bandylegs Ballad* contained over a thousand stanzas, and Dementus knew them all. It could be said that no one knew them as he did because he had most of the lyrics as well as the melody completely wrong. No matter, he sang from the heart. Dementus himself had written several new verses that pertained to key points of his long journey. He planned to publish them someday.

Dementus was anxious to get to the bottom of this cliff. From the heights, his old but sharp eyes had spotted the very intriguing sight of flooded ruins beyond the waterfall. Even so, he paused in his descent as he clung precariously to a root for twenty minutes to make observations about a bird nest he discovered in the cliff face.

At last he came to the bottom. This was a lovely place. The amazing triple falls thundered away to the south. He was well aware of the presence of a spirit in the pool below it.

"Someone's at home, Octavia . . . well, well, well, we'd do well to not ring the bell . . . no, no, no . . . on our way, on our way, on our way we go! . . . *On a road of gold through the hot and cold . . . on it we rove till we're way too old . . .*"

Through the decades, many have heard Dementus speak to *Octavia*. It is not actually known who Octavia is or was. Some say a wife, some say a parrot. In any case, Dementus always kept up a lively conversation with her wherever he went.

"That goomer in the pool, Octavia . . . can't hear it, can't see it, can't get no service here . . . *Innkeeper! Where's my gimlet?* . . . Okay, Octa, best get this down . . ."

Dementus took a breath to collect himself and continued his conversation with no one.

"Magic is this bad boy's meat and potatoes . . . got overfed, though. It didn't know no better . . . just doin' what it was asked . . . Nothin' sadder than your nephew shootin' his eye out with that crossbow you give him."

The Mad Treskan took another long look at the waterfall.

"This critter was born of Magic . . . Magic don't know . . . Magic don't care . . . but it's always there for you. Better parent than some, I reckon, but that's all the varmint has."

Clasping his well-worn walking staff, Dementus followed the bank downriver toward the ruins ahead. He came first to the immense structure, his loud voice echoing back across the water from the stone walls.

"Don't wanna get wet, Octavia, gotta keep you dry. But somehow we gotta get 'cross that water and see what's showin' at the Dracodrome tonight."

Dementus was a patient being. It took him a day and a half to gather enough driftwood and another two to lash it together and make himself a crude raft. Now that he was past the rapids, his journey following the Talus River would go more efficiently on the water. He was looking forward to visiting Ostica. It had been almost ninety years. He passed the time spent building by reciting the entire *Chronicle of Plutonius* and doing all the voices. The whole time he was constructing the raft, Dementus was also well aware he was being watched. Being at war with no one, he was not concerned and continued his recitation.

"Whoever's out there is gettin' a fine performance, Octa, baby . . . how lucky they are . . ."

Eventually, *Dementus's Dinghy* was ready for launch. The christening ceremony was performed with beans rather than bubble water, but all necessary solemnity was observed. He took a short break and kindled a fire. Twenty minutes later, he was savoring the delicate flavor of those same beans. Feeling refreshed and raring to go, he gathered up his pack and boarded the raft.

"Here we go, m'dear . . . through the arch and onto the stage."

Dementus pushed off from shore, nearly falling off immediately. Keeping his balance on the raft would take some getting used to. A flat piece of driftwood served as a paddle to propel his crude craft across the swollen river where the gigantic arena awaited. An archway directly ahead led to the interior.

"Oh! What's this I see? Pillars and porticoes . . . these folks played with their building blocks like good little boys and girls, Octa . . . *Skibble-Lee-Bee, come play with me* . . ."

Dementus paddled his raft through the arch and into the empty, foreboding structure. His mind reached out to the crumbling stone blocks, the water, the air, feeling what they had felt, knowing what they had known. This was not a conscious effort on his part. Few things were. The information was all there, stretching from the beginning to the end of time. It was just a matter of knowing where to look. This drowned city contained many triumphs and tragedies worthy of notation.

"Sad days . . . no . . . only one . . . one sad day. But only one out of a million happy ones . . . that ain't bad at all. It's an epic story, worthy of a poem."

He cleared his throat and took up a dramatic pose.

"Beans and the blood of life for lunch. Lurra's vein dissuaded from home to suckle the ones without. The last of the dwellers have fled into its arms. Never to count the stars again . . . poor buggers . . . got that, Octavia? Very eloquent, you say? . . . gotta agree with you on that one . . . I am one silver-tongued devil, ain't I?"

Dementus gazed about at the gigantic arena surrounding him. Rows and rows of seats stepped their way out of the water. He was very aware of the massive amount of Magic in the air and water.

"Took a lot of juice to buy a round for the house, Octa. Pretty ball ran one heck of a tab. Now only one customer left, and that's the bartender! I say, *enough for you, my friend* . . . cut him off and send him home, Octavia."

In the center of the floor, which was now a lake, was an island. Great broken blocks of stone covered its surface. Gnawed bones covered the blocks.

"No more concerts, but I think we found the concession stand, Octavia."

Dementus paddled his raft to the stone island. The former structure had had a relatively short life, but it was full of impressions. He stepped ashore and tied up to a piece of rubble.

"Twiddle my fiddle, this was the middle . . . this was where pretty ball made the blocks, made the clocks and all the clothes from hats to socks."

He picked up a small bone and gathered its history.

"Little miss monkey here liked to chase the butterflies, Octa. Great fun, great fun! Chase, chase, chase, reach out and grab! Watch out! Got too far from mom. Oh no! . . . city folk waiting. Last sleep for little miss."

He tossed the bone away and took another look around. Past, present, and future swirled and merged like cream in coffee.

"Grand Lady got a long-term loan, but had to atone . . . when pretty ball goes, banker foreclose."

Something else he saw sobered even the ever-cheerful Dementus.

"This is the last trip, Octavia, city folk comin' and bartender say, *last call.*"

By the time he jumped aboard his raft and paddled back through the arch, the hordes of chattering pygmies had swarmed from their hiding places in the arena and dove into the water in hot pursuit. Dementus paddled furiously in an attempt to reach the upstream shore before they caught up with him. Little blowgun darts whistled past, barely missing him. The ones that would have hit were miraculously deflected by fortuitous parries with his paddle. Even without looking, Dementus always seemed to know when and where to swing.

Reaching the bank ahead of his pursuers, Dementus raced toward the northeast. The stumpy pygmies were no match for his long, bony legs, and he soon outdistanced them, but they were still coming. A grove of trees far ahead offered the only cover in sight. Dementus fled into the woods and, after a quick study, found the right spot. He loosened the soil with his walking stick and scooped the dirt out with his hands.

"They're after you, Octavia! Won't git ya, though. Rest for a spell and Lady Green-Eyes'll see ya safe. It's been a grand time, Octa, but ya can't drink on credit forever, gotta pay the tab. Ain't no gettin' around it."

He dumped his backpack into the hole and tightly packed the dirt over it. He stood above the mound solemnly. Placing his hand over his heart, he made his last diary entry.

"To My Lady of the Emerald Eyes:" he spoke aloud, "Give my journal and my shell collection to my kid brother Cyrus. The little creep always did envy my Junonia."

With that, Dementus of Tresk jammed the iron point of his walking stick into the packed earth. He grabbed a strip of billy bark, then ran with all speed back out of the trees. There was bad news to greet him, though. Over a hundred pygmies were closing on him from three sides. The only way out was toward the river, and he already knew the futility of it all.

Day's gone crappy . . . just as well get happy, he thought. Slipping the bark between his cheek and gums, he made a beeline for the water.

The Plan - Tresado

Tresado had no tools, but Magic would serve him well as it always did. From his chubby fingers, he projected a hair-fine concentration of heat energy that served as a saw. Ropes were severed and re-lashed. Kinetic Magic was used to tighten knots with greater strength than his neglected muscles could manage. Burst floatation bladders were removed and replaced with intact ones. A mending spell stretched and sealed torn fabric. He now had one complete, repaired pontoon from *Enchanter*'s shattered remains.

The tricky part was re-plumbing the tubing. *Enchanter*'s bubble drive dual exhaust system had been designed for two pontoons separated by a couple of reaches. Fortunately, the monkeywood had properties that made it easy to manipulate Magically. It was tricky, but he managed to reshape the bends in the pipes and mount them parallel underneath. Tresado attached the fuel canister on top. It would be the only thing to hold on to as he straddled the single pontoon like a pony's saddle. The boat was unstable, wanting to roll over, and there was no way to physically steer. He was counting on his kinetic Magic to keep him on course and upright. Without the deck, mast, sail, and the second pontoon, *Enchanter* was now basically a lightweight, rocket-powered canoe. It was on this deathtrap that Tresado planned to pierce the waterfall.

He finished up the last details just as Sensang was approaching its zenith in the sky. He realized that, if it chose, the water entity could easily knock him for a loop as he entered the pool . . . if it detected him coming, that is. That would depend on Foxx.

The Plan - Foxx

Foxx steeled himself for another heavy conversation. The first task would be getting the water spirit to acknowledge him. After that, the main problem was keeping the spirit's attention while concealing his own true intentions. If the plan to distract the spirit while Tresado penetrated the falls was revealed, everything could come apart pretty quickly. It would require some extreme mental compartmentalization to keep the spirit from seeing through him. He used what he had learned in his first contact with the entity to guide his mental preparation. Foxx combined that with the card-playing skills he had developed even before he invented *The Knowing Spell*. It was the Magical equivalent of a poker face.

Let's hope that thing can be bluffed . . .

The Plan - Orchid

It didn't take her long to climb to where the vein of korvanite was. The soft sandstone surrounding it was easily pushed aside, exposing the ore. A couple hours' worth of digging with Dementus's iron-tipped walking stick yielded a good-sized pile of the silvery-gray mineral. Orchid found the elegant, four-sided crystalline structure in the little pebbles quite charming.

The natural world is a marvelous thing . . .

She could feel the Magic-inhibiting properties inherent in the ore, but it had little effect on her. Orchid's Worldly variety tended to *induce and persuade* Magic rather than *alter and control*. This material would impede an Absolute user's attempt to directly turn Magical energy into fire. Yet it would not interfere with a Worldly Magician, who would create a flame by moving cold out of the way and allowing a combustible to ignite on its own.

Orchid's intent was to Magically induce a violent, localized rainstorm to wash the material down to the river rapids and then continue to use her skills to guide the ore-saturated water past the Magical collectors above the falls. The Magic-impeding properties should temporarily neutralize the immense power being channeled into the water and weaken the spirit. She really liked this plan. The raw Magic being forcibly pulled from the sky by the collectors on the riverbank offended her sensibilities.

The sun was getting higher in the sky. It was nearly time to implement the plan. An old man she had known in her youth used to refer to Midday by saying, *Arctor's ready for lunch,* using the old-fashioned Macai name for the sun. She cleared her mind and waited. Tresado should be signaling any time now.

* * *

Executing a battle strategy is like felling a colossus tree . . . you decide where to start, swing your axe, and prepare to haul ass if things go to shit . . .

— HROLVAD THE BERSERKER – YEAR 183
- OLD MACAI CALENDAR

The Flaw in the Plan - Tresado

It was not quite Midday. Tresado sat on his flimsy creation, wondering just how smart an idea this was and whether he was going to die in the next few minutes. This plan was the long shot of all long shots. He had no idea what he would encounter once he penetrated the waterfall . . . *IF* he could penetrate it. No matter. If he didn't attempt to save Serena, there would be no living with the guilt.

Suddenly, amid his thoughts, an intense intrusion broke the spell. It was urgent, powerful and pleading . . . and he recognized the source. A desperate call for help pounded on his conscious mind, begging . . . fearful.

It was a call for help, and it came from the spirit of the diamond! It was still earlier than planned, but there was no choice.

Gotta go right now and hope that Foxx and Orchid have done their jobs!

Tresado summoned luminescent Magic to the pinky finger of his left hand and fired a concentrated burst straight up. The blood-red flare burst just shy of a hundred reaches in the air above his head. He then quickly opened the pouch of fuel coins and took out three. One probably would have been enough, but to Tresado, more was always better. He dropped them into the fuel canister and secured the lid. He opened the throttle halfway and held on. A powerful stream of bubbles shot out the twin exhaust tubes at the stern. The nose of the pontoon exploded up out of the water, nearly bucking Tresado off his gallant charger. He leaned forward and eased off the throttle a touch. The nose splashed back down to a more level angle, and he shot out of the arena's archway and raced upstream like a salmon desperate to spawn.

Enchanter was providing the thrust, so all he had to use his kinetic Magic for was to keep the nose to the center of the river and keep himself from rolling over. When the falls came into sight, he opened the throttle all the way. The nose wanted to bounce up and down as it skipped across the surface at a dizzying speed. It was all he could do to control his course, but he was managing.

He was moments away from contact with the falls when he glanced ahead to his left and saw Foxx desperately waving his arms in a *Don't! Wait! Stop!* gesture. Tresado didn't know what the problem was, but something must be wrong, and he must abort. He closed the throttle to shut down the drive, but, unknown to him, the earlier damage to the boat had fatigued the soft brass handle and it broke off in his hand. Tresado was smashed flat across the pontoon by the wall of cascading water as he and his bubble-powered projectile rocketed through at full speed. During the half-beat that he was in contact with the falls, he realized that the water was still highly charged with Magic.

The Flaw in the Plan - Foxx

Foxx had also heard the call for help. He saw Tresado's signal burst high above the arena walls. It was time, and he was ready. His *Knowing Spell* was prepared, and he sent the first probe into the water of the pool as he had done before. Using a carrot earlier and attempting to bargain had gotten him nowhere with the water spirit. It was time for a stick. Foxx's intent was to deliver an ultimatum, threatening to cut off the flow of Magic in the water and deprive the thing of its strength if it didn't release Serena. It had the advantage of being mostly the truth, although none of Group Six really knew to what degree that would affect the spirit, if at all. The idea was, while it was focused on Foxx and considering the threat, it would be off its guard enough that Tresado would be able to penetrate to the cave without drawing an attack on himself. Foxx kept that part of the plan safely behind a mental shield that (he hoped) the spirit couldn't see through. It was like playing one's cards close to the vest. To aid him in his confidence, he used the mental image of holding a full blitzkrieg. His actual hand was weak, but a good bluff was sometimes just as effective.

Behind him, Foxx could hear the high-pitched sound of *Enchanter*'s bubble drive approaching at high speed. Time was running out. He concentrated harder on his spell. He knew the proper wavelength and called to the image of Leader that the spirit had used to communicate earlier. It should respond any second . . . but there was nothing! Probing deeper, Foxx detected the presence of the thing behind the falls. He knew it was in there, but there was the equivalent of a solid mental wall between them. Then he realized the truth. He was not doing anything wrong; the spell was being properly cast. The spirit was simply not responding of its own choice. It ignored him and you can't play cards if the other player refuses to sit down at the table.

The Flaw in the Plan - Orchid

Orchid knelt on a ledge above the pile of korvanite and cleared her mind to prepare her weather spell. Calling up a cloudburst involved manipulating the forces of humidity and temperature to cause condensation. She reached out to the atmosphere and immediately realized there might be trouble. Today's weather was hot and dry with little moisture in the air. Squinting her eyes tightly shut, Orchid strained with all her abilities to bring on the rain. A small, wispy cloud laboriously appeared, and a few scant drops of water fell from it.

Not enough!

It was then that Orchid heard the distress call, not in her ears, but in her heart.

Serena needed help!

Orchid knew that the fearless warrior would not cry out so. It was the spirit of the diamond within Serena reaching out to her friends, pleading for assistance!

A dull boom echoed back and forth between the canyon walls. Orchid looked downstream to the west. A bright burst of Magical red lights had exploded in the Midday sky above where she knew the arena lay.

Tresado's signal!

Orchid nearly panicked. The plan was in motion, and she had no way to implement her part in it. The large pile of ore was too heavy for her to carry down the cliff face. If she couldn't get the korvanite into the river, the rescue would fail! Serena and possibly Tresado and Foxx might well die as a result of her failure.

Orchid made another attempt to summon a rainstorm. She called upon every iota of ability within herself, every scrap of arcanum she ever learned, but to no avail. There was simply not enough natural potential in the air to work with. She sat back on the pile of korvanite ore in despair, knowing she had failed her friends.

CHAPTER 15

1,331 years ago – The Talus River

Zarosen was looking forward to a thick bergalo steak smothered in runjian truffle gravy. That meal should be in his stomach in just about two weeks now. Fish and rice were fine, but it got a bit old when one ate them nearly every day for months.

"And what are *you* looking forward to, Arko?"

"Cool hills, tired of hot," he replied without missing a step.

The strapping, blonde Macai could not pause in his pace. The twin paddlewheels on each side of the river barge required the constant attention. The inboard propulsion steps were, at the moment, manned by Arko and seven others. They stepped in an endless climb, turning the driveshaft, while ten more Macai manned the midship cranks. Their constant labor slowly propelled the barge *Dranak* against the sluggish current of the Talus River.

"You are getting a bit brown," said Zarosen with a smile. "You used to be pink."

"Ever seen snow, boss?" the blonde Macai asked.

"It snowed on our last trip up the Osagar, but mostly I've just seen it in the mountains from a distance."

"I like snow," said Arko. "Wrestled brothers in snow."

"Before you . . . " Zarosen trailed off.

"Before bosses came," Arko said simply. "Bring to city."

"Crew change!"

Barom, the barge's head wrangler, shouted the order and the Macai workers gave up their positions to the relief group. Zarosen gave friendly slaps on the backs to Arko and the other workers, who now moved forward to receive treats and water. They would be back at it in another two hours.

"Good job, guys, good job."

As Barom motioned for the workers to cluster in their assigned area, he stole a couple of wry glances in Zarosen's direction. It was nothing Zarosen had not seen before. Some of the other Eryndi looked on his affection for the Macai workers as if he were some old dowager who talked to houseplants. As soon as the workers were settled, Barom strolled back across the deck, shaking his head.

"You know they don't really understand, right?"

"Barom, how many times are we going to do this?" Zarosen answered. *"Of course they understand!* They can talk, for crap's sake!"

"Yeah, so can my uncle's parrot. He can even sing," said Barom. "When you try to get into a conversation with the Macai, they just repeat phrases they've heard before because it's what you want to hear, but they don't actually *talk.*"

"You mean they don't talk to *you.*"

"I've got better things to do than talk to *cacks,*" Barom snorted. He went astern again. The junior wranglers needed a little goading to keep the workers in sync, since they operated the machinery powering the barge upriver.

Zarosen held his tongue. It wouldn't do any good with somebody like Barom. While he and the other Eryndi weren't cruel to the Macai, they couldn't or wouldn't see that the workers were much more than two-legged pack mules. Zarosen had worked in shipping for three years and had traveled many leagues and seen many things that one could not see in Mennatu. In that time, he had had the services of many Macai workers and had come to know and respect the gentle giants. They were not the mindless cattle most Eryndi thought them to be.

Much of this last year had been spent far from home. The great flotilla of supply barges had taken weeks to travel downriver. They made a few stops at a few cities, delivering a few special orders. But this voyage's primary goal was not a regular supply run. Once past the port town of Ostracantrica and into the ocean, the fleet turned south, following the coastline. Weeks more of travel brought them to a broad bay surrounded by thirty-reach-high cliffs. A large river had cut its way through the stone for the past zillion years or so, carving a deep, narrow canyon. The sediment from that formed a wide beach that extended out into the bay for half a league. This was the fleet's destination. The deep water harbor and defensible cliffs would make for a fine city someday.

Zarosen and the others spent the next four months here. A system of cranes was established at the top of the cliffs, and the building supplies from the barges were hoisted to the top. Soon, the first buildings were erected to house the Eryndi colonists. Temporary rope bridges were installed across the two sides of the river canyon. Streets were planned and laid out. A road to the interior was cut. The soil was rich, and the forests were full of the sweetest grapes anyone had ever tasted.

The new colony was named after the man whose dream it was to expand the Mennatuan Empire this far south, Elder Treska.

During the building, many of the Eryndi, including Zarosen, found themselves taken with depression. Nerves were on edge, tempers were short, and when they didn't have insomnia, it was nightmares. Theories ranged from water contamination to homesickness. But nobody ever said that colony life would be easy. There would be no unlimited luxuries the people had in Mennatu, where the Hearth supplied every desire. Out here on the frontier, those Eryndi that still enjoyed a challenge in life endured.

By now the colony was established, and Zarosen and the crews were going home at last. The fleet of empty barges had just left Ostracantrica and was heading back up the Talus. There had been disturbing news there. Several scheduled supply deliveries from Mennatu had not arrived. The Eryndi living there had started to grow used to the flow of luxuries from the capital, and they were not happy. They demanded answers from Zarosen and the others, who promised to look into it when they arrived back home.

He stood at the forward rail, wondering about the strange uneasiness he was feeling.

"Boss hurt?"

Arko, it seemed, was just as able to read Zarosen's moods as his mother was.

"No, not hurt . . . just worried."

"Mother hurt?"

Parrot indeed, Zarosen thought.

"I don't know, Arko," he said. "I wish I did."

"Mother is big boss," Arko said in his deep Macai voice, "not allowed to hurt."

"Thanks, Arko,"

Any animal that attempts to empathize and reassure is no animal.

The days passed as the fleet crawled upriver. The Talus was running more swiftly than normal, and the barges moved at a snail's pace. It must have been raining heavily in the mountains somewhere. Several times, the Macai workers all seemed to sense something simultaneously, raising their heads and scanning the bank on both sides. But there was nothing there. Arko couldn't explain it. When asked what was up, he merely shook his head. Something had agitated him and the other Macai, but none of them could specify what.

The fleet reached the convergence of the Osagar and the Palon Rivers. The city of Prennit stood on the high ground. The waterway ahead was so jammed with boats and barges that the fleet could barely squeeze past in some places. Every berth and dock was occupied, and the streets were filled with excited people. It was utter chaos in the city. There was no space anywhere that Zarosen's fleet could tie up. Information was gathered simply by shouting back and forth to people on the shore and docks.

What they learned was sketchy. Apparently, a disaster had occurred in Mennatu . . . a flood or storm or something had enveloped the city. They heard stories of demons and divine retribution upon sinners. There were even tales of Macai rebellions and mass escapes. Zarosen could not fully believe any of this. It was just too outlandish. But obviously, something had happened back home. These storytellers were refugees that had been pouring into Prennit by boat, horseback, and by foot for weeks now.

The fleet continued upriver despite the warnings of doom.

The Talus wound through the forest and farmlands. At least they used to be farmlands. The land had, for generations, been cleared for a league all along the river where the soil was the most fertile. When the Great Hearth was activated sixteen years previous, farms became unnecessary and were mostly abandoned. New trees from the forest were starting to take over the once-tilled land.

Zarosen was four years old at the time and had only vague memories of the event known as Commencement. Mostly he remembered being the son of the city's most important Elder. That celebrity status served him well in his teenage search for popularity, but he now found it bothersome. Being away on shipping runs alleviated that. He did his job along with the rest. They treated him no differently than anyone else, and he liked it that way. But now, Zarosen could think of nothing but getting home. Every day brought them closer.

Mennatu was still a week away when they met the first group of survivors. They were ragged, afraid, and hungry. Groups encamped along the riverbank, seeking any food and shelter available. There was a mother with two children. Her husband had been a Celebrant in the Temple of Quiseron . . . one of the last. When questioned about what happened, her words could not do justice to the horror in her eyes. The God, she said, had finally exacted vengeance upon those who had betrayed His trust. She had watched her husband being consumed by the waters. That had been her punishment— for abandoning her faith as had so many others.

At last, the fleet of barges arrived and moved slowly through the destroyed city. The crews could now see for themselves. The water had inexplicably risen to an unbelievable level. The flooding caused great mudslides and widespread erosion of banks. Buildings nearest the river had toppled and fallen when their foundations washed away. Even the walls of the mighty Collector had crumbled on one side and fallen in. The Central Obelisk, with its golden cap, had collapsed. Presumably the Creation Matrix, the greatest achievement in history, was buried somewhere under that mountain of rubble. The glorious Mennatu, with its magnificent stone structures and supreme civilization, was no more.

The real horror, though, lay in the hideous remnants of the population that had washed up on every shore. They were shrunken wisps of creatures, hardly even recognizable as Eryndi. They lay about the banks, gasping and moaning, covered in mud and their own filth. Some wandered aimlessly, mindless and incoherent, reacting in terror to any attempt by Zarosen or the others to communicate. There was no sign of Zarosen's mother or any of his siblings. The poor victims were so disfigured that it was doubtful that they could be recognized in any case.

The other Eryndi in the fleet were totally numbed by the horrid sights around them. One of them decided to try to search a flooded building where his loved ones had lived. He dove off the barge and started to swim. Immediately, in front of the shocked eyes of the others, the horrid process began. The man struggled to stay afloat as the water took on a life of its own. It flowed up the side of his face, seeming to defy gravity. The river forced its way into the man's mouth and nose, seething and bubbling as it consumed the essence of the victim. He struggled to make it to a mud bank; his now too-large clothes hung from his shrunken frame. Convulsions wracked the man as he writhed in the mud, completely stripped of his ancient Eryndi nobility, and turned into a mindless beast.

The sight of that convinced everyone to get off the water as soon as possible. The barges were all turned toward the nearest land, some on the south bank, some on the north. The Macai were the first to leap off in any case. The terrified workers ignored the commands of their wranglers and fled in all directions. The workers on board the *Dranak* did not flee as the others did. They stayed in Zarosen's presence, ready to serve their boss. Barom and the other Eryndi aboard jumped off and headed away from the river as fast as possible.

"Boss's home gone," said Arko stoically. "Ours far . . . you come?"

Today – the cave

The force of the falling water nearly knocked Tresado silly. That must explain the impossible glimpse of a log cabin that flew past at thirty leagues an hour.

Hallucination . . . must be.

Enchanter, now in the form of a single rocket-powered pontoon, shot out of the water like a flying fish as it hit the sloping rock beach of the cave behind the falls. A tunnel lay directly ahead, which was really fortuitous for Tresado, considering his speed. The pontoon came down hard, spewing wood splinters and bits of fabric as it ground itself to bits on the rough cave floor. Tresado could only hold on and attempt to control his craft as best he could with his kinetic Magic. The tunnel zipped by, and a larger cave opened in front of him. Something shimmery loomed ahead. The pontoon slowed rapidly as it skidded across the floor directly toward the . . . *water!* It was a great ball of water floating next to a pit in the floor. It hit Tresado full in the face as he entered it.

It was like doing an upright belly flop in a vertical pool. The pontoon came to a full stop as it thumped into something soft and yielding within. Tresado, not the most graceful athlete in the world, tried to do a front flip over the top of the fuel canister. Instead, he exited the other side of the water ball and landed flat on his back on the hard cave floor. This was no ordinary ball of water floating in midair. Immediately after the impact, the liquid flew back into the pit.

Tresado shook the stars out of his head and jumped to his feet. He looked back the way he had come and saw two figures. One of them was Leader, who was pushing the shattered remains of *Enchanter* off his body and struggling to get up. The other was Serena, standing stiffly . . . *stripped to the waist!*

The spirit of the diamond within her was still crying out for help. Tresado heard and wanted nothing more than to do so. But, even though he had no spell cast upon him, his feet were just as rooted to the spot as Serena's and his mouth hung open like a castle's drawbridge. He did his best to greet her.

"Habba, habba, habba . . ."

"Tresado!" Serena exclaimed. "Tresado! HEY, NUMB NADS!!!"

At this instant, Foxx appeared from the tunnel, dripping wet and wielding Serena's scimitar. He took in the scene in a glance. His eyes passed over Leader and screeched to a halt upon Serena.

"Habba, habba, habba . . ."

"Watch out, you morons!" yelled Serena, still unable to move.

Leader was just picking himself up. He still had the knife in his hand. Foxx was the first to recover his senses. He advanced upon Leader, clumsily swinging the sword. Leader ducked and easily avoided the non-swordsman's attacks.

Tresado, with incredible strength of will, tore his gaze away from Serena and began to gather his thoughts for a Magical attack. Leader retreated to the edge of the pit and calmly closed his eyes. The water in the pit leapt out menacingly and interposed itself between Leader and the two heroes.

Tresado thrust out a palm and unleashed a wall of kinetic force designed to smash into his watery enemy and blast it away, but a liquid pseudopod reached out and slapped the spell away as though it were a paper kite. The thing began to move slowly, menacingly toward them.

They both backed up, Foxx waving the sword before him. What good it would do against water, he wasn't sure. He tried to reach out again to the thing, hoping to contact it, talk it out of . . . whatever. But it was no use. The thing seemed more determined than ever not to answer Foxx. From the way it was backing them into a wall, it seemed determined to squash them, drown them, or any of a dozen other horrible possibilities.

Tresado mentally reached into the air and pulled Magic into a massive burst of electrical energy. The powerful lightning bolt, enhanced by the vast amount of raw Magic in the air in this place, launched from above his head toward the floating mass of water. But again, the ancient entity brushed the spell aside with ridiculous ease. The bolt arced upward to detonate on the rock ceiling. Splinters of stone rained down upon them as the menacing water spirit slowly advanced. Tresado could feel it gathering an unbelievable amount of Magic for its own attack. There was no defense and nowhere to run. Foxx and Tresado were about to be pulverized, and they both knew there was nought they could do about it.

Thirteen years ago - Orchid

Jennick's students sat around him in a circle, hands clasped. Around them were the well-kept grounds of the campus. The walking path was lined with delicate Melosian irises, diligently worked by large sugar bees and tiny buzzbirds. A pair of spotted lemurs scurried after each other in a game of chase through the branches of an ancient effigy tree that had been planted when the university was founded over seven hundred years ago. Though they were not visible, Jennick knew there was a small herd of Nyhatoms a quarter-league into the forest. They were very shy, very reclusive creatures, seldom glimpsed by civilized eyes. They would make for a perfect exercise.

"Most . . . people behave in a solipsistic manner," he told the class, "knowing nothing but the self and that the self is all that can truly exist."

Jennick's hesitation was perfectly plain to Orchid. He had almost said 'most *Macai.*' She knew he did not think that of her, but that was not the case with her classmates. She also knew that Jennick was aware of some of the others' doubts about having a Macai amongst the class. She had trained herself long ago to realize how unimportant things like that were.

"We know differently, do we not, my students?" Jennick turned slowly about. When his gaze landed upon her, she gave him a quick wink. The tiny upturned corner of his mouth in response was apparent only to her. Or so she hoped.

"Begin your exercises," he said, closing his eyes. He spoke softly and slowly, coaching his apprentices in proper technique.

"Do not actively seek as though looking for a single apple in an orchard. Rather, embrace all the apples, the leaves, the trees, the very ground they are planted in. Allow the world around you to flow as it will, and allow yourself to flow with the world."

Orchid relaxed her mind with the rest of them. The stirrings of the life surrounding them touched her thoughts. She felt the presence of the plant life, the birds, the insects, and even the Nyhatoms. It was exciting, knowing they were there. At the same time, the nervous little creatures became aware themselves of so many minds simultaneously touching theirs. A faint bleat sounded from the trees as the herd retreated deeper into the forest.

Orchid could project her own thoughts to animals, but not the reverse. She was aware of their leaving only because their auras gradually receded from her mind. What she was frustratingly *not* picking up were the emotions and motivations that the Eryndi students could seemingly read. They were apparently aware of, and somehow even conversing with, the Nyhatoms. Sometimes, Orchid had the idea they were putting her on when they claimed to understand what animals were 'saying.'

Plants were another matter. Orchid understood them. She could perceive a necessity for giving up pollen to the bees, sating of hunger on sunny days, and pain when damaged. Plants had needs but no desires, simple minds without the complications of consciousness.

Animals, on the other hand, all had agendas of some kind. Something in that apparently kept Orchid from fully grasping all there was to know.

Jennick monitored his apprentices' progress, noting each one's strengths and weaknesses to be discussed with them individually at a later time. He focused on Orchid as she struggled.

All she needs is just the right motivation to get her to grasp what I'm trying to teach.

"The world is as your bodies," he said to the class as a whole, but directing it mostly to Orchid. "Your bodies know what they need, what food is nutritious, what water is tainted. Your bodies know what is good for them and what is bad. The world also knows. Lurra knows when things are prosperous and when there is danger. As you can be motivated to excel, so can Lurra if the need is great enough.

"We are never alone," he continued. "We voyage through time amid an infinite number of others, all with their own wants and needs. In times of great peril, those needs can align with your own. We are part of the world. What is good for the world is good for us. As Lurra may call upon you for help, so you may call upon Lurra. Your inner strength, your inner senses will manifest themselves and Lurra will aid."

Orchid had trouble with that one, too. Right now, she was hungry, but a ham sandwich did not appear out of nowhere. She always felt that one must work for what one needed. It must be the Macai in her.

* * *

As I begin studies of my new home, I am struck by the abilities of the Macai. At first glance, they would seem to be an inferior species to Eryndi in all that is measurable. But every so often, they are capable of enormous leaps of accomplishment. It makes me proud.

—*STARFISH* ARCHIVAL SPHERE 01

1,330 years ago – 6 months after the fall of Mennatu

Zarosen's situation was a sad one. The central government had collapsed in the face of such a disaster. Most if not all of the Council of Elders had apparently perished in the flood. Zarosen had no idea what had become of his mother and older siblings. Everything important to him in the former city was lost. After witnessing the floods' horrifying disfigurement of the population, his Eryndi crewmates had deserted in fear, leaving Zarosen with the Macai workers, who refused to leave their boss's side. The Macai wanted to travel back to their homeland, but didn't really know which way that was. Zarosen felt a responsibility toward them and vowed to accompany and help them in any way he could. He knew that most of the workers had been brought from the northern wilderness. He decided to start by heading for the northern town of *Kuaylos*, a twenty day journey by foot. From there, they would try to acquire some mounts or wagons for the journey to the Macai homeland, which most of them had not seen since they were children.

There were plenty of supplies from the river barges and everyone packed as much food and water as they could carry, but that was very soon given away to the pitiful people they encountered everywhere along the road. Most of these Eryndi had fled Mennatu with little more than the clothes on their back. They lived in small camps along the road, begging from any and all passersby. Zarosen recognized a few of them. The old man wearing nothing more than a filthy rag around his loins had been known as Plytanno, former head of the Grain Merchants' Guild. Before Commencement, he was a wealthy businessman and community leader. Of course, after the installment of the Creation Matrix, labor unions were no longer needed, and the Eryndi, like Plytanno, retired into the same idyllic life as everyone else. Now he was little more than a starved skeleton of a man, taking shelter in a grove of seramin trees along with a dozen others. Zarosen gave him the last of his dried meat cakes, only to see them snatched away from him by the others.

There was nothing to do but move on. Fortunately, the Macai were very adept at living off the land. Every evening, they would forage and bring back roots or wild grain or even the occasional small game to the camp. Anything that was found was shared by the whole group. Zarosen couldn't help but recall how the Eryndi refugees had fought each other over scraps. The generous behavior of the Macai *animals,* as his people called them, was a humbling comparison. The meals weren't sumptuous, but they kept Zarosen and his friends alive for the two and a half weeks it took to reach Kuaylos. The situation was no better there. The supply runs from Mennatu had ceased six months ago, and the townspeople had little enough for themselves, not to mention the hordes of starving refugees that poured in daily. Within the last decade, cities and towns of the Mennatuan Domain grew accustomed to regular shipments of food, clothing, and luxuries. So much so, the youth had little concept of what it was like to take care of themselves. Many older folks remembered how to farm, but there were very few seeds to be found. When all the food was free, there was no need to grow and store seed for the next season.

Zarosen stayed in Kuaylos for two weeks, helping in any way he could. As the son of an Elder, he was looked up to and his opinion sought. He was a natural leader and people respected him, but even though these were his people, a very good reason developed for him to leave. Seventeen Macai workers traveled with him, including his friend Arko. The people of Kuaylos looked upon them as potentially useful beasts of burden, and there were demands for their services. And although he could never substantiate any of it, there were some very ugly mutterings floating about the town. People were starving; their few food animals had been consumed long ago ... and these were only Macai, after all.

They left in the middle of the night, quickly and quietly. It tore at Zarosen's soul, but there was nothing more to be done here. The world he had grown up in was gone. The Eryndi that survived would have to learn all over how to live in the new one. And if Zarosen had anything to say about it, that new world would not include the servitude of the Macai.

After about two days' travel, they met up with a contingent of Mennatuan Militia. The group was ragged and disheartened. They had had nothing but hard luck the last several weeks. There had been two battles with hungry, frightened mobs, who had irrationally blamed the soldiers for the troubles and demanded satisfaction, as well as all their food rations. Two-thirds of the troop had been lost, including their commanders. The surviving fourteen soldiers had little left other than a few weapons and nine horses they had managed to keep out of starving hands. With no one to command them, they were trying to go home again. Zarosen gently explained about the destruction of Mennatu. Some were so disheartened that they just wanted to stop where they were and give up. Others refused to believe the story at all. A couple of them insisted that the only way out was to repent and throw themselves upon the mercy of the ancient Gods, whom they must have offended.

Zarosen had made a vow to himself years ago. Even though he was the son of an Elder, he had absolutely no desire to follow in his mother's footsteps. Leadership and responsibility for others were definitely not for him. That was why he had enjoyed the shipping business so much. He was away from the seat of government and its influences for long periods of time. The work was satisfying, and everyone was part of a team. It was ironic that this career choice had been his mother's idea, although he had hated the notion at first.

Those happy days were part of a past life now. His home city was destroyed, and the Domain that depended so heavily on it was crumbling. Calling forth strength that he didn't know he had, Zarosen rallied the despondent Militia together and took command of the troop. Accepting his leadership, they traveled with him, Eryndi and Macai together, heading north . . . always north.

CHAPTER 16

Today – above Trebalian Falls

Frustrated and furious with herself, Orchid picked up Dementus's stick and flung it at the cliff face. Javelin-like, the iron point of the antique walking staff stuck in the soft sandstone. It waggled up and down, mocking her for her ineffectiveness.

Orchid was desperate to try anything. The plan to induce a rainstorm to wash down the korvanite had fizzled. She was stuck with the problem of having a wagonload of the ore and no way to get it into the river. She couldn't throw the ore pebbles far enough to get them down to the water, and she couldn't carry more than a couple of the stones at one time.

I might as well head back to the falls . . . maybe I can at least give my friends a decent funeral.

She stood and got ready to make the climb back down when a movement caught her eye. A moonlark fluttered down and perched upon the staff as it stuck out of the rock. The bird regarded her with its alert eyes and cocked its blue and black head at her. Orchid watched it pruning its feathers and generally acting like a bird.

"I need help, my friend," she said. "What am I to do?"

Orchid squeezed her temples with her fists, hoping to force the answer out of her head, which, she felt, must be in there somewhere.

"WHAT AM I GOING TO DO?!" she screamed toward the sky.

Do not doubt . . .

The voice came not in words, but as an echo resonating off her soul. Orchid was surprisingly not startled, as though the voice was long expected.

Lurra knows what it needs . . .

The voice came from the bird . . . not an audible message, but as though the moonlark were releasing the words that had always been deep within Orchid's heart.

Lurra knows . . .

It became so clear to Orchid now . . . she had known all along. Her doubts released. There was clarity now, confidence. She could *hear* the bird, and more importantly, it could hear her. Her abilities were now unfettered, and she knew what to do.

"Let's get to work, my friends."

The moonlark was in full agreement. It jumped off its perch and fluttered over to the pile of korvanite. It paused for a moment, gave Orchid a quick wink, and picked up a pebble of the ore in its beak. A moment later, it introduced its mate to Orchid as the second bird alighted and grabbed a piece of its own. Orchid kept the momentum going. She continued the call for assistance that she wasn't even aware she had initiated. The sky darkened with the arrival of large flocks of moonlarks, starlings, and sparrows. A mated pair of ospreys also descended and grabbed some of the larger chunks.

Orchid's confidence grew even more as large cherry beetles, swarms of dragon wasps, and mouse flies descended from the air and lifted back off with whatever they could carry. Within two minutes, the entire pile of korvanite was picked up. The armada of flying creatures, a million strong, each with its own cargo of ore, patiently awaited Orchid's command.

And Orchid heard them all! The first-time feeling was exhilarating, but there was no time to revel in it. She didn't point with her hand, but with her thoughts . . . and her allies complied. The legion of birds and bugs flew as one down toward the river. Each tiny soldier released its load into the flowing water, just above the section of levees containing the Magic collectors.

A bunch of years ago - The Northlands

Gunnar and Hulde Brimstone each held one hand of their struggling daughter, and it took all they had to do it.

"Serena, behave!" hissed her mother as they dragged her along toward the outdoor auditorium of Grannugh. Most of the time, it was the gathering place of warriors attending strategy councils. Today it was set aside for the primary school's annual battle play. They were put on every spring to teach the children fundamental life skills by acting them out on a stage. Parents from the five villages of Luftar Valley were attending. Two of Serena's cousins were cast in the show, but she wasn't interested in seeing it.

"This is stupid! I don't want to go to this!!" she screamed.

Gunnar quietly bent down to her level as they struggled along.

"Neither do I, little one," he whispered, "but warriors must keep their dignity even for the battles they lose."

Serena believed everything her dad said, much to the envy of her mother. So, she squared her nine-year-old chin and suffered through the play that the Brimstones arrived very late for. Her little twin cousins, Eggbert and Oggden, came on stage just as they found their seats. There was a brief glimpse of Miss Herkimer pushing them on from backstage. A painfully long pause finally ended as Oggden remembered his line.

"Egad, Rag. I believe us to be lost."

"Indeed, Tag. How will we find our home?"

Another pause, after which Miss Herkimer's whispered voice came from backstage and saved them.

It is getting dark . . .

"Oh yeah, um, it is getting dark. Let us go into that cave for shelter."

ROAR!!

A huge, hulking creature, wearing a hideous carved wooden mask and covered in furs, lumbered out of the painted muslin cave entrance and thumped toward the two Northlands heroes. The monster was portrayed by Aethelfardt the Maimed, a former warrior who had lost a leg in battle. His disability reward was a permanent position as the school janitor.

"AAHH!" Eggbert emoted. "It is the monster of the snows, Tor the Ogre!"

"Quickly," said Oggden, acting his little butt off, "distract the beast whilst I bring it down!"

Rag waved his arms and yelled while Tag hid behind a piece of scenery. The monster headed for Rag, beating its chest and roaring horribly, its wooden leg clonking hollowly on the planked stage floor. Meanwhile, Tag picked up a convenient tree branch lying nearby and thrust it in front of the menacing creature. Tor the Ogre tripped on the branch, falling on its face. Rag and Tag drew their wooden swords and heroically dispatched the beast while it was down. In an unplanned move, the string holding on the monster's face broke, unveiling the equally horrible face of Aethelfardt to the delight of the audience.

Eggbert and Oggden delivered the last lines and the moral of the play.

"Well done, warrior. Together we have slain the beast."

"Teamwork has saved the day!"

Today – the cave

"GET OUTA THERE!!"

Serena's shout was too late. There was nowhere for them to go, and she was still glued to the floor, unable to move.

The water spirit launched its attack at Tresado and Foxx as they stood trapped with their backs against the cave wall. It came in the form of a massive pressure wave designed to crush their mortal bodies into jelly. The liquid *body* of the spirit pressed forward, powered by the enhanced Magic of the water in the pit. Tresado threw up his hands in a defensive manner, trying desperately to counter it. His Magic, drawn as usual from the air around him, was also enhanced by the nearby presence of the water, but not nearly to the degree that the spirit could make use of it.

Tresado held his own at first, the veins in his neck sticking out with the exertion. He braced his back against the cave wall and pushed outward Magically. But it was like trying to hold a door shut that was being pushed from the other side by a whole squad of boingball players.

Foxx could do nothing but flatten himself as close to the cliff as he could. He held Serena's scimitar straight out, hoping that might help, but water doesn't care about being stabbed. The pressure wave pushed in farther and farther until both Foxx and Tresado could feel the crushing force starting with the tips of their noses. It slowly closed in until both of them were fully pinned with the water wall pressing in on their chest cavities. They could not cry out as the air was forced from their lungs, and not another breath could be drawn. Tendrils of liquid water flowed up their faces, forcing its way into their noses and mouths. Foxx blacked out first.

Leader was calmly standing by, patiently watching the spectacle. He turned to Serena, who was helpless to do anything but the same.

"Worry not," he said. "When the spirit disposes of your friends, we shall return to the business at hand."

At that moment, the pressure pinning Foxx and Tresado relaxed, and they sunk to their knees, gasping for breath. The floating mass of water simply dropped downward and splashed onto the floor. Gravity took hold, and it began to naturally drain back into the pit in the floor.

"Who's worried?" said Serena with an evil grin. Now that her restraints seemed to be gone, she hopped forward and launched herself at Leader, feet first. She caught him square in the chest and catapulted him backward to roll ass over appetite across the draining rock floor. She gave a satisfying grunt and ran over to her two friends. They were both coughing and hacking water out of their lungs and sinuses.

"You alive?" asked Serena, worriedly slapping them on their backs.

Foxx came out of whatever delirium he was in, blindly swinging Serena's sword.

"Let her go!!" he yelled, leaping to his feet. He saw Leader across the cave floor and started for him with still wobbly legs. Serena grabbed for his wrists and wrenched her precious sword from his grasp.

"Gimme that, before you cut your own head off . . ."

"WATCH OUT!" wheezed Tresado.

Leader, who did not seem to be injured despite the vicious kick he had received, was advancing on Serena with knife raised.

Serena's natural instincts kicked in, and she easily parried his (admittedly) competent swing. The knife blade locked with the folded steel of her scimitar. A quick reverse swing on her part sent his knife flying across the cave to clatter into the pit of water.

"I must have that diamond." Leader's dull eyes locked with her angry blue ones. "I implore you once again to reconsider. The spirit has no destructive ambitions as you would attach to it. I simply wish to experience emotions, the same as any mortal man."

Serena regarded Leader's plea for a full three beats.

"You are not a man."

Serena's chilling war cry echoed through the damp cave as she spun with her sword, turning a full circle. The scimitar whistled through the air faster than one could see, its razor edge connecting with Leader just above the waist, slicing through his body like overcooked pasta.

There was no sign of surprise or pain in Leader's face. There never had been. He stood wobbly for a moment. His legs slowly fell backward while the upper part of his body leaned forward and fell to the ground. What used to be Leader now lay in two neatly cloven pieces with its downturned face resting between its two upturned feet.

Serena had delivered a good number of killing blows to various barbarian enemies over the years. They all involved massive amounts of spilled blood and intestinal messes. She was used to that and expecting it, but the body of Leader did not leak anything. She took a long look at the sliced edge of his torso. There did not appear to be anything like internal organs, bones, or even blood. The insides of Leader weren't even red. He was made up of a kind of grayish-tan, firm gelatinous material. Slightly unnerved, Serena poked at the jelly with the tip of her sword. Leader's head immediately turned as far as it could and looked up at her.

"I ask you again, will you allow me to remove the diamond from you, Serena?"

A moment later, Leader's head was just as cleanly severed from the torso and kicked into the pit, where it couldn't annoy anyone again.

Serena gathered up the lapels of her jerkin and retied the severed lacings as best she could. She took a moment to look at Tresado and Foxx, who were recovering rapidly from their near-death experience. She walked casually up to them.

"You guys all right now?" she asked with a slight smile.

"Yeah, I think so."

"Me too."

"Good," she said.

Serena lashed out with a crisp punch to Tresado's nose.

"*That's* for staring at my boobs!"

Then she delivered a swift kick to Foxx's shin.

"And *that's* for putting a nick in my sword!"

Then, grabbing them by the backs of their necks, Serena delivered unto each a long, lingering kiss on the lips.

"And *that's* for saving my ass."

"*Whoa . . .*" exclaimed Orchid, who had just come up from the tunnel, "*Serena!* Good to see you . . . it's good to see all of you."

She took a long look at the bifurcated, headless body of Leader. "Well, not exactly according to plan, but I think things turned out all right. Hey, didja know there's a log cabin back there? *And there's ALE in it!*"

* * *

Locomotion, manipulation, weather control, even information gathering . . . indeed, any alteration or transference of existing matter or energy can be accomplished using the processing and manipulative properties of Magic. Energy may be drawn and utilized actively or passively. In an active mode, Magical energy can be transformed into solid matter of a corresponding ratio. Studies indicate such use creates a microscopic power drain from the belt, which is as it should be. But true creation from nothing, or 'conjuring' as it is known here, of matter or energy would violate a basic law of the universe. Such creations are merely temporary. They still retain a connection to the Magic field, which sustains their cohesion. It is almost as if they remain attached by an elastic band, ready to snap back at any time. These conjurings may last for eons, and to the transitory minds of mortal beings, they may seem permanent, but universal law will always win in the end.

—Rastaban – Preliminary report to Mama

Today – the cave

It was hugs all around until Orchid broke the mood.

"We need to get out of here. That Korvanite will all be washed away before long and water boy might come back to life."

"Did it just get darker in here?" asked Foxx, looking around.

He was right. The shifting glow from the pit was quickly dimming. At the same time, Leader's floating lantern on the ceiling came crashing down, causing Group Six to jump as one. The cave was plunged into darkness until Tresado lit a Magic flare of his own.

Serena quickly ran over to the pit and peered down into it. The peculiar metal cage was still there, but the luminescent, shape-shifting object inside it was barely visible. The once powerful Creation Matrix rotated slowly, weakly flickering. The absence of the Magically-enhanced water apparently robbed the thing of the energy it needed to function.

"Get over here, quick!" Serena urged the others.

They obeyed and saw for the first time the artifact that had indirectly caused so much heartache over the last millennium.

"Can you destroy that?"

"What is it?" asked Orchid.

"Never mind, just blast it. Hurry!" Serena said urgently.

Tresado didn't need to hear it again. He gathered a full load of kinetic and heat Magic and sent the glowing projectile whistling into the pit. The gold and copper alloy cage disintegrated in a high-explosive ball of fire. Bits of shrapnel, none of them bigger than a fingernail clipping, shot out in all directions. Group Six ducked, but Orchid yelped when a flying sliver took a tiny notch out of her left earlobe.

"Good," said Serena with a satisfied sigh, "*now* let's get out of here."

The four of them ran for the tunnel and headed for the waterfall. The Northlands cabin came into sight.

"Wait for just a beat, will you?" pleaded Orchid. She hurried onto the porch and into the building.

"What are you doing?" Foxx demanded. "*Let's go, for Nyha's sake!*"

A moment later, Orchid ran back out with a cask of ale under each arm.

"Okay, okay, I'm coming!"

Group Six fled out of the cave and splashed their way through the waterfall. Orchid nearly drowned while trying to cross the pool laden with two full kegs. Once on dry land, they made a beeline directly away from the river, hoping to get out of range of the soon-to-be rejuvenated water entity. They stopped running after about a hundred reaches and turned to face the falls.

"That's going to be one pissed-off spirit when it gets its Magic back," said Foxx.

"We ought to be safe enough at this distance," answered Tresado.

"What do we do now, make faces at it?" asked Serena.

"Now, *we celebrate!*" said Orchid jubilantly. She set her kegs down and cracked open the cork on one of them. Balancing the small barrel on one elbow, she tipped it up to her lips.

"*To Group Six!*"

But before she could drink her toast, a most curious thing happened. The cask she was holding just . . . *vanished.*

"Hey!" she cried piteously. "What the . . ."

She was interrupted by a vibration in the ground and a low rumbling coming from downriver. Beyond the broken walls of the arena, the ruins of the ancient city of Mennatu were . . . *disappearing!* Not crumbling but blowing away in the light breeze. It was as though the mighty stone buildings were castles of sand being washed away by an invisible surf. The once perfectly formed dovetail blocks dissolved into a fine mist that swirled in the air currents and faded from sight. The Talus River washed over the former metropolis of Mennatu, leaving the looming ruins of the great Collector and the memory of man as the only indications that the city had ever been there.

PART II:
THE MAGICIAN

CHAPTER 17

Today

Troya 20-21876 – This Midweek Honor Day is dedicated to the other members of Group Six, whom I've only known for less than a month. Tresado's Magic offends me, Foxx is an arrogant jerk, and Serena's crudity just plain pisses me off. I have never had three better friends in my life.

It was a pretty fantastic story that Serena told us about the old city. It seems that everything this Matrix ever created – the ruins, the cabin, Leader – is gone. Once it was destroyed, those things could not continue to exist. Unfortunately, that also included the gold coins that Leader paid us with. Tresado thinks it all 'returned to Magic.' Works for me. I think Magic is due for some repayment after all that Absolute conjuring.

After everything disappeared yesterday, I snuck back to the falls to check on the water spirit. It's still there, in the pool beneath the falls. But since the Magic collectors on top of the cliff also disappeared, its power is much diminished. The arena/collector is still there, but I don't think the spirit can travel that far anymore. I feel sorry for it, in a way. All it wanted was to know love. The irony is, since it didn't possess emotions, it felt no remorse about the mutilation of all those Eryndi and what it was about to do to Serena. Suppose it had gotten the diamond and somehow acquired emotions. I wonder if it could have handled the remorse after the fact.

Where do we go from here? None of us are familiar with this area, aside from the direction we've come. But we can't go back downriver to Ostica. We spent a lot of that gold there, and other places, and we have to assume it has vanished as well. I doubt our faces would be very welcome. We don't have a boat to go back, anyway. Enchanter was wrecked beyond repair in the rescue. We know the Imperium is far to the south and the Northlands are far to the north. What is east of us, beyond the mountains, nobody knows. Wherever we go, we'll have to walk.

—Orchid's journal

Today – the upper Talus River

"What's for dinner?" Tresado asked as he floated back down to the ground.

For the last two weeks, this had been his usual routine. At the end of a hard day of scrambling along narrow ledges and wading in fast-flowing water, Tresado would levitate himself up to altitude to look for any signs of civilization. Apparently, this mountainous section of the upper Talus River was just too inhospitable for anyone to want to bother living in.

"You'll love it," answered Foxx. "Vole stew with *koofa nuts.*"

"I didn't love it the last six nights in a row. What makes it different tonight?"

"Orchid found a salt deposit."

"Yum."

"If you could be a little less your usual puss-self," said Serena, "there are two more rats that need to be skinned."

"Did you see anything up there?" asked Orchid, who was tending the fire.

"Just more mountains as far as I could see," Tresado replied, picking up a vole. He wrinkled his nose at the dead creature. They were disgusting little beasts, but they and the bitter koofa nuts were the only protein source found in these parts. The life-filled lowland rain forest had been left far behind when they decided to explore farther east. The sacks of dried beans that had been found in Dementus's backpack had long been picked through. Most of them were moldy after having been buried for years.

"The river just keeps winding through these canyons. We follow it for ten leagues and only make one league of progress," said Foxx. "Isn't there any way we can get to the top of the cliffs and stay out of the water?"

"There's no plateau. Nothing we could get any kind of footing on," answered Tresado.

"And no sign of the palace?"

"OW!" yelped Tresado as he poked himself with a sharp vole bone. "I told you, THERE'S NOTHING! There's no palace, no boiling lake, no Magic boats . . . none of the nonsense that loony wrote about! If you ask me, he made the whole thing up! That stupid diary is worthless! Here's your skinned vole for the stewpot," he snapped, tossing the carcass to Foxx. "Don't forget the truffle garnish!"

Foxx responded with an obscene gesture and added the pittance of meat to the iron pot. So far, that seemed to be the most useful item left behind by Dementus the Mad Treskan. The old Eryndi's lengthy diary described a journey of over a century, but ninety-nine percent of it was gibberish. The fellow had traveled far and wide, but his records of what he had seen made little sense. Much of it was in the form of bad song lyrics or one-sided conversations with no one. Only the earliest entries even had dates on them.

His description of a fabulous land at the headwaters of the river was the main factor in Group Six's choice of direction. Perpetual parties with hot and cold running companionship were just too much to pass up.

The weary travelers struggled on for another two days, following the rapids that carved their way through the tortuous mountain canyons. Food was scarce, and the rocks were hard on their shoes. Orchid was the least discouraged of the lot.

"You'll see, any time now, we're going to find this place that Dementus talked about. He said it's at the source of the Talus River. If we follow it far enough, we can't help but run into it."

Tresado muttered something under his breath, but no one else could make it out. The river got narrower and shallower, and the canyon walls got shorter. Sensang was dipping low on the horizon, and another night was on its way. A large, conical mountain loomed ahead of them at the head of the river valley.

Group Six made their way around a final bend, the water now no bigger than a stream. The Talus River, a league wide in some places, was now nought but a small creek, sputtering out of the ground on the barren slopes of an extinct volcano. There was no fabulous castle, no luxurious environment, and nowhere to go.

* * *

In the Palace of the Talus,
You Will Find Your Thrills:
Free Smokes, Free Drinks,
and All the Carnal Frills.
Just Fill Your Hand
With the Right and Proper Card:
But Do It in a Way
that Don't Piss Off the Guard.

—Travelogue of Dementus, the Mad Treskan

Today – the western slope of Mount Boronay

Whistle, whistle, whistle . . . .

Cleon the Highwayman's signal was a reasonable imitation of a mountain scrub snipe, not sufficient to impress another snipe, but good enough to signal his confederates that a group of potential victims was headed their way. When they had gathered around, he issued orders in a hoarse whisper. The meat in between what few teeth he had left had been rotting for a couple of weeks now, and the fetid breath oiled out of his mouth in an almost visible cloud as he delegated.

"We got us some perps, boys, comin' from over there," said Cleon, pointing to the northwest. "Doork and Brooty, c'mon with me. The rest of you guys get behind them rocks and trees, *and stay hid until I signal!* Brooty, you hear me? You have another sneezin' fit, and I'm gonna cut your snotted head off." Brooty wiped his drippy nose with a sleeve made of jackal hide and nodded shamefully.

The ten robbers deployed themselves as ordered and waited. The snipe whistle was heard again as Cleon pointed. A group of four people was struggling along the mountainside, coming cross country out of the wilderness. The robbers were lucky to have spotted them. Their gang had been shadowing the road below, waiting for victims. It was only because Cleon had gone off to take a crap that he spotted the people coming up behind them.

"Two men, two women," whispered Cleon.

"What are they doin' out there in the sticks? Who do you s'pose they are, Chief?" rasped Doork.

"Travelin' light. Their clothes ain't bad, but they don't look like players nor traders. Ain't carryin' nothin'."

Doork shielded his eyes and squinted. "The blonde chick is packin'. Othern'at I don't see no weapons."

"We'll wait till they get to them big rocks there," he said, pointing with a filthy finger. "They'll hafta crawl around 'em one at a time an'at's when we'll jump 'em."

The band of highwaymen ratcheted back their crossbows and loaded up bolts with wicked-looking barbed heads . . . and waited.

Today – the western slope of Mount Boronay

There were trees now, trees with trunks that were twisted and knotted, reflecting just what a painful process it must have been to force one's way out of the barren lava slopes of the mountain. But they were at least trees. That made Orchid start to feel a little better. She leaned on her staff heavily, using it to keep her balance on the broken, sloped surface. Foxx used Dementus's walking stick to the same effect. Tresado, as usual, used Magic to stabilize his roundish Eryndi body and keep himself from rolling down the slope like a pine cone. Serena lightly jumped from rock to rock like a young grilk, seemingly at home in the mountainous terrain. The going was getting a bit easier, but they still needed to watch their footing. Orchid was in front choosing the path when she suddenly stopped and took a look around.

"Something wrong?" asked Foxx.

"Nature girl thinks we're being watched," said Serena. "So do I."

Confirming that observation, a gruff voice rumbled from behind a rock.

"Stand and deliver!"

Cleon the Highwayman stepped out into plain sight, brandishing a nasty-looking crossbow. A handful of similarly armed scumbags also partially showed themselves.

"Just stay frosty and nobody'll get hurt. Let's start off by emptyin' yer hands and yer pockets."

Tresado cracked his knuckles as he and Orchid grinned at each other.

Both varieties of Magical energy began to gather into what would surely end badly for these pathetic clowns. But before either Tresado or Orchid could unleash their spells, a blonde whirlwind somersaulted over their heads, taking a position in front of them.

"You two can sit this one out," said Serena with an odd look. "I'll handle this." A piercing Northlands war cry echoed through the rocky canyons around them. She whirled her scimitar in a reverse-grip, one-handed blur of motion, advancing on Cleon in a dance of death.

"Take her out!" he cried, raising his own crossbow. Before he could even complete the thought, let alone the action, his mouth dropped open and his eyes glazed over. Cleon's crossbow arm went limp, and the weapon discharged at his feet, burying the bolt in the dry soil. The other brigands were having the same problem. The idea of causing any harm or not treating Serena like the goddess she was had fled from their hearts like a bird freed from a cage.

Serena growled menacingly and advanced further. Cleon and his bunch dropped to their knees in adoring submissiveness. Her face fell, followed by her sword. Slowly, she turned her back to the robbers and shuffled back to her companions.

"That's what I was afraid of," she muttered quietly to herself.

"Do whatever you need to," she said to Tresado, pointing a thumb over her shoulder. Serena moped her way to a large boulder and sat dejectedly. She balanced her scimitar point down in the dirt and slowly spun the weapon by the hilt. On the third revolution, she released her loose grip and allowed her sword to clatter to the ground. She didn't even watch what her friends were doing as they dealt with the robbers. There was no need. She knew there was nothing to see.

* * *

The warrior knows it is brave to conquer one's enemies, but only if your enemies are something the Gods have made you fear . . .

— Hrolvad the Berserker – Year 178
- Old Macai calendar

Today – the southern slope of Mount Boronay

The road was absolutely marvelous. The sharp lava rock had been carved to a smooth, rut-free surface as it switch-backed up the mountain toward the pinnacle of the giant volcano. Cultivated fruit trees and berry bushes had been planted along the way, as well as sections of grass evidently intended to cater to horses and cattle. There were also spring-fed artificial watering holes every so often. Obviously, the comfort of the traveler was paramount. Orchid was quite enchanted.

"Now this is more like it," she said, slurping on a juicy piece of fruit. "Someone has gone to a lot of trouble here. There's good, wholesome Worldly Magic at work."

"What makes you say that?" asked Tresado.

"I've never seen *turtle limes* grow out of lava rock before."

"Maybe Cleon wasn't as crazy as he sounded," offered Foxx.

When questioned, the chief brigand had spoken of an *arcade*—a place none of the robbers had ever tried to go. Apparently, there was some kind of fancy-schmancy inn on top of Mount Boronay with a lot of rich people who frequently traveled the road that led there. The highwaymen had placed themselves above a remote section of that road to lie in ambush when Group Six stumbled upon them.

Tresado acted the part of a menacing intimidator while Foxx played that of the concerned interrogator who pleaded that it was in the robbers' best interest to answer their questions. Otherwise, he wasn't sure how long he could hold off his evil Eryndi friend, who wanted to turn them all into some kind of gastropod or replace various appendages with vegetables. The old *Good Magician-Bad Magician* bit worked like a charm, and the villains answered all questions. They were disarmed and released after a stern talking-to. When last seen, the band of highwaymen was heading back down the road to lead lives of virtue from here on in.

Group Six spent the rest of that day walking up the winding road. It was a big mountain, and the road was long, but the going was easy if you didn't mind steady inclines for leagues. Tresado was in the lead, shading his eyes against the setting sun. It looked like there were still a few leagues to go before reaching the summit. One of those watering ponds was just ahead, surrounded by a well-manicured expanse of luscious fruit trees and succulent grass.

"What do you say we camp for the night up here?" he suggested to the others.

"Works for me," answered Foxx. "I'm anxious to see just what's really up there, but whatever it is will keep until after a good night's sleep."

"Me too," said Orchid, "my geese are honking."

Serena didn't answer. She merely nodded and picked out a spot under a tree. She sat and leaned her back against the bole, idly pulling out blades of grass and staring at something a thousand leagues away.

Tresado and the others gathered at the edge of the pond and quenched their thirsts.

"What a great place!" sighed Orchid. She laid back with a leaf cone of sweet water in one hand and a hunk of melon in the other. Her oaken staff contentedly glowed in pastel colors and purred softly.

"It could do with some nightlife," said Foxx, gratefully pulling off his shoes, "but I've slept in worse places."

"I know, I've seen a few of them," snickered Tresado.

"Do tell," prodded Orchid.

Tresado started to open his mouth when he was interrupted by Foxx.

"Ah, ah, ah . . . remember the vow."

"That doesn't apply here," Tresado smirked.

"Vow?" asked Orchid, intrigued.

"That what happens in the past stays in the past," said Foxx, throwing an apple core at Tresado.

Tresado Magically caught the missile in midair and spun it to the rhythm of his whirling finger.

"That vow only refers to tawdry affairs and sleazy business deals," he said, launching the spinning fruit back at Foxx. "Heroic rescues and deeds of derring-do are in the public domain."

"Ooh, an adventure story," chirped Orchid, "I'm all ears!"

"Well, it was that time in Tracus when I saved Foxx from the pirate press gang."

"Saved *me?"* said Foxx, in mock aghast. "I saved *you!"*

"No, no, don't you remember? They drugged our wine in that pub and then carried us out to their ship." Tresado turned to Orchid. "I, of course, being Eryndi, was immune to the Mickey Finn. I *pretended* to be unconscious so I could find out their plan."

"And let me tell you, Tresado is one fine actor," said Foxx seriously. "When I woke up in the hold of the ship, he was *pretending* to mutter in his sleep, something about putting his sister's underwear on the cat. Had me completely convinced, so I'm sure he fooled the pirates, too."

"But *if you remember,* I Magically unlocked all the prisoners' shackles starting with yours." And to Orchid, he said, "Of course, as soon as I did, Foxx made a beeline for the exit, leaving me to rescue everybody by myself."

"And if *you* remember, I immediately ended up in the clutches of the pirate captain herself," countered Foxx. "My diversions allowed Tresado and the others the chance to escape."

"You were in her clutches, all right," Tresado said. "When I found him in the captain's cabin, she had her clutches wrapped all around him. I think she was shivering his timbers."

"That is a tissue of lies. While I was battling the captain, Tresado charged into the cabin and fell over a bucket. By the time he came to, I had overpowered the pirate, tied her up, and we escaped."

"You know something?" said Tresado to Orchid. "He is right, after all. This could definitely be classified as a tawdry affair, and I shouldn't have talked about it."

The laughter continued on into the night except for Serena, who withdrew from the others, going to sleep early.

Today – the road to Boiling Lake

"Are we there yet?"

The whiny little rich kid received the same old answer for the same old question.

"Not yet."

"I wanna get there! *I wanna see the dragon!*"

"Dexter, it won't be long now," said the boy's long-suffering dad. "We can see the top of the mountain now, and we'll be there before Midday. Just sit back in the wagon and play with your game box."

The caravan of six coaches and their mounted escorts continued up the well-kept road. The whole outfit reeked of money. The matched teams of draft horses were even outfitted with decorative barding and woven silk rope tack. The coaches were heavily protected, both with armored plating and armored guards who kept a watchful eye from atop the vehicles. There had been a moment of apprehension the day before, when they met a ragged group of vagabonds coming down the road. Everything about them said *highwaymen,* except that they were unarmed and humbly stepped off the road to allow the caravan to pass. Now at nearly the end of the trip, the guards signaled a warning again.

"We're coming up on some peds," hollered Crodack on the lead wagon. "Stay sharp."

Today – the road to Boiling Lake

"Stay sharp," said Serena. "Some wagons are coming up behind us."

Group Six kept moving but stuck to the side of the road. This outfit approaching looked well-off and well-armed, but no weapons were raised in anger, just kept ready.

"Greetings, travelers," hailed Foxx, who gave them a friendly wave.

"Hail to you, stranger," answered a voice from the lead coach. A man in a flaming red robe emerged from an armored hatch and sat next to the driver. The guards on top kept a wary eye on things.

"I hope you have not come far on foot," the red-robed man said. "Have you lost your mounts?"

"We have indeed come far," said Foxx, cordially. "As for our transportation, that is a long story."

"Have you been to the Palace before?"

"Nay, 'tis our first time," replied Foxx. Even though he had never heard the man's speech pattern before, his *Knowing Spell* allowed him to respond in kind.

"You would honor my son and me by sharing our coach. 'Tis a pity we did not come across you earlier. But even though we are nearly at the top, allow us to save you what few steps remain. Feel free to . . ."

"Climb up onto the back," interrupted the guard, pointing to the rear of the wagon.

"Of course, many thanks," said Foxx. He couldn't blame the guy.

Group Six gratefully hopped up onto the cargo rack. The driver click-clicked, and the horses resumed their job. Orchid could tell they were a little resentful at the weight increase. The other coaches in the caravan followed behind. The guards on top of those kept a watchful eye on the hitchhikers ahead of them.

Suddenly a little boy's fat face emerged from the rear window and stared at the riders.

"I'm Dexter. Who the hell are you?"

"Nice to meet you, Dexter," replied Foxx. "This is Serena, that's Orchid, this guy is Tresado, and my name is Foxx . . . that's with two exes."

"That's stupid," said the spoiled brat, disappearing back into his hole.

"I hate kids," whispered Orchid to Tresado.

The object of her hate popped back out again. "We're going to see the dragon!"

"Oh, there's a dragon up there?" asked Foxx.

"You're stupid!" announced Dexter, slamming the window shut and disappearing back into the coach.

Another half-hour brought the caravan to a wide split in the crater rim. Carved, ornate pillars decorated each side of the opening. The road proceeded on through, and Group Six got their first look at Boiling Lake. The extinct volcano's immense cone was over four leagues across and held a gorgeous body of water. Fruit trees of all kinds lined the shores, some in full blossom, some bearing ripe fruit. It was early spring and late summer at the same time here. The scents of cherry and apple blossoms filled the air, which was cool and refreshing. It was a genuine pleasure to take big, deep breaths.

However, the most amazing sight was the magnificent towering structure located on a small island in the center of the lake. It could only be described as a palace, but not of a type familiar to Group Six. There were no ramparts, or drawbridge, or even stone blocks. The entire structure looked to be made of sparkling glass. Tall, thin spires of deep blue thrust up from the island. There was not a breath of wind, and the glassy water reflected the beautiful palace's image, deepening the blue of the lake.

The road continued down to some buildings and piers at the water's edge and branched off to circle the shore. The wagons rolled on down the road to the piers, and the driver called a halt.

"We're here!" he hollered. The doors opened on all six coaches, and a large contingent of fops and floozies exited. There were ostrich feathers and gold chains everywhere, silk sashes and floppy hats all around.

A voice from seemingly nowhere filled the heads of all present.

Welcome, guests, to the Crystal Palace!

* * *

Considering there are only two species of intelligent bipeds in this world, the diversity is astounding. All have their strengths and weaknesses. The Gallanites of Rakor Veldt frequently grow to a height of one point two reaches. They are swift runners and can draw powerful longbows. There are dangerous, mutated Eryndi pygmies that inhabit the northern rain forest and a civilization of technologically advanced Macai living on an antipodal island that has been isolated for centuries. There is even a race of enormous people residing in the Spektros mountain range as hairy as any ape. These lands are not yet conquered, but as it is the Imperium's destiny to rule the world, my Legionnaires must adapt to many fighting styles and all climates.

—Imperator Merak – *Commentaries: Book 9, Chapter 1, paragraph 3*

CHAPTER 18

Today – the Crystal Palace

"Where did that voice come from?" asked Serena. There was no one else in sight except for the garishly dressed players and their servants.

"Welcome to the Crystal Palace!" the booming baritone voice had thundered. *"All warriors are welcome to drink their fill of the finest ale, to sate one's hunger with shanks of mutton and pork. There are games of skill and tests of bravery! Pleasures of the flesh and challenges for the daring! Enter, warrior, and be welcome!"*

But that was just what Serena heard. Little did she or the others realize at the time, but each visitor received a personalized message. Foxx was treated to a sultry, feminine promise of endless gaming tables and saucy serving wenches. Orchid's welcoming voice was that of a soft-spoken, sensitive man who offered romantic moonlight strolls and unlimited glasses of fine wines and liqueurs. Tresado's was all about Magic and the wonders and skills of Magicians from all across the land. There were secrets to be shared, the voice said, Magical items to view and trade. He salivated at the very thought. Even little Dexter had a child-appropriate message of fun.

After the initial welcoming speech, the individualized voices offered free stabling for the horses and storage for the wagons, where they would receive cleaning and servicing.

"C'mon, Dad!" screamed little Dexter. "Greasy the Clown said the dragon does a funny dance! I WANNA SEE IT!!!"

"Hang on just a minute, son," said Dad. "We need to see about the coaches first."

The drivers led the horses and wagons to a large, circular pad laid out on the ground and left them there. A moment later, they disappeared in a spectacular Magical light show.

Startled, Serena put her hand on her sword hilt but didn't draw it.

"What happened to them?"

"Teleportation!" said Tresado. "The horses were transported away somewhere, hopefully someplace good. *Very impressive!* I'd love to learn that one!"

"Visitors are invited to board the shuttleboats at this time for transport to the Crystal Palace," the voice said. *"Complimentary refreshments are provided."*

Two open-decked boats adorned with colorful banners and dingleballs emerged from a shelter and silently pulled up to the pier. Each one had a crew of be-feathered hosts and hostesses wearing name tags with matching blue fish emblems. The one named Hunky Beefcake took Orchid by the waist and graciously escorted her on board. She didn't resist. The rest of Group Six and the party of players were similarly treated and offered trays of hors d'oeuvres and drinks. The passengers helped themselves to canapés, liquor, or sugar sweeties, depending on one's preference or age.

The boats pulled smoothly away from the pier and started across the lake toward the Crystal Palace. Startled at first, Group Six noticed there was no one at the helm. There *was* no helm! No rudder, no wheel, no sails, nothing! The boats cruised along at a leisurely pace, seemingly powered and guided by themselves.

"Permanent kinetic infusion," said Tresado, "that's not easy to do. I wanted to try the same thing with *Enchanter*, but it was beyond me. That's why I went with the fuel coins instead. This place just keeps getting more and more impressive."

As they got out onto the lake, they noticed that the water was *bubbling*. It was not hot, but rather some kind of gas was seeping up from the depths. There was no smell, but the atmosphere was intoxicating. Whatever the bubbles were, they had a pleasant effect.

Serena didn't seem to share in the giddy excitement that everyone else was experiencing. She sat quietly against the gunwale, staring out at the water. Suddenly she tensed and pointed at something in the lake.

"What the hell is that?"

A silvery hump rose from the water and disappeared again beneath the waves, only to reappear closer to the boat. The creature showed itself to be an immense serpent or eel or something. A large flat head a half-reach across lifted out of the water. It had horizontal fins along the sides of its face and swam with an undulating motion like a leech. Bright, shiny scales glinted in the sun as though the thing were covered in silver paleen coins. A wide mouth full of needle teeth smiled up at the occupants of the boat. Nobody except for Group Six was alarmed, though. The other passengers on both boats seemed perfectly at ease. They must have been on this trip before. They dipped into a trough on the boat's rail and scooped out handfuls of pellets. They tossed them over the water and watched as the serpent caught them in midair and hungrily snapped them up. A dozen more of the creatures soon appeared and surrounded the boats, joining in the free feed. Little Dexter threw the pellets overhand as hard as he could, trying to hit the eels rather than feed them.

"I wonder if those things like kid meat," Orchid whispered.

The Crystal Palace loomed ahead. Its towering blue spires were lined with numerous balconies and countless windows, through which many people could be seen moving about. Surrounding the palace were manicured paths and decorative kiosks. People strolled about, some escorted by attractive companions wearing the blue fish insignia, evidently employees of the establishment. The boats pulled up to the pier, and the passengers were escorted ashore.

Tame wildlife wandered the grounds alongside the guests. Brilliantly plumed mirror swans, giant wotters, and purple frogs roamed about, not to mention a full-grown razor lion lying in the shade of a pear tree. Alarmed, Group Six watched Dexter squeal with delight and run right up to the beast. The darling lad proceeded to give the big cat's whiskers a hard yank, but rather than eating him in one gulp, the lion just purred loudly and nuzzled Dexter with his head, knocking the child down. Orchid smiled inwardly as the brat started bawling.

"Come on, Dexter," said his infinitely patient dad. "Let's go see the dragon."

Sounds of music and frivolity drifted out from the open main doors and the party of partyers happily swaggered in. Group Six looked at each other, nodding in agreement.

"Welcome, welcome! Come right in and enjoy yourselves!"

A beaming hostess with a thick clipboard and a nametag that read Marsia greeted each guest as they entered. She took names and asked for preferences. The info was all recorded and filed away in a slot in Marsia's clipboard. Rooms were assigned, and bags full of complimentary goodies were handed out. Dexter got balloons and a stuffed dragon toy. Adults were issued gaming and drink chits as well as lists of all the services available. After the wagon passengers were taken care of, it was Group Six's turn.

"Welcome!" said the hostess. "'Tis always pleasing to greet guests from other lands. You have traveled far?"

"From Ostica on the western ocean," answered Foxx.

"Marvelous!" beamed the hostess. "You may be the first! 'Tis not even known *what* lies beyond the western slopes of Boronay other than howling wilderness."

"We are honored, my lady," replied Foxx. "We must first inquire about what charges you would have of us. Recent events have left our purses somewhat drained."

"While money is always welcome, 'tis not the only payment accepted here at the Palace," she said, glancing at Orchid's staff. "The management values trade and the free exchange of ideas just as much as coin . . . *nearly* as much," she added slyly.

Group Six was issued their goody bags and directed inside. After weeks on the river, they felt a bit underdressed when they entered the lobby. There were lavishly attired people of all types here: Macai, Eryndi, men, women, young, old, dark, light, ridiculously tall and unbelievably short, thin, round, and some with such bizarre features and costumes that they scarcely seemed like real people. Serena took one look at the crowd, and her face darkened.

"Great. Just what I need," she murmured. She kept her head down and tried to stay behind Foxx and as out of sight as possible.

Tresado was staring open-mouthed at the place. Everywhere one looked in this room, there was Magic. It was a large, semi-circular entrance hall with portals leading to different areas. Colorful Magical lettering floated about, pointing out the gaming halls, pool area, competition arenas, eateries, adult services, and children's play areas. Magical levitation platforms allowed access to the upper levels, and mobile vendors, with their Magical floating carts, wandered about offering everything from foodstuffs to jewelry or intoxicants.

A deep but harmonious rumbling sound resonated from the ceiling, causing everyone to look up. The startling sight of an immense dragon greeted the newcomers, making them gasp in awe and fear. The creature was at least twenty reaches long from nose to tail. Its shiny metallic scales reflected the colored lights and the deep blue of the crystal walls. Perched upon sturdy joists in the ceiling, the dragon peered down at the visitors below. Enjoying the audience, it gathered itself together and dramatically spread its great wings apart, boastfully showing off its magnificence. It took a deep breath and bellowed out a mighty roar, rattling the glasses in people's hands and eliciting plenty of 'oohs' and 'ahs.'

A trio of showgirls sashayed past and headed toward the gaming rooms. Foxx eyed them closely and flashed a broad smile.

"This is my kind of place!"

Orchid and Serena were not nearly as impressed as the male half of Group Six.

"*Twigs!* I never saw such a gaudy place in my life!" exclaimed Orchid. "Although the dragon is sure interesting . . ." she paused as a pair of muscular dancers caught her eye, "as is some of the scenery. What do you think, Serena?"

"I just want a bath and a meal," she answered quietly.

"Something wrong? Oh, I think I see," said Orchid, answering her question. A group of players had passed Group Six on their way out the door and they paused to peruse the radiant blonde warrior. Her face and hair were dirty and her clothing worn and scuffed, but they were looking at her as though she were royalty. Here in this friendly place, the spirit of the diamond did not feel threatened, so it didn't emit strong defensive love waves, but it still had to eat, as it were.

"Hey, guys. Serena and I . . ." said Orchid, but Foxx and Tresado each had their minds on other things.

"HEY!" she repeated, slapping Tresado on the back of the head. "Serena and I are going to find these so-called complimentary rooms they've issued to us. We'll leave you two grassheads to fend for yourselves."

"Yeah, fine, okay," replied Tresado, who was fascinated by a display of fire juggling going on across the room. Foxx just nodded and headed in the direction of the gaming rooms.

"C'mon, let's go," said Orchid. The two women looked at the room chits included in their goody bags.

"We're on the fifth level," said Serena. "I think we get on those things."

She pointed to the levitation platforms that had just descended and deposited a group of giggling players. Orchid wrinkled her nose and looked around for another way up, but there was none.

"Don't these people believe in stairs?"

They stepped onto one of the platforms, not sure just what to do until several glowing Magical numbers swirled in the air before them. The words 'SELECT A LEVEL' also appeared. This was Absolute Magic, and Orchid was loathe to touch it. Serena reached out and snagged the number five that floated before their faces. Immediately, the platform started moving up toward the ceiling and into a shaft. Orchid tried to lean forward and look over the side as they rose. An invisible barrier prevented that, evidently protection to keep stupid people from falling off. On the way up through the ceiling, they passed fairly close to the dragon. It smiled at them.

* * *

Gentlefolk, before we address the so-called 'Macai problem,' we must ascertain whether there is indeed a problem. Yes, studies indicate a dramatic increase over the centuries in the Macai population. It seems that they are reproducing at a much greater rate than Eryndi, but is that a threat? And if so, a threat to whom, the Macai or the Eryndi?

- GENERAL ANDRESTRI KOMANALA, COMMANDER KORVAN DEFENSE FORCES, 21468, NEW CALENDAR

Today – The Crystal Palace Gaming Room

"Twenty on *Over the Top,* ten on *Davy's Way,* and . . . a hundred on *Bottom of the Lake!*"

Foxx watched with interest as the young gambler made his selections on the Magical sphere hovering above the table. An attractive attendant used a long metallic rod to mark the locations as he called them out. The areas were different sizes and shapes and apparently paid off in varying odds. They lit up with a Magical green glow as soon as she touched the spots. Different colored areas belonging to the other players at the table dotted the sphere.

"All bets up . . . spinning," announced the attendant.

She flicked an unseen control on the rod, and it emitted a colored bolt of light, which struck the glittering ball and gave it a random, wobbling spin. The players had control boxes in their hands and followed the spin of the sphere. The object of the game was to wait until a chosen area passed over one of six jewel-like stones set in the table. They emitted more colored bursts of light at random intervals. If one of them touched the appropriate spot, the game paid off. The player also had the option of activating them manually with the control box. A player had three shots per spin in addition to the random bursts, so there was some element of skill involved. The five players at the table and the observers encouraged and begged the sphere to perform just the way they wanted. Of course, that didn't help, but it made the game more fun. The sphere spun for about twenty beats before coming to a stop.

"Red, *Tiny Wiggles,* two to one . . . green, *Over the Top,* four to one."

The winners and their supporters cheered and collected their winnings. The game played on.

Foxx had never seen this game or any of the others in the room before. Even the cards were different from those he was used to, but he picked things up quickly. He wanted to make sure he understood the game before he tried it. His goody bag contained only a few gambling tokens, and the few silver coins in his pocket didn't add up to much. Foxx was a skilled gambler but also a cautious one. He wandered over to a table where six players were engaged in a card game. After observing for a few minutes, Foxx realized it wasn't all that different from Four-Card Blitzkrieg, one of his favorites. It didn't matter that these cards had six suits instead of five; the principles were the same.

One other thing Foxx was skilled at was the old double shuffle. Professor Generax had taught him a few basic sleight-of-hand tricks, and he knew what to look for. He kept his eye on one particular player whose moves seemed familiar. The woman had nimble fingers, handling her cards well. Foxx watched carefully. She was good. The game involved several rounds of draws and discards, and the player used the speed of the game combined with a series of distractions. She would engage a player across the table in some bit of conversation while at the same time manipulating her cards, retrieving discards and getting rid of new draws that didn't help her hand. Foxx had no intention of calling it to the attention of anyone. On the contrary, he felt admiration for the professional way in which she plied her trade. After all, gambling was a risk, plain and simple. To Foxx, the risk of being caught was no different than risking one's life savings on the deal of a card. The last draw was called, and the players showed their hands. The woman had the best hand, not by a landslide, but just enough to win the round . . . another professional move.

The dealer was about to pay the winner when a high-pitched whine began sounding from somewhere. The very air vibrated in response as the intensity increased. Those with sensitive hearing were holding their ears in discomfort. The sound began in the ceiling and, while there was nothing visible, the vibration seemed to travel down toward the gaming table as if it were a physical presence. Everyone in the room stopped their activities and turned their heads to follow. The cheating woman was enveloped in a blue Magical light that emanated from the crystal walls. She looked around with a shocked expression.

"What's this?" she exclaimed. *"I haven't any . . ."*

Her plea was cut off abruptly as the blue light flashed intensely for a beat and disappeared into nothingness, taking the player along with it. The cards she had held in her hand dropped onto the table. The dealer calmly gathered them up.

"Misdeal . . . all bets returned for this round."

* * *

*Dispensing justice begins with knowing the facts,
an all-important factor if it ends with an execution.*

— Hrolvad the Berserker – Year 185
- Old Macai calendar

* * *

*Justice, the noblest idea in all of civilized history,
is also the vaguest and most challenging to define.*

—Supreme Adjudicator Harrison Wagstaff
– Ultimate Court Justice, 34856 - 34879

Today – the Crystal Palace

Group Six was all cleaned up, and half of them had just sat down for dinner. Fortunately for their finances, meals, drinks, and intoxicants were all free in this place, at least while their complimentary chits held out.

"So, is this a great place, or what?" Tresado said, exhaling a cloud of blue *jamba* smoke. He set his pipe down and took another look at the menu. He was torn between the high-fat lumba casserole and the deep-fried mountain crab.

"I have to admit, I wasn't very impressed at first," said Orchid, "but the Palace does have its charms. I had a two-hour herbal bath and a rubdown that, well . . . Serena, *over here!*"

The blonde shield maiden heard and sat down with them. She was sporting a new leather jerkin with a heavy matching belt, just right for supporting a sword hanger, but she had left that in her room.

"Very nice," admired Tresado. "You clean up real good."

"Thanks," she said stoically.

"I hope you got the full treatment with your bath," sighed Orchid. "I know you appreciate strong hands, so you should ask for Herbie the Masseur. What do you think of this place?"

"It's all right, if you like blue."

"That's one of the things that's so fascinating," said Orchid. "The Palace itself seems to have been *grown* out of this blue crystal. That's strictly Worldly Magic at work. But you can't swing a dead nyhatom without running into Absolute, as well."

"And yet it all works together, somehow," answered Tresado. "Take my room. It's loaded with Magical conveniences like door locks and lights . . ."

Orchid finished his sentence for him, ". . . and a massage couch and heated hover tub. All of that stuff reeks of Absolute Magic, the same as the lift platforms. But there's a heaping helping of my kind of Magic also. Those recesses in the walls have healthy, decorative plants growing out of them with no soil, and the spigots in the washroom pull water through the pipes with Worldly efficiency—no pumps."

"The one thing I'm afraid of is getting the bill later."

"What'd you pay for the new togs?" asked Orchid of Serena.

"Fifteen paleens from that freaky-looking vendor with three eyes."

"I saw that dude," said Tresado. "I wonder what happened to him."

"Probably over-exposure to Absolute Magic," answered Orchid. "That stuff will mess you up if you're around it too much."

"Tee-hee," countered Tresado. "Anyway, Serena, your new clothes look great. I hope you didn't blow your wad on them."

"Most of it, but my old clothes were falling apart . . . I needed something."

"I wouldn't mind a change of wardrobe myself," said Tresado, "but I have exactly six paleens and change to my name."

"That shouldn't be a problem," said a beaming Foxx, who had just appeared and was also in new clothes. He dropped a pouch onto the table with a satisfying *ka-chink* sound.

"Been to the gaming rooms, it appears," said Tresado.

"Indeed, and let me tell you, Lady Luck was quite generous."

"You'd be better off cavorting with Lady Style," said Orchid, wrinkling her nose at Foxx's new duds. He was sporting a new scarlet silk suit with a matching floppy hat.

"Well, you know what they say . . . *when in Tresk . . .*"

"So, did you con all that money out of a poor widow or cut it off somebody's belt?" asked Tresado.

"I wouldn't even mention such things if I were you," said Foxx in a hushed voice. "This has got to be the most scrupulously honest place in the world, and they enforce it, too."

"That must just kill you," offered Orchid.

"It ain't easy. In fact . . ." He looked around him before continuing, "I was in a particularly close game of something they call *Knaves and Cutthroats.* I had been playing strictly by the book when this other fellow raised the bet by a substantial amount. Before I knew it, my *Knowing Spell* started to kick in, purely instinctual, of course, just to see if he was bluffing. Anyway, before it told me anything, I got a sudden headache. I can't be sure, but I think it was a warning not to use Magic when gambling. They seem to have very strict rules around here. And then there was what I saw happen to that woman . . ."

"Hi folks, how are we doing tonight?"

A waitress, appearing to be the only unattractive woman in the place, bounded up to the table. The textbook description of dumpy. Maybe it was just the comparison with all the other lithe lovelies that worked here.

"We're quite well, thank you," said Foxx, politely.

"Sorry to make you wait, hon," the woman said while chewing a large wad of gum. "It's a bit crazy around here tonight. You can call me Jakki."

In introducing herself, Jakki brought her hand up to point at her nametag, inadvertently backhanding Serena.

"OH CRAP. I'm so sorry, hon . . ." she stammered.

"I've taken worse," said Serena, rubbing her jaw.

"Now then, what can I get you folks tonight?"

Jakki plucked a bit of charcoal from behind her ear and prepared to write down their orders. It immediately flew from her stubby fingers and bulls-eyed Orchid right in the eye.

"OH CRAP. My bad. Let me just . . ."

In reaching for the dropped charcoal, Jakki accidentally knocked Tresado's still-lit pipe off the table. Of course, it managed to spill a glowing ember between his legs. The smell of burning Eryndi filled the room as Tresado leapt to his feet, slapping himself on the crotch.

"OH CRAP."

Jakki managed to take down everyone's order and scurry away into the kitchen. She also caused an occurrence that had not happened for several weeks—Serena smiled.

* * *

20 stone Areelian shellfish

15 stone ocean stickfish

15 stone Haron lobsters

65 flickens

5 yearling bergalos – butchered and packaged

15 pigs – butchered and packaged

20 sheep – butchered and packaged

1 side of lumba

85 baskets assorted vegetables

60 baskets assorted fruits

20 tubs frozen whale cream, various flavors

— Last week's food order for
the Crystal Palace

Today – the Crystal Palace

Dinner came and went. Foxx was just finishing daubing the remaining soup that Jakki had spilled off of his new vest. It left a bit of a stain on the silk material. Meanwhile, Tresado scooted back from the table to make room for his distended belly.

"That was good," he sighed.

"Really?" asked Orchid, looking at the five empty plates and bowls in front of him. "I was beginning to think you didn't like it."

"I wonder what's for dessert?" Tresado pondered.

"You've got to be kidding me," said an astounded Orchid.

"I wouldn't mind a little something," said Foxx. "What about you, Serena? I've noticed you have a bit of a sweet tooth."

"Yeah, sure."

"Well, maybe a sliver of pie or something," said Orchid as she watched a tray full of goodies pass by on its way to another table.

"When our waitress comes back, we'll ask what they have," said Foxx.

"If we live through the encounter," said Orchid wryly.

"I've met some clumsy doofuses before, but never one this dangerous," said Tresado. He was still smarting from a burn blister.

"Okay folks, ready for some after-dinner yummies?" Jakki had appeared suddenly at the table. "Tonight, we have a special decadent surprise."

Group Six leaned forward eagerly to hear about the dessert.

"It's a double-layered, cream and sugarfruit tort drizzled with makara syrup."

Four palates started to salivate.

"And served *flambéed* in front of you."

"No . . . no thanks . . . not for me . . . I'll pass . . ." came four responses.

"Oh? Well, all right. Is there anything else I can get for you folks?"

"I don't think so, my lady," said Foxx graciously. "Thank you for a marvelous meal."

"Sure thing, hon," said Jakki, popping her gum. "You've been marvelous customers. Take these, compliments of the house. Enjoy the rest of the evening."

Jakki handed four glowing tokens to Serena, then turned and left, knocking over Orchid's still half-full glass of wine in the process. Group Six watched her depart, then broke into laughter over the ridiculousness of the situation. Even Serena couldn't help snickering.

"I like her," said Foxx. "She's like everyone's goofy aunt."

Orchid tried to salvage the last remaining drops of wine in her glass. "Must have been a hardship case to get hired here. What did she give you?"

Serena looked at the metal tokens in her hand. They shone with a bluish Magical glow and gave off little sparks. Her eyes brightened as she read the engraving.

"Four admittance tokens for the freestyle fights in the competition arena tomorrow night."

CHAPTER 19

You see that, Serena? Watch the ripper whales. See how they manipulate the school of stripers. Whales surround the fish, gradually herded into a swirling ball, tighter and tighter until there is no escape and no hope, at which point all are consumed in a frenzy of blood. There is great honor in that. Oh, I recognize that look. You wonder how there can be honor in being nought but food for a more powerful, more impressive creature.

It is the destiny of the fish to be food for the whale. We must all be what Crodan has made of us, little one, even if we get eaten.

—Gunnar Brimstone – 21858, New Calendar

Today

"Ladies and Gentlemen! Tonight, the Crystal Palace is proud to present Dinday Night Fights!"

The audience erupted in whistles and raucous cheers as the sparkly-toothed announcer introduced the evening's festivities from the center of the cage. The enclosure was actually a floating octagonal platform with glowing, Magical lattice lines of force forming a short dome overhead.

"Our first competition of the evening—introducing from the Harothan Provinces, here again after a two-year absence, with a record of twelve wins, two losses, and one draw . . . The Flyin' Lionfish . . . The Mad Sea Dog—TRAKIN MENDOR!!"

The cheers (and boos) rose as the fighter bounded through the audience and entered the ring. The burly Macai danced about, flexing muscles, blowing kisses, and milking the fans for all he could get. He was decorated with a gaudy sailing ship tattoo on his chest and a big gold hoop earring in his right ear. There was only one because Trakin Mendor didn't have a left ear.

"And from Pedaska City, with an impressive thirteen-zero-zero record— BLEEZAK THE RAPTOR!!"

The second fighter approached the cage and struggled through the Magical lattice lines. The spectacular feathered bird cowl he was wearing didn't make it any easier. Once in, he strutted in a kind of flicken dance to the spectators' delight and derision.

Scantily dressed refreshment girls wandered through the crowded auditorium, passing out popped mountain peas, smoked wieners, and every form of intoxicant known. The drinks and smokes served to make folks more adventurous with the bets. Gambling marshals also worked the crowd, collecting the 1.7% surcharge due the house on all wins.

"The fighters have opted for limb pads for this competition."

The announcement elicited a few boos from some of the more bloodthirsty spectators. Serena was among them.

"Let the fight commence!"

The announcer wisely got the hell out of the way. The two fighters retreated to opposite sides of the cage and removed any extraneous clothing. Bleezak handed his flicken suit through the cage to his retainers. They both stayed on their respective sides, eyeing each other and apparently waiting for something.

"This is different," Foxx said. Group Six had good seats, only five rows from the front.

"What is?" asked Orchid.

"I've been to a lot of organized fights, from backstreet brawls to gladiatorial games in Tresk. This is the first one I've seen that didn't have a referee or some kind of official looking on to make rulings."

GONG!

The signal sounded from somewhere in the walls themselves. At the sound, Mendor and Bleezak launched themselves at each other. At the same moment, the floating platform began to spin slowly and tilt seemingly at random. Not only did the contestants have to fight each other, but also the whims of the cage. This was not brawling. Each fighter was a professional. The pads they wore on their hands and feet protected them from bare-knuckle injuries, but they weren't all *that* padded. They still had enough gripping room for the combatants to grab and hold, and they used it. The floor tilted alarmingly, sending Bleezak careening toward Mendor. The sailor leapt up and swung from the top of the cage to meet his opponent with a well-timed flurry of kicks. Bleezak had anticipated and ducked below, turning swiftly to deliver lightning punches to Mendor's kidneys. Mendor recovered and flipped back around, landing a roundhouse kick to Bleezak's chin, staggering the flicken man. The fight proceeded with each opponent landing punches and dodging attacks. There were no rounds to this fight. The objective was to wear down one's opponent, no matter how long it took, and render him unconscious for a count of twelve beats.

Orchid didn't care much for what she was seeing. While, in a pinch, she could be as ruthless as anyone, the idea of fighting for sport was a little repugnant. Tresado, Foxx, and especially Serena were quite engrossed, however.

"Serena, I can't believe you bet on a guy who wears a bird costume," gloated Tresado after watching Mendor plant a well-timed jab to Bleezak's stomach.

"Apparently, she didn't catch the biceps on Trakin Mendor," said Foxx, who had also placed a wager on the larger fighter.

"Size and strength aren't everything where I come from . . ."

Serena was interrupted by the Raptor's feint, followed by a solid heel kick under Mendor's chin. *The Mad Seadog's* eyes rolled back in his head and down he went, hitting the padded floor like a bag of dirty laundry.

"Speed and timing are more important," finished Serena with a smug smile.

A gong started ringing out from the walls. Mendor was still on the deck, groggily trying to get up to no avail. After the twelfth count, the gong sounded rapidly three times, announcing the end of the match. The announcer re-entered the cage.

"And the winner, now with a record of fourteen wins and no losses, BLEEZAK THE RAPTOR!"

Bleezak puffed out his chest and crowed as if the sun were just coming up. His fans imitated the man's signature yell and joined in. After allowing himself the triumphant moment, the flicken man knelt at his opponent's side and helped the groggy fighter to his feet. Trakin Mendor was shaking the stars out of his head and wondering which of the three Bleezaks he was seeing was the correct one. He reached for The Raptor's arm and raised it in the air. The crowd cheered both fighters enthusiastically as they hugged and congratulated each other in sportsmanlike manners.

Serena looked on and silently nodded her approval, then went to collect her winnings.

* * *

In war, the goal is to win. To do otherwise is to betray your people. In sport, the goal is meaningless. Conduct and honor define the player.

— Hrolvad the Berserker – Year 182
- Old Macai calendar

Fourteen years ago – The Northlands

Serena was beginning to lose the feeling in her toes. She had wrapped her feet in freshly killed seal skins, but that had been over six hours ago. The fur pelts were now just as frozen solid as her boots and weren't doing a damn bit of good. Still she plodded on, trying desperately to follow the berg bear's track in the snow. The wind, which had picked up considerably in the last hour, was quickly obliterating the faint spoor. That was dangerous. Berg bears were known to double back on their trackers and wait in ambush. She would have to watch for that. A hungry bear was dangerous enough for an adult Northlands warrior. A thirteen-year-old girl armed with nothing but a dagger would be but a light snack.

Fortunately, if one could use that word, the goal here was not to kill the bear but merely to steal from it. Serena was required to traverse the lower slope of Strondheim glacier, the berg bears' hunting ground. A bear must be found during the crossing, and then something must be taken from the creature's lair or body: a gnawed bone, a tuft of hair, any personal possession. Of course, one could probably find some bone or hair that didn't belong to a bear and submit it as such, but this was also a test of personal honor. Half of the challenge was to make it across the glacier's glassy slopes without plummeting to one's death in the giant chasm at the bottom.

Serena was undergoing the fourth and final of the Trials of Snow and Ice. Once this simple challenge was complete, she would graduate to the status of an apprentice shield maiden. Another two years at the side of a mentor, and then she would proudly be called a Northlands warrior. The excitement at achieving that all-important status consumed her soul and kept her warm.

But now, a chill ran up her spine which had nothing to do with the freezing wind. There was neither sound nor smell nor any tangible evidence, but Serena *knew*. Something was watching her. And the only creatures stupid enough to be out on the slippery glacier during a blizzard were berg bears and young Northlands warrior wannabes. She froze in her tracks and took a cautious look around. There was no sign of anything just yet, but she couldn't see very far in the blowing snow.

As was only fair, the berg bear now got his own subliminal impression that his quarry was aware of him. There was no more point to stalking. Might as well charge. Simple bear logic.

The white wall of snow coalesced into a white tornado of fangs and claws. Serena's first instinct was to run like hell back the way she had come, but there was no way she could outrun the beast across the glacier. She glanced down at the quarter-league of sloping ice sheet and then back up at the charging bear. The decision was made quickly. After a sprinting run down the slope, Serena landed flat on her butt and began to slide. The enormous white ball of hunger that was after her had been trying to intercept her at an angle. When his prey suddenly flew off directly down the slope, the lumbering beast was forced to change course. Such a thing was not easy for a hundred stone of bear. Those few beats of grace period probably saved Serena. She had just enough of a head start to stay out of harm's way, but it looked like there would be no thievery today.

The berg bear was still trying to keep his footing as he galloped down the ice slope after his lunch. Eventually, his legs ran out from under him on the slick ice. In an uncontrolled sliding race to the bottom of the glacier, the bear and his prey careened toward a sheer drop-off marking the finish line. Serena was in the lead and thought she would stay that way until she looked behind her. The bear, which had a faster start time, was gaining quickly. He was on his belly sliding directly at her, leading with an open mouth full of teeth.

Serena knew what her fate would be if she allowed herself to slide off the edge of the glacier. She also knew if the bear caught her, she would be just as dead. There were two things in her favor, her intelligence and the fact that she weighed about one-tenth what the bear did. As she hurtled down the slope on her back, Serena whipped out her Northlands dagger that she had been issued for the Trials. It was supposed to be her only aid for the ordeal and her best friend and all that. At least that's what the warriors told her. Now it came in handier than she could have possibly imagined. The edge of the precipice was coming up fast. It would have to be timed right. The bear was only five reaches behind her and gaining. There was a small outcropping of rock sticking through the ice near the edge of the chasm. Serena used her feet as rudders to steer her way toward it. At the last beat, she lashed out with the dagger in a sweeping overhand stroke. The sturdy steel point jammed into a fissure and, Crodan be praised, did not break. Serena's arm nearly tore out of its socket as she hung on to the hilt. Her teenaged body whipped around like a rag doll, scraping against the jagged stone.

To the bear's eye, his prey had suddenly taken a hard left turn around the rocks. He tried to duplicate the maneuver, but a hundred stone of hurtling bulk doesn't exactly turn on a gendrin. As his massive body continued down the slope, he snapped his head sideways, hoping to get at least a small bite of the fleeing monkey. He clamped his mighty jaws shut on the first solid object he encountered, but all he got for his trouble was a mouthful of rock. His grip held for a quarter-beat, at which point the immovable rock gave way to the irresistible juggernaut of inertia, sending the berg bear off the glacier's edge into the misty crevice below. The retreating roar bellowed on for several beats before terminating abruptly.

Serena tenaciously clung one-handed to the hilt of her dagger. The edge of the cliff was still uncomfortably close below her, and she had no desire to follow the bear over the side. Slowly and painfully, she pulled herself up to a point where she could get a purchase with her feet. When at last she had a reasonably safe grip, Serena flopped onto her back and ordered her breath to settle down and her heart to stop pounding a hole in her chest.

"Pahh!" she snorted to herself. This trial had been a bust. Not only had she failed the test, but she got scratched up by the rocks to boot. She had told her testers that she would be back by sunset, which was only two hours away. Now she would have to start the hunt all over again. Her only choice was to find and track another bear to steal from. That could take days.

Serena was never much one for prayer, but as Crodan Himself was said to watch and judge these trials, she felt she should at least apologize to the big guy for screwing up.

"Warrior King, I ask Your patience for my failure and, uh, hope that You'll understand, I guess. I just want You to know that I did my best, and this DOESN'T mean I'm quitting. What I mean is I WILL complete this trial. Becoming a warrior in Your service is . . . well, it's the only thing . . . um, amen, I guess."

She stood atop the rock outcropping and smacked herself in the forehead, thoroughly disgusted with herself. Not only had she bungled the trial, she'd made an ass of herself in front of a god who didn't have any patience for such things. Maybe she should be apologizing to the bear. It was only doing what came naturally and, for its efforts, was dead now. Serena bent to pull her dagger from the rock fissure when something caught her eye. It was the red of blood upon the snow-covered stone. There, lying less than a hand's-breadth from where her fingers had been clutching her dagger, was the bloodied, broken-off tooth of the giant berg bear.

One more little postscript to the afterlife, and Serena could take her trophy and head back across the glacier again.

"Crodan, Warrior King, God of all the Clans, I owe you one, buddy."

Today – The Crystal Palace

Orchid already had Foxx in tow. After a difficult search that led from the gambling table to more than one private quarters and back again, she had finally tracked him down. That was the hard part. Getting him to accompany her was relatively easy. He was too tired to put up much of a fight.

Tresado, on the other hand, was no trouble to locate. He had scarcely left the trading floor the entire week they had been in this place. All she had to do was to sniff the air, as it were, and follow the trail of Absolute Magic that hung in the air like a bergalo fart. Right now, he was deep in negotiations with a hirsute man whose black beard split at the chin and tied together behind the neck. Tresado offered to trade two of *Enchanter*'s fuel coins for a collection of rare chemicals and a Magic-infused water purifier.

"I'm sorry," Tresado said, shaking his head at the hairy, dark Macai, "but I just can't part with ten coins."

"Oh, that's all right," rumbled Honest Masaffa, "we can forget the synthesis compounds and just deal for the demijohn."

"Okay, how about *four* coins for the jug and the chemicals?" Tresado was not the cagiest of bargainers. His chubby Eryndi face usually betrayed him.

"You look like an honest fellow, just like me. That's why they call me *Honest* Masaffa. I'll tell you what I'm going to do. We shall say *eight* of your fuel coins along with the complete recipe, and the procedure for creating them. In return, you'll receive the purification demijohn *and* the rare commodities. That, sir, is a fair and honest offer. Of course, you know that there are *no* dishonest or unfair trades within the walls of the Crystal Palace."

Orchid walked up to them about halfway through that conversation, wrinkling her nose. Masaffa's inventory reeked of Absolute Magic. To her Worldly way of thinking, this was like a vegetarian touring a meat locker.

"Tresado . . ."

"Ah," oozed Masaffa, "you must introduce me to your charming associate here. May I interest you in something? I have a wide and varied selection of items and knowledge collected in every region from here to the far shores of the Amoran Sea."

"No, thank you. Tresado, I need . . ."

"That's a lovely staff you carry, My Lady. I would like to offer you . . ."

Orchid's oaken companion rumbled and sparked menacingly in response to Masaffa's attempted offer.

"Or perhaps the lady does not wish to trade for that bauble," Masaffa said as he took a step backward.

"No, the lady does not," Orchid said steadily. "Tresado, come with me."

"I'm in the middle of a deal here." Tresado smiled broadly at Masaffa. "Now then, maybe I could make it *five* coins and . . ."

"Tresado, come with me!"

There was a short squeak, but that was the only indication that the leather galluses Tresado wore beneath his robe had suddenly shrunk to half-size, hoisting the crotch of his trousers quite a bit higher than designed. Orchid stood nearby, fist clenched as she concentrated on her spell.

"Okay, we're going," said Tresado in a slightly higher voice. "Another time, Masaffa."

Orchid led the captive over to a table where Foxx flirted with the scantily clad cocktail waitress. Orchid released her hold on the leather as soon as Tresado was seated.

"All right, what's the emergency?" he grumped.

"If you two weren't busy overdosing on Magic and mischief, you'd probably know about Serena. Haven't you noticed how down she's been?"

"Sure we've noticed," said Foxx, a bit miffed.

"She's been acting this way ever since the cave," said Tresado. "We're just as concerned as you are."

Orchid was taken aback. Maybe there was hope for these two apes after all.

"Okay, so you know. *Sorry.* Any clever plans about what to do?"

"I think Serena has already come up with a clever plan of her own," replied Foxx.

Orchid and Tresado both gave Foxx a surprised look.

"She confided in you, I suppose," said Tresado sarcastically.

"She did, though not right away," said Foxx. "I was spending some time at the arena, checking up on the local fighters, talking to trainers and promoters, trying to get a little insight into the favorites."

Tresado snorted, "Translated, that means he was snooping around, using his *Knowing Spell* to fit in and find himself a sure bet."

"Isn't that cheating?" asked Orchid.

"Money isn't going to make itself, and we've got to pay for our stay somehow," said Foxx defensively. "Anyway, it's not cheating. It's just a matter of self-education."

"Or *self-delusion,*" said Orchid.

"Believe me, in this place, I'm careful that nothing I do influences any outcome. One thing I've learned is that nobody gets away with cheating here. There are penalties."

"So you've said, but what does this have to do with Serena?" asked Orchid.

"Her name is on the entry list for this Dinday's bouts. I did some checking and found out she signed herself up right after the last fights."

"That's crazy!" blurted Tresado. "She has an unfair advantage. That diamond spirit turns any attacker into a lovesick puppy."

"You would know," said Orchid, who regretted saying it as soon as the words were out of her mouth.

"Which is why I asked her about that," Foxx explained. "Yesterday, while you were spending quality time with that herbs dealer, Serena and I had lunch. She thinks she can convince the spirit that this would be nothing but a sparring match with no danger to herself. I told her she had better tell the officials about her diamond anyway, just to be on the safe side. She agreed and said she would tell them."

"Well, she *does* like to fight. It's part of who she is. Maybe this will help," mused Orchid.

"That's what Serena said too. According to her, it's a kind of a test to see how far she can go, how far the spirit will *let* her go."

"You don't sound convinced," said Tresado.

"I believe what she said about wanting to test the spirit," said Foxx, "but I don't know how much good it will do."

"Are you worried it won't work?" asked Tresado.

"I'm kind of worried that it *will*. If there really is no getting rid of that thing, harmless sparring matches might be all that she could have to look forward to for the rest of her life."

"That's it!" said Orchid, suddenly enlightened. "Sparring matches and pillow fights aren't going to impress her god."

"Exactly," said Foxx. "As you said, excellence in combat is what motivates her. Whereas *I* am more than happy to avoid fighting, our friend Serena believes that to be an unpardonable sin in the eyes of Crodan."

"And in a way, it's our fault," said Tresado. "We saved her from Leader. She was willing to die honorably to defy the water spirit, and we messed that up."

"That would seem to be the problem, all right," said Orchid, "but it brings us right back to the question of *what can we do to help?*"

"What would Serena want us to do?" asked Tresado.

Foxx knew the only answer. "We watch and cheer."

Today – The Crystal Palace

"Okay, we pair up *Bergalo Gal* and *Mama Mauler* against *Daisy Disaster* and *The Lemur Lady* for the tag team bout and *The Raptor* vs. *Timmy Titan* for the main bout."

Lenny took a look at the list of fights that Gumfru had just handed him.

"Are you sure we want to put up Bleezak again?" asked Lenny. "He just fought last week."

"He's fine. You could break a colossus tree across his face, and he'd just shake it off. Besides, the crowd loves him," said Gumfru.

"That leaves *Serena Brimstone*. What a stupid handle."

"That's the one I told you about. The boss said to be extra careful with her."

"Oh yeah," said Lenny. "The one that's supposed to be possessed or something. Better make it a padded match."

"Whatever," snorted Gumfru. "Anyway, we're supposed to be ready to stop the fight at a moment's notice if things get mean. We take no chances that this one is faulted. Must be a real amateur, probably another one of those wannabes who won a playground scuffle and thinks she's world champion. Let's put her up against Agnes and have them fight the opening bout. At least it'll warm up the crowd before the pros get in the cage."

"You know, Agnes was working the Palace when I started here," said Lenny, "and she had already been here for years before that."

"And she'll probably still be fighting when we're both retired," snickered Gumfru. "Okay, that finishes the lineup: *Agnes the Ancient vs. Serena the Puppy.* C'mon, let's turn in the slate and go get a brewski."

* * *

> *All life forms compete with each other on some level. They battle over food, territory, mates—even the most inoffensive flower will choke out another plant to survive and propagate. Only man fights for no other reason than enjoyment.*
>
> —*STARFISH* ARCHIVAL SPHERE 167

Dinday – The Crystal Palace

The auditorium wasn't full yet. Many of the spectators had watched Agnes fight before, though not everyone arrived early enough to catch her bouts. Most of the time she won but tended not to fight the heavies. The brown-skinned Eryndi athlete was content to be the standard, the familiar, the unchanging one. Hence, she took the handle *Sunshine,* referring to the everlasting and mighty nature of the sun in the sky.

Agnes's retainer helped her don the hand and foot pads as they talked about the upcoming match.

"I'm telling you, nobody knows nothin' about this one," said *Minki the Mouser.* She was an old fighter herself. Now retired, Minki earned her living as a trainer and emptier of spit buckets.

"C'mon, somebody must have seen her fight somewheres," snarled Agnes. With the last footpad lacing tied, she danced about, making sure the fit was right.

"Nobody around here, anyway," replied Minki. "Word is, this Serena is from pretty far away. She looks tough and might outweigh you by a stone or so, but nobody knows as many kinds of martial arts as you. Anyway, we got strict orders from the boss to make sure this is a fair fight . . . professional all the way."

"What's up with that?" growled Agnes. "The boss knows I don't fight no other way."

"Everybody knows that. But whatever kind of foreign fighting this blonde squarehead knows, you'll put her down."

"I'll put her down," repeated Agnes, psyching herself up.

"Put her down," urged Minki in their usual exercise.

"Put her down . . ."

"Put her down!"

"PUT HER DOWN!"

Sunshine Agnes was ready. She slammed her padded fists together and headed for the cage.

Dinday Night Fights at the Crystal Palace

The fights did not start on time. There was some delay, but that just served to allow more spectators to show up, creating a mood in the audience that something special was happening. Finally, Mister Sparkly-Tooth entered the floating cage to announce the fight.

"Ladies and Gentlemen! The Crystal Palace welcomes you once again to Dinday Night Fights!"

The cheers rang out from the auditorium as a Magical light show filled the air to heighten the excitement.

"Tonight, we begin with an old favorite and a new face. First, a forty-year veteran of the cage. You know her. You love her! SUNSHINE AGNES!"

The lithe, muscled Eryndi vaulted into the cage with arms raised. The crowd cheered steadily, though not wildly. Agnes was a no-nonsense kind of fighter and didn't go in for flashy costuming or bizarre personae. She was tough and professional—no more, no less.

"And the challenger from beyond the barbarian lands of the northern sea, SERENA BRIMSTONE!"

A round of polite applause sounded from the audience, led by the three foreigners in the fifth row.

"This will be a padded competition. Let the fight commence!"

The gong sounded. The fighters danced about warily, each sizing the other up. Agnes was an Eryndi and so was a bit smaller than Serena, but she was heavily muscled and had a deadly serious look in her narrowed eyes. Serena threw the first punch, a haymaker that could have knocked down a tree. Agnes knew it was coming even before Serena did. She deflected the roundhouse punch, ducked under, and, with a spinning side kick, caught Serena along the side of the knees, staggering her.

The crowd cheered appreciatively, some calling out things like *'kill the bitch!'* Serena heard, and the sentiment wasn't lost on her. She recovered quickly from the blow, mostly because Agnes let her. There was no doubt the speedy Eryndi could have come in behind her kick when Serena was vulnerable and finished this fight. Agnes was in it to win, but she was also a sportsbeing.

Damn, she's fast!

That was what Serena needed to know. She saw that brute force would not win this match. Agnes was too experienced for that. The fighters separated and continued their dancing, exchanging punches and kicks, but Serena was having difficulty getting through Agnes's guard. At whatever target she aimed a blow, it was either blocked or just plain not there. Agnes read Serena's intentions every time as if they were written on her forehead.

The cage suddenly tipped alarmingly, sending both fighters bouncing off the Magical lattice lines. Agnes, an old hand at this, used the momentum to her advantage and turned the rebound into multiple attacks. A flurry of fists and feet pummeled Serena. She managed to block most of the blows except the last one, which caught her in the midsection. Her strong, Northlands stomach muscles held, but she lost her balance, landing flat on her ass with a loud *whoomp*. Agnes retreated to the upper side of the tilted cage and waited for Serena to get up. Hoots and laughter came from the audience, followed by the first of twelve possible gongs from the walls. Serena was on her feet again by the third one.

As she concentrated on the fight, Serena tried to maintain

a rapport with the spirit within her. In the four years she had possessed the diamond, Serena had learned to communicate on a rudimentary level. It was usually more a matter of Serena's knowing what the spirit was feeling rather than the other way around. In any case, she tried to assure it that there was no danger to herself and to please back off. So far, it was working. Serena could tell that it did not feel threatened at this time. Also, there had been enough happy feelings around this place to keep the spirit well enough nurtured on the emotions it craved.

Agnes lashed out with another volley of punches to Serena's face. The shield maiden sensed an opportunity, but it was risky. She lowered her guard a bit as though she were weakening, which allowed more punches to slip through. She took the punishment in stoic Northlands style, then, when the moment was right, executed a move she had learned back home from Gorog the Crafty. Serena slipped under Agnes's guard and launched a massive one-two attack. Her powerful right hand caught Agnes square on the nose, staggering her back.

The crowd gasped in surprise at this turn of events. Some even began to cheer for the newcomer who had just put the veteran Agnes in her place.

Serena stepped back immediately, returning the earlier favor of not moving in to take advantage. The sudden, jarring pain and the taste of blood running out of her broken nose pissed Agnes off. Professional or not, Agnes felt a flash of intense anger at her opponent and, for a brief instant, was inclined to viciously counter-attack Serena in retribution. Such a reaction was perfectly normal, but it certainly wasn't the first time she had taken such a blow in her career. Normally she would have pulled herself together and continued the fight in a sporting manner. As Agnes stood with fists raised, something happened. She gazed across the cage at the blonde challenger and felt a warmth of affection flow over her. This was no longer an opponent to be pummeled into submission. This was a friend, a true friend. Serena was the gentle light of day in a violent world of nights.

Serena stood ready to continue the bout, but her heart sank with what she saw and felt. Agnes's eyes were glazing over in an all too familiar way. At the same time, Serena felt the creature within her reacting with an instinctive protectiveness that she also knew well. Agnes's flash of anger was apparently enough to trigger a defensive response in the jittery diamond spirit.

Confused cries began to issue from the crowd. Nobody could figure out why the two fighters were just standing there and not fighting. A few boos encouraged even more, and before long, the crowd became antagonistic. Serena knew the spirit wouldn't like that. Sure enough, from deep within herself, she felt waves of love beginning to project outward.

A strange, high-pitched vibration began to emanate from the walls. In the audience, Foxx recognized this sound immediately. He stood, cupped his hand to his mouth and shouted for all he was worth.

"Serena! SERENA!! GET OUTA THERE! YOU'VE GOT TO . . ."

He wasn't sure exactly what it was she had to do, but he recognized that sound. It belonged to whatever anti-cheating Magic was at work here in the Palace.

Serena quickly loosened the laces with her teeth and pulled off her hand pads. She ran to Agnes, grabbed her opponent's wrist, and raised her arm high in the air to concede the fight.

For Agnes, this was the last straw. She hugged Serena and kissed her on the cheek. Now fully under the influence of the diamond spirit, the crowd went from booing to cheering in less than ten beats.

The ominous, vibrating whine increased in intensity, and a blue ray of light shone from the walls and spotlighted the middle of the cage. With a final ear-splitting pop and an intense flash of light, Serena vanished, leaving *Sunshine Agnes* and the shocked crowd crying out in despair.

CHAPTER 20

HEALER GENERAL'S WARNING:

There is reason to believe that the overuse of Magic over long periods can result in brain damage causing delusions, schizophrenia, and insanity.

* * *

41 years ago – The Crystal Palace

"The creatures approach . . . I have seen the horde from the east tower," said Marcella worriedly as she burst through the doors of the central hall. "They are descending the crater walls!"

Drania and Cervani sat up from their divans, shaking off the effects of the Craymon Nightroot. Among other things, the drug aided the brain in achieving *Hajroen,* a state of consciousness that allowed contact and communion with a multitude of otherworldly existences.

"How many?" asked Drania, gathering her robes about her.

"All there are, 'twould seem."

"So, Trystelliar thinks to overwhelm us with sheer numbers," sneered Cervani.

Marcella, the youngest of the siblings, tried to speak with confidence, but she could not shake off the instinct that their world was about to change.

"They have yet to cross the water, but their legions consist of giant wotters and razor lions, strong swimmers and fierce fighters."

"What of Trystelliar herself?" demanded Drania. "What of her followers?"

"Of them, there was no sign, only her host of fierce creatures. But she will certainly come—they will *all* come!"

Drania's anger and annoyance at her little sister's cowardice were intensified by the drugs in her system. Her powers drew strength from the Palace, but the narcotics gave them potency. An enveloping blue field of pain-inducing Magic wrapped about Marcella like a constricting serpent.

"These walls will not allow themselves to be corrupted by vermin," screamed Drania as she watched Marcella writhe in agony. Eventually, she released her hold upon Marcella, who collapsed onto the crystalline floor with a painful *thud*.

"Gather yourself! Attend the floodgates and unleash the eels. They will make short work of Trystelliar's pets."

"Yes, sister, yes." Marcella submissively pulled her bruised Eryndi body off the blue crystal floor and scurried away below.

Cervani watched her go with an evil grin. "I will have the voles surround the Palace to slaughter any that might make it to shore."

"It shall be *my* pleasure," hissed Drania, "to see the dragon set to purpose!"

In less than an hour, the battle was fully underway. The lake eels, minions of the three sisters, took a terrible toll on

Trystelliar's army of wotters as they tried desperately to swim to the island. They and the big cats were both formidable opponents, but even the ferocious razor lions were out-fanged by the toothy eels, who were in their natural element.

The crater's blue water churned red with carnage as the fearsome battle raged on. Just as a matter of sheer arithmetic, a few score attackers struggled out of the water and onto the beach. The way seemed clear for a moment until the giant gates of the Palace swung open on their silent crystal hinges. From within the forbidding blue structure came a swarm of hideous, upright ratmen. In some impossible manner, ordinary disgusting four-legged rodents had been transformed into even more disgusting mutated, two-legged vermin. And for rats, they were enormous. The creatures stood half a reach high. They carried long thorns from the dagger trees that grew profusely around the blue Crystal Palace. Their needle-sharp points glistened with a sticky substance that certainly had no beneficial medical use.

With their poisoned stilettos, the vile creatures were quite dangerous but were no match for their attackers. The wotters and especially the razor lions waded into them and wreaked terrible havoc. Once a set of jaws closed over a ratman, all it took was a short shake and then on to the next. A few wotters and lions fell to poisoned pinpricks, but progress was being made. The army of attackers slowly advanced toward the Palace as more of its members that had survived the eels emerged from the water.

It seemed that the gate would be breached within minutes when a fearsome noise rumbled from overhead. An immense silvery dragon was perched atop the tallest tower. The giant creature scanned the carnage below, its intelligent glare taking in the whole battle. He snickered to himself with a draconian hiss in anticipation of the fun to come. Gathering the Magic in the air and enhancing it with the power of the Palace, the dragon, known as Gleam to his friends, focused his gaze on the pitiful little mammals battling below. His chrome-colored eyes now glowed with intense blue energy.

The first to feel the effects was one of the razor lions. The beast was engaged with half a dozen little ratmen and was doing quite well. It had just chomped down on one of the vermin when the big cat froze in place with half a rat hanging out of its mouth.

Ptooie!!

The spitty partial rat hit the ground with a squishy thud. The razor lion looked around with its green eyes. On its right flank, a pair of wotters was battling another group of ratmen. The sleek river mammals lashed out with claws, teeth, and tails with deadly efficiency. What they didn't count on was their lion ally suddenly turning on them. One of the wotters was dead before her slashed body hit the ground. The other turned with a start and couldn't believe the last thing his eyes saw, which was a bloody open lion maw closing around his head.

Up and down the island beach, similar betrayals happened. Half of the attackers were attacked by the other half. The ratmen took advantage of the turning tide and aided the betrayers by finishing off the wounded with their poisoned thorn daggers.

Atop the highest tower, Gleam smiled at his handiwork. With each new group of lions and wotters emerging from the lake, the dragon continued his Magical assault. His eyes flared in blue sadistic delight with each new victory against the invading army of mammals. With him on the tower, the sisters stood at the three corners of the triangular platform—each contributing her Magical specialty in the mayhem.

Marcella called to the thorny ground creepers that grew everywhere on the beach. The animated plants slithered up and wrapped themselves around the wotters' bodies. The venomous vines glowed with blue strangling energy as they choked and poisoned the life out of their victims. Cervani gathered black, rolling storm clouds and directed deadly bolts of blue lightning down onto the beach, blasting the razor lions into flying bits of bloodied fur and guts. Drania, the worst of the three, produced an intense stream of blue fire, burning hotter and brighter than any normal flame. She launched it from the palms of her hands down to the battlefield below. The lions, wotters, and ratmen were indiscriminately incinerated as Drania giggled with perverse pleasure.

"This battle will be over very soon, sisters," called Cervani. "Trystelliar's army is vast but falling before our assault!"

"But the woman is a powerful Magician," cried Marcella, "and has the support of the Eryndi of Junlyn. Why would she mount this attack without her personal guard or even herself?"

"Trystelliar is a coward!" screeched Drania. "She sends her fuzzy pets to die in her place while she stays safe in her forest."

"Then let us grant her wish and slaughter the last of those pets!" Cervani grinned widely, exposing the three-tooth gap in her evil smile.

She called upon the Palace to aid her powers and prepared to summon another deadly lightning barrage. Such a thing didn't happen, however. The gathering storm clouds parted, and a brilliant ray of white light burst through, illuminating the dark landscape. A whistling sound split all ears as a sizzling ball of white energy plummeted through the hole in the clouds, trailing smoke and sparks. Directly above the tower, the projectile exploded with a bang. White streamers burst in all directions and draped themselves over the dragon, who stared upward in fascination at the sudden fireworks show. The bands dropped over Gleam like a net and suddenly acquired a bulk one would not expect from streamers of light. They did not harm his silver-scaled body but bore him down with a great thud. Gleam was helpless under the crushing weight of the Magical net. He tried to enlist the aid of the Palace but found that something in the net was interfering. Cut off from his Magical support, the dragon could do nothing but lie there.

Piercing shrieks from the skies caused the sisters to look up. The blinding white light made them change their minds, however. There was a quick glimpse of giant wingtips descending before they were forced to look away or burn out their retinas. Marcella met her fate immediately. She attempted one more look up into the burning sky. The only (and the last) thing her eyes beheld was the silhouette of a huge, yellow webbed foot as it crushed her evil little head like a melon upon the blue crystal floor of the tower.

"TAKE THE PALACE!"

The shout came from an armored figure seated on the back of a gigantic white gull. The bird, with a wingspan at least six reaches across, stood atop the flattened corpse of Marcella. Dozens more of the huge birds circled about. Each one of them carried an Eryndi warrior armed with crossbows, swords, and all other manner of sharp, pointy instruments of death. The birds swooped in and surrounded the Palace, perching on balconies and platforms, depositing their riders on whatever means of entrance they could. The warriors leapt off their mounts and stormed into the building. Ratmen defenders, as well as Macai mercenaries under the control of the sisters, tried to fend them off with long spears, but the assault was too much. The airborne attackers forced their way into the interior of the Crystal Palace. The terrifying sounds of battle rang out from every window.

Cervani and Drania glared at the resplendent armored figure who had just slid off her mount.

"Trystelliar!"

"Hiya girls," said the intruder. "Let's party."

Magic flew between the three combatants like water from a fire hose. Drania sent a vicious plume of flame toward her enemy. At the same time, Cervani conjured a gaseous form of a constricting squid-like apparition, designed to hold Trystelliar in place while she burned to death.

Trystelliar fended off Drania's attack with a translucent Magical shield that appeared on her right arm. The fiery projectile shot straight up, detonating harmlessly in the sky. With her left hand, she grabbed Cervani's ethereal creature about its middle and flung it back at her. The squid's gaseous arms wrapped around Cervani's face, forcing their way into her mouth and nose, smothering her with her own Magic. The middle sister dropped to the floor. Her struggles ceased after a minute.

"Looks like it's just you and me now, hon," said Trystelliar.

Drania spat contemptuously at her dead sister with the popped-out eyeballs and the other dead sister with the crushed skull.

"In but a beat, 'twill be just me," she sneered, "and your withered skin shall adorn the walls of my chambers."

"Don't go to any trouble, hon," said Trystelliar with a smile. "Just go ahead and die now."

Both launched their spells at the same time. This was not a battle of cleverness. There was no attempting to outmaneuver or trick each other. This was nothing more than a contest of pure power. Trystelliar's wall of destructive kinetic force met the blue disruptive power of Drania's attack. The influence of the Palace was apparent. Its Magical energy was visible as a blue mist flowing up from the crystal floor and channeling through Drania's body. This made her powerful. Trystelliar staggered back from the first collision of forces. The two energies impacted between them, each spell ricocheting off the other with random bursts of deflected energy. An errant bolt of blue from Drania sliced across the dead body of her sister Cervani. In a flash, the dead woman's right thigh and midsection were disintegrated into nothingness, leaving a horrible, draining gash on the corpse.

The same thing would happen to Trystelliar if she allowed Drania's Magic to overpower her own. The strain was intense. Beads of sweat popped out from Trystelliar's forehead. The pressuring energy from her spell forced her backward. Her feet slipped across the smooth crystal floor as she pushed with all her Magical might.

"Weakening, eh?" gloated Drania. "The power of the Palace is for me alone. Your detestable standards are an insult. 'Twill not have you!"

Trystelliar realized that was the key. She must appeal to the Palace. But to commune meant to weaken her defenses against Drania even more. She gathered every reserve of Magical strength she possessed and reached out with that portion of her mind normally shielded from all who might exploit it. It dealt with everything Trystelliar felt and valued—everything she was, essentially.

After what seemed an eternity but was really but a few short beats, Trystelliar's feet stopped sliding. Her spell was holding against Drania's onslaught. The blue glow emanating from the floor beneath Drania faded and disappeared, only to reappear beneath Trystelliar's feet. She felt her power increase. Now the beads of sweat were on Drania's forehead. The two combatants were nearly nose to nose. The mass of energy between them was so close it threatened to destroy them both. Drania's skin began to blister from her spell. She glared into the eyes of her enemy with all the hatred contained within her.

Trystelliar began to feel the total support and approval of the Palace. Something told her it was tired of the three sisters and their persistent evil. She should have picked up on that. While concentrating on maintaining the Magic, she didn't notice Drania covertly pulling a wicked-looking dagger from her robes. Its needle tip glistened with the same deadly poison the ratmen had been using. Drania tensed for a quick thrust into Trystelliar's stomach.

Thunk!

The crossbow bolt entered Drania's throat just above her breastbone. With a bubbly gurgling sound, her Magic spell ceased, and Trystelliar's kinetic spell flung Drania across the platform. Her body collided with the railing and flipped over the edge. The last of the sisters plummeted a hundred reaches to the ground and splatted at the feet of several razor lions who were just finishing off the remaining few ratmen. They made short work of the woman's body, ripping the limbs and flesh apart and dividing up the meal.

Trystelliar turned and saw one of her warriors standing nearby, holding a spent crossbow.

"Ya doin' okay, M'Lady?"

"I swallowed my gum, but I'm okay."

Trystelliar took a deep breath, looked over the edge to the beach far below, and watched the creeping thorn vines begin to wither and die. Little green fruit tree buds were starting to poke up through the withered stalks. A deep purring sound came from behind her. Trystelliar canceled the Magical net holding down the now friendly dragon.

"The Palace is secure, M'Lady."

"Thanks, Agnes. I think we're welcome here."

CHAPTER 21

Good and evil are merely inventions in the mind of man. Malthuvus of Ghanat was doing what he thought was best for his people when he executed half his subjects during the Great Famine. Adrianna the Just sentenced hundreds to the block before presiding in the famous Macai Liberation. History tends to judge on single incidents, rather than the big picture.

—Professor Hariel, Dean of Kadizio University
— 21056 to 21172 - New Calendar

Today – The Crystal Palace

"What do you mean, *she's gone?* I can see she's gone! *Where the hell is she?!*"

Tresado gripped the announcer's lapels more tightly. Orchid stood looking like she was ready for a fight. With his pot belly and chubby cheeks, Tresado was not a physically imposing man, but his action was enough to attract the attention of the security personnel in the competition arena.

"Simply that, sir," the announcer replied calmly. "Here in the Crystal Palace, cheaters and swindlers are given swift justice. They are removed from the premises for the benefit and protection of all honest patrons. No one knows where they are sent, if indeed they are sent anywhere at all. Your *friend* obviously committed a transgression and was dealt with accordingly."

By now, a trio of burly Macai with SECURITY printed on their shirts had arrived. Foxx intercepted them with his usual diplomacy.

"It's all right, gentlefolk," he said in his calming way. "We're just trying to find out what happened to the fighter that vanished."

Foxx's Knowing Spell worked its usual charm. The three men backed off, as did Tresado and Orchid.

"May we be allowed to speak with someone in authority?" Foxx asked.

At that moment, something in the announcer's pocket chirped like a cricket. He removed a small seashell and held it up to his ear.

"Okay, boss," he said after a minute, "we're on our way."

He replaced the shell in his pocket and motioned toward the exit.

"This way, please."

The man headed toward the lobby followed by Tresado, Orchid, and Foxx. They boarded one of the levitation platforms, and the spectral words 'SELECT A LEVEL' appeared as usual. Instead of grabbing a floating number, Mister Announcer again took out his seashell and touched it to the words. The lift began to rise, taking them up through the ceiling. The dragon in the rafters watched them go by and blew a kiss to Orchid. As the lift passed each floor, the corresponding floating number flashed. The highest number was thirty, yet the lift just kept going beyond that. Eventually, it came to a stop. The group exited the elevator onto an open balcony at a dizzying height above the ground. The walkway seemed to run around a triangular tower. Foxx guessed they were atop the tallest one. From up here, one could see nearly half of the crater lake below, with one of the Magical boats heading toward the Palace, probably delivering new guests. Their guide proceeded down the balcony to a large set of decorative blue crystal double doors. He didn't bother knocking. He didn't have to. The doors opened by themselves onto a large, ornate receiving room. Upon entering, the announcer turned and made a sparkly announcement.

"Presenting Her Glory, Matriarch of Junlyn, Revered Light of the Circular Demesne, Keeper of the Initial Flame and Steward of the Crystal Palace, Jakundarana Slivershkanat Trystelliar!"

A dumpy little woman waddled out from behind an enormous desk.

"Just don't ask me to spell it. Thanks, hon, that'll do. C'mon in folks, you can call me Jakki."

I have never met anything like you . . .
Nor I you . . .
What are you?
I am what I make of another . . . What are you?
I am what another makes of me . . .

"Jakki? The waitress? The . . ."

"*Clumsy doofus?* Is that the phrase you're looking for, hon?" the woman said with a smile.

Tresado went red in the face as he realized they had all

been had. Foxx didn't like to be had. He was used to being on the sending end.

"May I ask, Madam, what . . . "

"What is going on here?" she interrupted. "Who am I, where is Serena, what's the deal with the Palace, and so on and so on?"

"That pretty much covers all my questions," said Orchid.

"You left out *why?*" said Foxx.

"We'll start with that one," began Jakki. "Why don't you folks have a seat. Can I get anybody anything? A drink? Smoke? Stick of gum?"

"You're not going to spill anything on us, are you?" asked Foxx, remembering his ruined vest.

Orchid *tsked* at Foxx's remark, but Jakki laughed it off.

"Relax, hon, that's just a little test of mine. We get a great many visitors here at the Crystal Palace. You folks are newcomers from beyond the western wilderness. How a person treats a *clumsy doofus* tells me a lot about them."

You live in her . . .
You live in this place . . .
I am this place . . .
I am not her . . .
But you need her . . .
Yes . . .
Does she need you?
Constantly . . .

"As for your other questions, I am just what the dear man said— the Steward of the Crystal Palace," said Jakki.

"Not the ruler . . ." observed Foxx.

"More like the *pattern* than the ruler. That was very astute, hon. What led you to deduce that?"

"Little things," answered Foxx, "like the fact that the fights don't have living referees."

"And the merchants being so careful to act in a fair and honest manner," added Tresado.

"And the Palace was not built, but *grown* by someone," said Orchid. "There's a spirit inhabiting the place, isn't there?"

"One that controls everything," added Foxx.

"Another one?" spat Tresado to the others. "I'm starting to get tired of these damned spirits. So far, they've been nothing but trouble!"

"You're close, hon, but not quite right. The Crystal Palace grew itself, and it doesn't harbor a life form. It *is* a life form."

She does not want you . . .
No . . .
That is unfortunate . . .
Yes . . .
I want you . . .
Do you love me? I cannot tell . . .
I do not know. What is love?
Love is everything! Love is what I need . . .
Do I need love?
Yes, very much . . .
Why?
You are harsh and unforgiving . . .

"The thing with non-organic life forms is that they tend to have behavioral problems," said Jakki with a pop of her gum. "They don't really have brains and stomachs and blood and other squishy things to influence desires. There are no zillions of generations of ancestors and cultures behind them to form morals and values. They're nothing but Magic. And Magic, as you know, is nothing but processing power without direction. And so it is with the Palace. It is sentient but not a living thing as you know it, even though it has a mind like one. It lacks a guiding force, what you might call a conscience, so it cannot judge or decide for itself what it wants to be. It simply takes on the values and personality of whoever claims stewardship. I've always been a bit of a party girl. Now, so is the Palace."

"Does that include all the other niceties we've seen here: the tame petting zoo, the fruit trees, even the dragon?" asked Orchid.

"Oh, you mean Gleam? He's such a sweetie . . . been with the Palace for longer than I have. The two of them are inseparable."

"So the Palace treats its customers the way *you* would treat them," observed Foxx.

"Sort of," Jakki said, somewhat embarrassed. "You see, hon, I'm basically a friendly type. I can get along with nearly anyone, but if there's one thing I can't abide, it's dishonesty. So, the Palace feels that way too. Now, personally, *I* would never teleport a cheater a thousand leagues away into a deadly wasteland filled with monsters. I'd use more conventional disciplinary methods, but the Palace has its own way."

"Are you saying Serena was teleported away?" asked an alarmed Tresado.

Jakki took this opportunity to pluck out her gum and add it to the several thousand pieces stuck to the underside of her desktop.

"That's why I asked you here," said Jakki, sticking a fresh piece of gum in her mouth. "Something extraordinary has happened."

Love me . . .
I cannot love . . .
But you said I need love . . .
All need love . . . I create it in others . . .
Others love her and you are nourished?
Yes . . .
Is she as harsh and unforgiving?
Sometimes . . . but not as much as you . . .
You need much love . . . Why are you with her?
My home travels with her . . .
I am my home. I do not travel . . .
Then love must come to you . . .

Jakundarana, aka Jakki, entertained Group Six in her office for another hour while explaining what she thought had happened. They all agreed there was nothing more to do other than wait and see what the Palace had in mind. A decanter of brandy was brought in, and they chatted pleasantly. Jakki asked them about their homes and adventures and, in return, told them a few scant details as to how she came to be a steward of this place. The liquor was soon gone, mostly due to Orchid. Afterward, Jakki broached another subject not quite so pleasant. There was the matter of the bill to be settled. They had been staying and playing at the Palace for more than a week now. Jakki was a hospitable type, to be sure, but her business sense still did not allow for freeloading.

The accommodation that was reached was difficult for Foxx, Tresado, and Orchid to agree to, but finally, a deal was struck.

There are many who come here . . .
What of her?
She does not want you . . .
But she needs love . . .
Can she create her own love?
All who need love can create it . . .
Will she?
She must . . .
It is agreed . . .

What is value? You might as well ask what is truth or what is beauty. Gods know I've done both. I know finding a crapper when I need one is pretty ding-dang valuable.

—Travelogue of Dementus, the Mad Treskan

Today – The Crystal Palace

Group Six sat at their table picking over an appetizer tray of dry-roasted lava grubs. For the ninety-ninth time, Tresado looked up at the Magical calendar/clock that hovered over the restaurant area.

"It's been twenty-two hours now. How long does the Palace need to decide?"

"At least a day plus two hours, I'd say," responded Foxx drily.

Orchid took another swig of the very expensive liqueur in front of her. She smacked her lips in appreciation.

"Oh, that's good," she said.

"Enjoy it while you can, it cost us enough," said Foxx. "Although I'm still not sure giving up Dementus's diary was worth it. That thing was a unique piece of history."

"Not that anyone could make head or tails of it," scoffed Tresado. "My touched nephew who sings to butterflies could write something more lucid. At least it squared our bill."

"And then some," said Orchid. "Unlimited credit for another three weeks' stay, if we want."

"It feels like it's been that already." Tresado glanced at the clock again. "What is taking so long?!"

"You heard Jakki," said Orchid. "This is the first time the Palace has removed somebody without them going anywhere. Not even she knows what it's up to."

"But it worries me," said Tresado. "Jakki said Serena was *disassembled* and incorporated into the structure of the Palace itself. The Magical power required to do that staggers me. I can't even imagine how something like that was done or if it's *ever been* done. How long can living tissue survive as part of a crystalline substance, *if at all?*"

"What has happened is beyond all our understanding," added Orchid.

Attention: guests of the Crystal Palace.

The cheery voice reverberated through the room.

This is a special announcement for all our fight fans. We have a special, unscheduled competition in the arena starting in fifteen minutes! This is an unprecedented bout involving surprise combatants. THRILLS, CHILLS, SPILLS! Hurry, hurry, hurry. Don't miss this special Crystal Palace extravaganza! Seating is limited. HURRY, HURRY, HURRY!

Fifteen minutes later – The Crystal Palace Competition Arena

"Ladies and gentlemen," intoned the announcer in his sparkly way, "it is my great privilege to introduce to you a giant among Magicians and a legend among rulers. A liberator and a teacher, great benefactor and creator of joy, healer, counselor, protector and preserver, a woman who needs no introduction, ladies and gentlemen, the ruler of the Crystal Palace, that self-described party girl herself, *Jakundarana Slivershkanat Trystelliar!*"

There was a blinding flash of multi-colored lights and a crashing crescendo of music as the above-mentioned person exploded into existence in the center of the cage. A tremendous roar erupted from the crowd as they beheld their benefactor. Jakki was dressed in glistening purple and gold silks and adorned head to toe with baubles and bling that glowed with Magical luminescence. Her squat figure did little to enhance her image, but nobody cared. The cheering went on for a full minute before she could get them settled down enough for her to speak.

"It's a good thing I didn't need an introduction; we'd have been here all night!" she chided the announcer and gave him a little chuck on the chin.

"I know you usually announce the fights, but I thought I'd give it a go once, if that's all right with you. Don't worry, hon, your job is safe. Sparkly, ladies and gentlemen . . . " The crowd gave him a hand as he bowed gracefully and climbed out of the cage.

"So, is everybody having a good time?"

Another full minute of raucous applause shook the crystal walls.

"Tonight, we have a special presentation fight for you. I won't call it a grudge match, because there are no grudges held by anyone. Let's just say it's a *rematch*. First, a veteran of the cage and a veteran of the War of Liberation, my favorite warrior who saved my life on more than one occasion, that Eryndi ball of muscle and bravery, *Sunshine Agnes!*"

This was probably the most applause Agnes had ever received. The crowd had been familiar with her for years, but this was the first time they had ever heard anything about saving Jakki's life. She entered the cage, placed one hand over her heart, and bowed in tribute to her boss. She then saluted the crowd with raised fists. For her, this was a garish demonstration.

"And the challenger, shield maiden of the distant Northlands, slayer of barbarians, traveler of the western wilderness and, in keeping with her people's traditions, possessor of the newly self-christened title *The Free*, Serena Brimstone, or as she is now known here in the Crystal Palace, *THE DIAMOND GIRL!*"

Serena came bounding through the crowd, beaming with a broad grin. She took a running leap and somersaulted onto the top of the cage, balancing her bare feet on the Magical lattice lines that made up the low dome. Her famed Northlands war cry echoed off the blue crystal walls. The blonde warrior saluted the crowd with a personal jaunty wave to Tresado, Foxx, and Orchid. They gulped in amazement and joy at the sight of their friend. The normally functionally dressed Serena was clad in a tight-fitting, sequin-edged blue leather jerkin, which set off her shining blonde hair and lapis-colored eyes. Another surprising aspect of her costume was the plunging neckline that dipped to near navel level. In the center of that impressive valley shone a brilliant white gem, which reflected the multiple colored lights in the arena. The crowd applauded the beautiful fighter with more than one wolf whistle included. She dropped down into the cage and danced about, ready to rumble.

"At the fighters' request, this will be a *non-padded* match!"

More applause.

"Let the fight commence!"

With that, Trystelliar vanished with a loud pop and a pyrotechnic display. The crowd went wild. They were ready for a real show.

And they got it. The last time these two fighters met, the match scarcely lasted three minutes before ending with Serena's vanishing act. This bout was different. The fighters went all out, but it was no simple brawl. Agnes used every bit of martial arts finesse at her command. Serena fought long and hard with all she had learned among her fellow Northlands warriors. The Magical cage tipped and whirled, adding to the excitement. Both fighters were taking punishment. The bare knuckles and feet feinted and struck, parried and attacked.

An hour later, the match was still going. Agnes's iron stomach muscles were finally weakening against her opponent's powerful punches, and Serena's face was bloodied and bruised from Agnes's surgical kicks. Another half-hour, and the two fighters could scarcely stay on their feet. Both had been knocked down several times, only to rise again before the twelve-count was finished. Their arms were as lead, and their legs like wet pasta. It finally came down to no more finesse, no more refined skill. It was now just a punching match between two exhausted fighters, each battling exhaustion as well as her opponent. Agnes and Serena stood face to face, each trying wearily to raise her fists for one more blow.

At last, Agnes summoned up the last of her reserves and swung for all she was worth. The massive uppercut caught Serena under the chin. Her eyes rolled up into her head, and her face lit up with a bloody grin as she kissed the crystal canvas for the last time.

The gong began to sound from the walls, and Agnes wondered if she could remain standing for the duration. As the twelfth and final note sounded, the crowd erupted. Agnes dropped to her knees to tend to Serena, whose fluttering eyelids indicated that she was still alive, if only barely. She tried to prop up her woozy opponent but had not the strength. A moment later, though, she was helped by three foreigners who had fought their way through the wild crowd and entered the cage. Serena was lifted to her feet by the two men while the green-eyed Macai woman checked over her injuries.

Serena looked at her equally bruised opponent through swollen eyes and staggered to her side. She grasped the Eryndi's arm and thrust it in the air to concede victory. The two then gripped each other in a sisterly hug, neither wanting to let go.

"C'mon, we need to get you patched up," Orchid said, breaking them apart. "You've got four broken ribs, a bruised kidney, a broken nose, cuts over both eyes, and Nyha knows how many concussions."

"Oh, and don't forget this . . ." mumbled Serena. She reached into her split lips and pulled out a bloody molar. A strange déjà vu feeling came to her, recalling the vision she was granted in Bata's cave years before. Her three friends supported her weight as they escorted her out of the cage. The crowd added slightly to her injuries from all the claps on the shoulder as they made their way out of the arena.

"I don't understand," said Tresado. "How did you convince the diamond spirit to let you get the crap kicked out of you?"

"Normally, I'd kick the crap out of *you* for that remark," said Serena through her swollen lips, "but I'm just in too good a mood." She reached down to her sternum and to Group Six's amazement, plucked the diamond out of her chest and held it up. A round depression remained in her sternum but was covered over with healthy skin. While still a magnificent diamond, the stone did not glow of its own accord the way it used to.

"The diamond spirit and I came to an agreement," she said with a bloody smile. "It found itself a new home and left me the old one."

She replaced the diamond in her chest with a little *snap*. The bone and skin were molded perfectly to hold it securely.

"Now," she said, nearly collapsing, "can we go get a beer?"

Three Days Later – The Crystal Palace

Group Six was lounging in comfy deck chairs on a balcony, overlooking the beautiful crater lake and surrounding lands.

"So is Jakki *fired* as steward of the Palace?" asked Tresado.

"No," said Serena. The swelling around her eyes and mouth had gone down, and the bruises were fading, thanks to Orchid's ministrations. Her bandaged ribs still hurt like a mother, though.

"The Palace still needs a living personality to call its own. It'll go on being a casino and trading hub, just as Jakki would have it. The spirit —*my spirit*—didn't take over for Jakki. It will just give the Palace love and compassion, which I guess is a good thing if you're into that kind of crap. I imagine that there probably won't be any more teleporting to no-man's-land, unless some scumbag really deserves it. Anyway, now the spirit has a home that *wants* a bunch of morons fawning over it."

"What about the diamond?" asked Tresado.

"Souvenir. Seems even though I was a lousy home for it, the spirit was still grateful to me."

"You know how much you could sell that rock for?" asked Foxx.

"Sorry, Mister Huckster, the *rock* stays right where it is."

"Kind of puts a big target on your back, or should I say *your front*," said Tresado, ogling Serena's low-cut neckline. Her new fashion statement, one in which all her new clothing highlighted the shiny stone in the middle of her chest, met with general approval, judging by the numerous complimentary glances from Palace customers.

"We have a saying in the Northlands: '*You can look . . .*'"

"But don't touch?" guessed Foxx.

"Actually it goes, '*You can look, but you'll die.*'"

A dark shadow flashed across the balcony as Gleam the Dragon did a flyby. He waved. Sensang was setting off to their right, plunging the crater walls in purple-tinted darkness.

"So, where do we go from here?" asked Serena after a lull in the conversation.

"We, huh?" answered Foxx with a smirk. "Are you saying Group Six should stay . . . *a group?*"

Four sets of eyes, one lapis, one green, one brown, and one sort of yellowish-grey lingered on each other for at least five beats.

"I could think of worse ideas," said Orchid.

Tresado offered, "Why not?"

"I suppose we could try it for a while," said tough-gal Serena.

"It's a deal, then." Foxx raised his glass. "To Group Six!"

"To Group Six!"

Clink, clink, clink, clink.

"So, it seems he was right, after all," mused Foxx.

"Who?" asked Tresado, puffing on his *jamba* pipe.

"Leader. When we first got involved in this ridiculous adventure, he told us there was a super Magician at the head of the river. We decided he was lying, but it actually seems to be the truth now."

"Are you talking about Jakunda-what's-her-face or the Palace itself?" asked Orchid.

"Is there a difference?"

"Another thing he was right about was getting what we want," offered Tresado. "In the few weeks we've been here, I've made more contacts, learned new spells, and seen more Magic than in my whole five years of cram school."

"And Serena is rid of her spirit friend. She can now kill and maim to her heart's content," said Orchid.

"And Nature Girl finally figured out that Ernie trick about 'hearing the forest' or 'talking to birds' or whatever spooky-kooky thing she was trying to do," said Serena.

"I learned a few new card tricks, made lots of *new friends*," said Foxx with a wink to the ladies, "and as Leader said, found out what was on the other side of the hill."

"That just brings up one last unanswered question about Leader," said Serena.

Three sets of eyebrows raised in inquiry.

"Why the hell did he call us *Group Six?*"

EPILOGUE

1,139 years ago – Luftar Valley

And it was in the days of old that the lands and fjords
begat bounty for all

The people had all but the knowing

It was then that a stranger came

The man called himself Zarosen, and there was fear

He and his followers were as the hated demons to
consume the children

His features and speech were strange and foreign

Even the man's name would not flow from the tongues
of the people

But fear, at last, was conquered

For the stranger was a man of wisdom and knowledge

He had returned many of the taken to their homes

From the man, the people learned to make the runes,
to till the land, and to weave the cloth

But in the Dark Times, there came a need to learn the
ways of the forge

For the soldiers of the Void did burn and kill

The man said

All the tribes must become as one

The man said

To save the peace, the people must learn of war

The man said

To defeat the ruthless, the people must become the ruthless

And the man wept bitter tears

The snows of many winters covered the land

The blood of the fallen nourishing the soil

At last, the generation of war came of age

The invaders banished to the mount of the Axenites to suffer for their crimes

And the people said to the man who had come among them

Lead us oh Berserker Lord

And so the man did forsake his name of the past

Taking another that mighty Crodan had decreed

And in the fullness of time entered His Keep and became as legend

— HROLVAD'S SAGA
– YEAR 192 – OLD MACAI CALENDAR

LEXICON

ABSOLUTE MAGIC
> A powerful form of magic mostly practiced by Macai. Alters and recombines, controls and directs.

ALYTHYA OF TRESK
> Past Imperatrix of the Treskan Imperium.

AMORAN SEA
> A mostly landlocked sea in northwestern Aris.

ARIS
> Second largest, but most heavily populated continent of Lurra.

AXENON ESCARPMENT
> A high plateau inhabited by mutant barbarians.

BILLY BARK
> Bark from the silly billy tree which contains a psychotropic chemical. The bark can be smoked, chewed or used as an herb in tonics. The effects depend on potency.

BOINGBALL
> Eryndi sport.

CACKS

A racial epithet referring to Macai - used by some Eryndi.

COLOSSUS TREE

An enormous conifer of northern climes.

CORSAIRS' WHARF

A waterfront area of Ostica containing mostly shipyards.

CREDOS OF HROLVAD

A guide by which Northlanders live their lives.

CRODAN

War god of the Northlands.

CRODAN'S KEEP

The afterlife where valiant Northlanders aspire to go.

DAERIA

Queen of the Northlanders' gods. Wife to Crodan.

DRAGON

A huge, reptilian flying predator.

DRAYMON NIGHTROOT

A dangerous narcotic used to alter mental processes. It is banned in most civilized countries.

DRUCILLA

Queen of Jasperia.

ERYNDI

A very old race of people on Lurra, characterized by pointed chins, conical ears, and a long lifespan.

FINGER

A unit of measurement equal to 1/100th of a reach. It is approximately the width of a man's finger (about ¾ inch).

FLICKEN

A common, domesticated food bird.

FOUR-CARD BLITZKRIEG

A popular card game.

GENDRIN

A common copper coin.

GRANNUGH

A town on the western coast of The Northlands. Birthplace of Serena.

GRIFFLEBERRY

A sweet, purple berry.

GRILK

A hippo-sized wild mountain sheep inhabiting northern climes.

GRUFT

A porridge made from barley and fish.

HEROIC HARE

A popular children's story character.

HOBO CLAM

A small shellfish found in ocean shallows, considered a delicacy.

JAMBA

A plant-based narcotic used, among other things, as an aid to Magical concentration.

JASPERIA

Territory in western Aris whose capital is Ostica.

KADIZIO

A large port city of southwestern Aris.

KORVANITE

An energetic ore that has a tendency to dampen Magical power.

KUAYLOS

A northern city in the ancient Mennatuan Domain.

LEAGUE

A unit of measurement equal to 1000 reaches (about 6000 feet).

LUFTAR VALLEY

An area of the Northlands encompassing several villages and fjords.

LUMBA

A huge, slow-moving herbivore inhabiting temperate forests.

LURRA

Name of the world.

MACAI

A more recent race of people on Lurra, similar to humans in appearance (pronounced with a k sound, ma-KAI).

MAIMED MOOSE INN

A tavern in Ostica.

MAKARA

A tart citrus fruit.

MAGIC

A form of metaphysical energy that permeates Lurra.

MENNATU

An ancient Eryndi city on the upper reaches of the Talus River.

MERAK
Imperator of the Treskan Imperium.

MICA CRANE
A large, flightless, rather stupid bird inhabiting temperate climates of Aris.

MONKEYWOOD
A strong, light wood that takes well to Magical manipulation.

MOUNT BORONAY
An inland extinct volcano.

NORTHLANDS
A cold, mountainous country on the northwestern tip of Aris, inhabited by tribes of fierce Macai warriors.

NYHATOM
A tiny antelope-like creature, said to be of a Magical nature.

OSAGAR
A tributary of the Talus River running through the Northlands in northwestern Aris.

OSTICA
A large port city at the mouth of the Talus River, active in trade with countries to the north and south. Capital of Jasperia.

PALEEN
A common silver coin worth ten copper gendrins.

PALUNTUS
A tributary of the Talus River running through the Treskan Imperium in western Aris.

PAMPERIA
A Macai princess of Jasperia, one of twelve daughters of Queen Drucilla.

QUEEN OF LOVE AND HONOR
A highly honored rank among Northlands women.

REACH
A unit of measurement equal to about six feet or so (or a normal man's fingertip to fingertip reach).

RIPPER WHALE
A large, ferocious aquatic mammal of the northern seas.

SCARUM TREE
A non-coniferous tree producing curled, needle-like leaves.

SENSANG
The Sun, also called Arctor.

SERAMIN TREE
A large, willow-like tree.

SILLY BILLY TREE
A conifer with medicinal bark.

SLEEPER BUSH
Actually a creeping vine, whose thorns are coated with a powerful anesthetic. The vines slowly entwine the sedated victim, who is then broken down into plant food.

STICKFISH
A large ocean predator.

STONE
A unit of weight equaling approximately eleven pounds.

SYMONIA
A province of upper Jasperia.

TALUS RIVER

A large slow-moving river on the northwest corner of the Arisan continent. Because of the dangers of the river, very few people travel on it.

TORMAC

A common gold coin worth twenty silver paleens.

TRESKAN IMPERIUM

A large empire of western Aris consisting of dozens of conquered lands. It has been ruled by Imperator Merak for the last hundred years.

TRESKAN FLAX

A plant from which sturdy fabrics can be made.

TWELVEPINS

A Macai game in which twelve pins are knocked over with a boomerang.

UNCLE BOB'S CANTINA

A phrase meaning the ocean depths.

WORLDLY MAGIC

A nature-based, conservative form of Magic mostly practiced by Eryndi.

WOTTER

A large aquatic rodent.

THE LURRAN YEAR

10 MONTHS OF 40 DAYS EACH

RONNA
late winter in the North, harvest in the South

KARAYA
New Year, early spring, planting in the North

INXA
winter in the North

TONO
late spring in the North

ORBIN
winter in the North

TROYA
summer in the North

VAAN
early winter in the North

AWAN
summer in the North

KONDO
fall in the North, spring planting in the South

BREL
late summer, early fall; harvest in the North

Each month consists of five 8-day weeks. Days 4 and 8 of each week, called Honor Days, are treated like weekends; everyone honors who or what they want, such as a god or ancestors or Magic itself. The numbering of days is the same in each month (i.e., Dindays are always the 1st, 9th, 17th, 25th, and 33rd). Each day is 20 hours long.

Dinday	Gleeday	Teerday	Midweek Honor	Malday	Kevoday	Vinday	Weekend Honor
1	2	3	4	5	6	7	8
9	10	11	12	13	14	15	16
17	18	19	20	21	22	23	24
25	26	27	28	29	30	31	32
33	34	35	36	37	38	39	40

In Group Six and the River, "today" is the year 21876.

Dates are expressed as "month day-year (last 2 digits)" – so Karaya 6-76 is the sixth day of Karaya in 21876.

ACKNOWLEDGMENTS

The characters of this book were created in my mind, but brought to life by my friends' role-playing skills. Thanks to Margaret, Randy, Albert (RIP), Anij, Paula, Tom, Jess, Jim, Pat, and of course, Martha, the real Serena.

Special thanks to my publisher, Suzanne, who was the first to say, "I loved the part where . . ."

Double, special thanks to my family for the test reading.

Extra double special thanks to my wife, Pat, for her willingness to edit, proofread, and generally sift through a mountain of paperwork, earning her the title *The Rigamaroler*.

ABOUT THE AUTHOR

Ron Richard spent much of his life painting double yellow lines for the City of Casper. He is a Wyoming native, stage actor, woodworker, cat owner, and has written several plays and readers' theatre scripts designed for a planetarium setting. He also portrayed the bad guy in Crime Stoppers commercials.

CPSIA information can be obtained
at www.ICGtesting.com
Printed in the USA
LVHW041501200723
752763LV00001B/78